The Dawn Timers

The Dawn Timers

Charles F. Hamblen

VANTAGE PRESS
New York

This is a work of fiction. Any similarity between the characters appearing herein and any real persons, living or dead, is purely coincidental.

Cover design by Susan Thomas

FIRST EDITION

Published by Vantage Press, Inc.
516 West 34th Street, New York, New York 10001

Manufactured in the United States of America
ISBN: 0-533-14476-0

Library of Congress Catalog Card No.: 2002095547

0 9 8 7 6 5 4 3 2 1

For Mom and Dad

"Come hither, Odysseus, famed in song, great glory of the Greeks! Bring your ship to, so that you may hear our voice. Never has any man voyaged past this place in his black ship without listening to our song. It flows like honey from our mouths. He who has heard it finds delight and learns wisdom. For we know all that the Greeks and Trojans suffered, by the will of the gods, for Troy. And we know all that happens on the earth, everywhere and at all times!"

—*The Odyssey* of Homer

Acknowledgments

I wish to thank the following for their valuable assistance and encouragement in the preparation of this book: Mike Bogdanski, Alan Driscoll, and Dottie Tedeschi for their detailed reading of the manuscript and their insightful suggestions; Frank Bean and Sue Nordoff for additional assistance; and all my friends at YRI for their unflagging enthusiasm and support.

A very special thanks to Bob Danielski for not only evaluating the manuscript but for lending me his much needed and appreciated cyber-expertise in readying the book for publication.

Finally, all my love to two wondrous ladies—my wife, Judy, and my daughter, Bethany—who continue to provide me day in and day out with awe, delight, and flashes of insight as to what women say and do and want.

1962

Boys will be boys.

True enough, but at the moment hardly a source of comfort for the twin fourteen-year-old sisters who lay sunning themselves on an isolated stretch of Connecticut beach on a sultry August afternoon in 1962. Hearing the raucous, profane shouts of a couple of teenage males, the girls hastily sat up on their blanket and fastened their swimsuit tops in place. They exchanged glances that might have been anxious or perhaps merely curious.

The boys were a hundred feet down the strand, playfully shoving each other in and out of the gently rippling surf. As they drew nearer, the girls saw that they were armed with beer cans and considered themselves drunk.

"Whooooooooeee!" hooted one of them.

"Christ! Are we cocked!" yelled the other.

Then they spotted the twins.

"Hey, look, Timmy!" shouted the first boy. "I must be really bombed. I think I'm seeing double."

"Damn! I think you're right, Steve! Either I'm as drunk as you are, or we got two mighty fine lookin' girls here."

"One for you an' one for me!"

The kid called Timmy turned and looked down the beach behind him, where a third boy lagged behind. "What about my little brother?"

"Brian? Way too young! He wouldn't know what to do with a girl. Not like what WE'RE gonna do!"

"You got THAT right!"

1

The two girls stood up now, as the boys, squinting against the still bright late afternoon sun, weaved up the sand in their direction.

"Hey, girls!" said Steve with a smirk.

Neither of the twins said anything.

"Cat got your tongue?" Steve said, resorting to the ageless cliché. His confidence seemed to have ebbed a degree or two.

Timmy, too, seemed a little unsettled by the stillness and unflappability of the two girls. "Hey, Steve. They're a little young for us," he said, taking a swig of his beer.

"No such thing as too young, right, girls? How old are you, anyway?"

"Fourteen," said one of them.

Encouraged by this first sign that he was making his mark, Steve smiled magnanimously. "We can handle fourteen. What are your names?"

The one who'd spoken looked at her sister then turned back to her interrogator.

"I'm Pamela," she said.

"And I'm Teresa," said her sister.

The girls could see the youngest boy approaching as well, though he hung back a bit and seemed uneasy.

"Well, hey, Pamela and Teresa. You're very good-looking little babes. Ever fool around?"

Pamela glanced sideways at Teresa. "We've got to get going." She stooped to pick up the blanket and their towels. Teresa made a grab for their beach bag.

"Easy, girls!" said Steve. "Why break up the party before it gets going?"

Pamela tried to get around him, but he grasped her roughly by the arm. "Let me go!" she cried.

"Hey, Steve . . . " Timmy cut in nervously.

"You chickening out, Timmy?" Steve sneered.

"No, it's just . . ." At this point both girls tried to make a break for it, but Steve successfully blocked Pamela and hurled her to the ground. Reflexively, Timmy grabbed her sister and held her around the middle. In her struggle to break free, Teresa tripped up her assailant, and they also tumbled to the sand. Now all four teenagers thrashed around, the boys grunting with their exertions trying to pin their intended victims, the girls squirming and wriggling and lashing out with their nails.

At this point, Brian, Timmy's twelve-year-old brother, leaped upon his sibling's back and tried frantically to pull him off Teresa.

"Goddamn, it, Brian! Cut it out!" roared the bigger boy, flailing backward with one arm while trying to control Teresa's struggles with the other.

Then, "Stop it!" yelled a high, clear female voice. Everyone froze in place. . . .

Like all the others, young Brian looked up in the direction of the new arrival and found himself gaping at a beautiful blonde girl of his own age, wearing a pink one-piece bathing suit. She had evidently just wandered around the end of a grassy sand dune and held a pail in her hand. This she now set down, and in the sudden silence, her collection of seashells clattered softly.

"Stop it!" she repeated, fixing Steve with a fierce glare. Brian shivered, partly at the unnatural authority of her tone but also because a stiff breeze had sprung up out of nowhere, riffling the wavelets of Long Island Sound and kicking up little swirls of grating sand around his feet.

Steve recovered his composure. Holding Pamela's wrists firmly, he looked up appreciatively at the newcomer. "Well, now. This must be little sister. Hey, Brian, you just got lucky! Grab her and join the fun!"

An ominous, smoke-colored cloud as newly arrived as the breeze now blanketed the sun. Teresa, still lying under Timmy, craned her head up and back. "Beatrice, get away!" she called.

"Let my sisters up," said the little girl, evenly, directing her comments to both Steve and Timmy. Then, oddly, she began humming a song. Behind her, the thickening cloud cover above was racing eastward toward them at an alarming rate. A low peal of thunder rumbled, as Brian fought hard to suppress a surge of panic. What was happening? Rain began to splatter, scouring chunks out of the sand at his feet.

Now it was Pamela who addressed the girl. "Beatrice, no! You can't control it!"

Then a hideous, livid streak of lightning forked the dark slate sky, followed instantaneously by a shattering bang of thunder. Everyone leaped up from the sand, stunned, as they began to be pelted by a sudden downpour. Beatrice now looked as frightened as the rest. Suddenly, she pointed at Brian.

"You, boy! Get to the pavilion!"

She thrust her arm in the direction of the boardwalk promenade a hundred feet away. Then, before he could react, he saw the three girls turn and race—TOWARD THE WATER! Reaching the surf line, they leaped into the rolling whitecaps and dove like a synchronized swim team, striking out for the dimly visible beach raft, which bobbed and lurched against the restraint of its anchor.

Another insane burst of lightning and thunder! Brian saw that Timmy and Steve, rendered immobile both by their fright and their unaccustomed liquor intake, were in a stupor.

"Timmy! Come on!" he screamed and then bolted for the boardwalk and the minimal safety of the roofed pavilion, which seemed a million miles away. What little reasoning ability he could summon at the moment reminded him of his earth science lessons in avoiding lightning strikes—crouch low and head for cover! Praying the others were behind him, he staggered

4

clumsily forward through sheets of drenching rain and turgid mounds of sand.

Another yellow-white flash—crash!

Finally, his wildly pumping legs brought him to the sandy wooden steps of the boardwalk, and a moment later he gained the pavilion. Staying well clear of the metal supports, he turned and peered back through the torrential rain, straining to see Timmy and Steve. His heart shrank when he saw how little progress they had made. Suddenly, Steve slipped and fell—and Timmy turned back and frantically grabbed at him, pulling him to his feet.

And that was that. In a hellish, apocalyptic burst of yellow-purple light, Brian saw his brother and Steve transfixed in stark, upright rigidity, clasping each other like embracing statues. Then they dropped lifeless to the sand.

"Timmy!" he screamed and—heedless of his own safety—raced back onto the beach. When he reached the spot where the dead boys lay, he smelled the scorched ozone that permeated the air all around him. Wailing, he fell to the sand and beheld the staring eyes of his brother fixed on eternity. The faces, torsos, and legs of the two boys were shadowed with livid burn marks.

Mindless now with shock and grief, Brian looked out over the water and his gaze unconsciously sought out the raft. Through the driving curtains of rain he could make out three small female figures, like dim and ghostly sentinels, standing on the raft looking shoreward.

One

Forty Years Later

Brian Ames sat on a red wooden bench under the pavilion that stood at the end of Crown Point Beach, part of the little coastal city of Evanston, Connecticut. He had visited the spot hundreds of times over the many years since he had witnessed his brother's violent death here on that long ago day in 1962. At first, his purpose in coming here had been clear-cut—to honor Timmy's memory. But as the recollections of his older brother inexorably dimmed over time, he'd acknowledged a deeper, darker, more obsessive motive. He desperately wanted—needed—to conjure up the lovely little demon/sprite who had, he was convinced, by preternatural means ended Timmy's life while simultaneously saving his own. He'd told himself a thousand, thousand times that he hated her—but that just wasn't so. In fact, he loved her with a longing that had become for him an exquisite torment without end. And so he kept coming back here—to the only place on earth where he'd ever seen her. He had to.

She was the only woman in his life.

Now the thought of her prompted him to take again the crumpled note from the breast pocket of his polo shirt. The brief message written in an attractive female hand on ordinary, unmarked stationary had arrived in the mail two days earlier and had consumed him ever since. It read:

Dear Mr. Ames,

I have been aware for a long, long time that you have been searching for me. I am sorry that personal circumstances have up till now prevented me from contacting you. However, I now believe that the time has come when it would be appropriate and mutually beneficial for us to meet. I have business in Evanston this coming weekend. If you agree to see me, I will be at the pavilion at the end of the Crown Point Beach boardwalk Friday afternoon at 5:45 P.M. I hope with all my heart that I will see you there.

Regards,
Beatrice Beaumont

Beaumont. The only scrap of new information he'd attained in four decades—and the name had been singing melodiously through his mind for the past two days. But to what end? The woman was obviously just another charlatan—one of a dozen or so "Beatrices" who had sought to claim his attention (and ultimately his sizeable fortune) over the years. But this one at least had the adroitness in her introductory letter to provide herself with a surname. The others had just melodramatically pronounced themselves "Beatrice." And this woman also had a finely honed, if possibly sadistic sense of chronology in fixing an assignation time forty years to the moment after the tragic instant that had immutably transformed his life. She'd clearly done her homework.

Nervously, Brian checked his watch. Two minutes to go. He turned around and scanned the length of the quarter-mile boardwalk behind him, back to the cluster of concession and amusement stands, with the new, eight-story Radisson Hotel rising behind the beach complex to the east. He could see tiny bunches of people in the distance, but no one was approaching the pavilion. That figured. Another fraud, after all. Obviously, Beatrice Beaumont had had second thoughts about her ability to carry out a convincing scam. Too bad. He might at least have bedded her for the night, as he had several of her predecessors. A shabby practice, to be sure, but fair enough payback for their greedy, opportunistic charades directed against him and the memory of his brother.

Without warning, a shadow joined his own on the boardwalk in front of him.

"Mr. Ames?"

He jumped. Jesus! *Where had she come from?*

When the woman moved around into his line of vision and sat down a few feet away on his bench, he didn't know whether to laugh or cry. Whatever else Beatrice Beaumont had in mind, she certainly wasn't intending to seduce the gold from his pockets by her appearance. She was a very diminutive woman dressed in white shorts and an abbreviated aqua top knotted at the midriff. So far, so good—and he could see that her legs were more than attractive. No, the problem lay with the ludicrously large wrap-around shades that made her eyes invisible—and the wide-brimmed straw sun hat that totally hid her hair. There seemed something faintly buglike about her—or maybe it was E.T. that she brought to mind?

Beatrice, if that's who she was, placed her bag on the bench beside her and sighed contentedly, stretching her legs out before her.

"It's a beautiful summer evening, isn't it? Not too hot—just right."

As unprepossessing as her appearance was, Brian found her voice to be sweet and delectably musical.

"I'm glad you came," she said softly.

"I hope I won't regret it, but I have no great expectations for this—little rendezvous," Brian said stiffly.

"I can understand that. I know you've been taken advantage of a number of times."

That was startling. "How could you know that?"

"Oh, we 'deadly mermaids' have our methods," she chuckled. She was twitting him about the precocious article on their long ago fateful encounter that he'd sold to *Reader's Digest* at age nineteen—the article that had launched his career as a best-selling author in the field of what charitably could be termed scientific speculation, or more harshly, mind candy for the terminally gullible. Brian had written half a dozen successful books that regurgitated mix-and-match "theories" published by similar authors on everything from alien abductors and early astronaut-gods to prehistoric lake monsters and the Shroud of Turin.

"So what is it you want from me, Ms. Beaumont?" Brian asked.

"Actually, two things, Brian . . . may I call you Brian?"

"Mr. Ames will be fine." *Christl What's WRONG with me?* he thought. *Have I really gotten that small?*

Beatrice smiled, apparently taking the rebuff in stride.

"I'm sorry," Brian said. "That was uncalled for. So what TWO things, then, do you want from me?"

Beatrice sighed then and said. "Absolution and assistance."

"Absolution for . . . ?"

"The death of your brother and the other boy. I swear to you, Brian, things just got away from me. I was a frightened, stupid little kid playing with the biggest book of matches in the world."

Brian gaped at her and let her amazing assertion of paranormal abilities sit there. When he'd recovered a little he said, "So astound me further, Beatrice—since we're on a first name basis. Give me some unpublished detail of that afternoon that will convince me you're the real deal."

She chuckled. "Ah, so we're going the 'oh, ye of little faith' route! Okay, what if I debunk your sanitized little narrative of what Timmy and Steve were really up to?"

Brian felt himself flushing. He knew where she was headed.

"I don't suppose, though, that *Reader's Digest* is big on articles detailing the attempted rape of minors."

Brian was silent.

"Then, of course, it was the fact that I saw you jump on your brother's back to try to free my sister from him that made me warn you to safety."

He was stunned. None of what she'd just said had ever been published. He could doubt no longer. This really was Beatrice.

Hoarsely he said, "I see." Then after a moment, he thought to ask, "So how may I be of assistance to you?"

"THAT's going to take a lot of detailed explanation—and I'm pressed for time right now. I'm here on . . . business, and I have to make a presentation to some clients in a couple of hours. I should be through by eleven-thirty, though. I'm at the Radisson. How about meeting me in the lounge there for a nightcap? Say midnight?"

"Midnight," repeated Brian, still trying to rally his senses.

"The witching hour," laughed Beatrice, obviously much amused by his discomfort. "Is it a date?"

Brian nodded.

"Fine!" said Beatrice. "See you then." She picked up her bag and stood up. As she rounded the bench on her end, she began to hum (very prettily) the old Lena Horne classic, "Stormy Weather." Before she'd gotten very far, Brian felt a sharp breeze rustle by him, followed by a thudding rumble far to the west. He hoped it was a sonic boom, but somehow he knew it wasn't. Astonished, he gazed at the retreating figure of the odd-looking woman.

Without turning around, she sang out gaily, "See you at midnight, Brian!"

The Nathan Hale Room at the Radisson Hotel was an elegant, softly lit, darkly paneled lounge that Brian had already patronized on several occasions, even though it had been open only a month. Bars were a specialty of his, and about the Nathan Hale Room he had only good thoughts.

Although it was Friday night, the place was only half occupied, but as he entered at ten of twelve, there seemed to be a flurry of excitement over by one of the little wall tables. Eight or ten people, some in formal evening attire, were clustered around a very attractive blonde, who chatted graciously with them and seemed to be signing some autographs. Bemused by the scene, Brian made his way over to the rectangular bar and took a seat facing the door. He wanted to be sure to catch Little Miss E.T. when she made her midnight entrance.

Ordering a Dewar's on the rocks, he asked Dan Perry, the sixty-something bartender, who the celebrity was.

"Daisy Crandall, the musical star," said Dan. "She opened the new Civic Center theater tonight. Quite a little looker, isn't she? Seems nice, too."

That's right. All week Brian had seen ads in *The Evanston Chronicle* heralding Daisy Crandall's three-night engagement inaugurating the town's opulent new theater. He knew she was a major Broadway star a little past her prime—and he'd thought she'd done a few movies, but he wasn't a show business enthusiast and had never actually seen her perform or even given her much thought. *Maybe he should rectify that?* She really was a visual treat.

Eventually, her fans began to drift back to their own tables leaving the star sitting alone. Too bad he already had a date, he thought, emboldened by his drink—which was far from his first of the evening. Trying not to be obvious and failing, Brian glanced sideways at the petite blonde and saw her giving him a big smile. Damn! He could happily drown in the deep azure pools of those eyes. Was it possible this famous actress was coming on to him?

Without quite realizing what he was doing, Brian got down from his stool and walked toward the woman's table as if drawn by a magnet. He stopped in front of her, not at all sure how he'd ended up there.

Gracefully, the actress extended her palm toward the empty seat opposite her and grinned.

"It's midnight, Brian. Time for our date."

Daisy Crandall.

Beatrice.

Two

Brian eased himself into the chair across from Daisy Crandall, having not the slightest notion of what to do, say, or think.

Daisy laughed. "Sorry about the disguise thing earlier. I was just having a little fun. Also, I didn't' want to come on to you as I'm sure others have—as your typical *femme fatale.*"

Brian tried to regain some lost ground. "Is that how you see yourself?"

"Not at all. There's nothing typical about me—as I'm sure you realize."

"Care to explain? I'm not very good at word games."

"*Au contraire,*" said Daisy smoothly. "Anyone who can gull several million readers into buying the same book six different times is a master. Change the title and the cover and they will come."

"I am sorry you have such a low opinion of my work."

"And I'm sorry that YOU do," Daisy said with some asperity. "It's always sad to see talent frittered away. Your youthful essay 'Deadly Mermaids'—starring me and my sisters—was brilliant, if somewhat overwrought and inaccurate. And your first book, *More Things in Heaven and Earth,* was provocative and informative. Since then, unfortunately, you've been content to repeat yourself endlessly and to recycle the half-baked hypotheses of Erich van Daniken, Whitley Streiber, and others. Ancient astronauts? Alien abductors? Atomic blasts leveling Biblical cities? Undeniably seductive and entertaining notions, but not a shred of real proof—nothing that can't be explained away by dull, plodding, earthbound science. But then dull, plodding, earthbound scientists don't get to go on Oprah or to live off their royalty checks."

Why, you smug, little air-headed bimbo! thought Brian. He couldn't believe he was taking this from an actress, a singer, a ditzy little celebrity—listening to her reduce his life's work to rubble. He didn't have to sit here and be insulted! He wouldn't . . . oh, God, look at those eyes!

"How can you be so sure of yourself?" he heard himself ask in a small voice.

"You know the answer to that one, Brian. You have every reason to know that I'm 'the real deal'—as you phrased it earlier. There isn't a scientist in the world who can explain ME—at least not yet."

She fell silent as a waitress came to check on them. Daisy ordered another Chardonnay. Brian stayed with his half-finished Dewar's.

When they were alone again, Daisy resumed speaking in a gentler tone.

"Brian, I'm sorry. The last thing I wanted to do tonight is get off on the wrong foot with you. And yet here I've been tactless and insulting. It's just that I'm . . . very nervous. The truth is I need your help desperately—and I'm afraid I won't be able to persuade you to give it to me. I really admire your basic gifts as a writer and your sharp reportorial instincts. And if you've let them atrophy over the years—well, I guess I have to shoulder much of the blame."

Still somewhat ruffled, Brian said, "I don't follow you."

"Brian—because of who I am and WHAT I am, I've eaten up your life for forty years. I've drained you of your creative juices and your focus. How could you possibly do the research and the writing of which you're so very capable with my image haunting your every waking moment and many of your sleeping ones?"

14

Brian felt eerily faint and disembodied. "How. . . ?

"Brian, you thought you were being symbolic when you called me a mermaid—but you were so close, so very, very close to the literal truth. No, I'm not a mermaid, but for thousands of years, my sisters and I have been mistaken for them. Like them, we haunt the shores and waterways. Like them, we can raise storms and lure men inexorably to us with our songs. Brian, without filtering your thought, tell me RIGHT NOW—what are you thinking about?"

Like a frightened schoolboy, Brian heard himself murmur, "Your eyes."

"Yes, my eyes. And my voice, Brian. Even though you've never heard me sing, what do you think of my voice?"

"It's haunting, magic. It's irresistible."

Daisy looked at him levelly.

"Odysseus thought so, too," she said quietly.

The waitress returned with Daisy's wine. Snapping out of his trance, Brian downed the rest of his drink at a gulp and pointed wordlessly at his glass for another. When the waitress had retreated again, he said, hearing the rasp in his voice, 'You were a Siren?"

Daisy nodded, taking a sip of her own drink. "Still am."

Had he missed something here? Had CNN reported earlier that evening that the Earth had slipped its moorings and been whisked through a black hole to re-emerge as a hybrid fantasy land where mortals and mythical beings sociably commingled? Or were he and his late night companion both certifiable?

Brian cleared his throat. "I assume that means that reincarnation is a reality. I mean, you're not claiming you've lived one continuous stretch for thousands of years. You were only a child when I last saw you."

"True. I'm not sure how it works for the common run of humanity—but, yes, I've lived many lives down through the ages." Daisy seemed to turn inward now as she contemplated her lengthy existence. "And men have not dealt kindly with me, Brian. They have sought after me and lusted after me, and when they've found me unattainable, they've turned on me. Then they have reviled my name and called me temptress and witch. They have driven me from their villages, stoned me, stretched and torn apart my limbs in smoky dungeons, and burned me at the stake."

Brian noticed that she'd turned pasty and was perspiring. Feeling ill himself, he instinctively reached across the table and covered her hand with his.

"Can you imagine being burned alive?" she whispered.

For the first time in his entire life, Brian visualized the meaning of that phrase. He was suddenly filled with horror and sick with shame at the abysmal bestiality of his own species.

"Surely when you . . . envision it now, you can't feel the pain?" he asked softly, not knowing how he could go on with his life if she said yes.

"Thankfully, no," she said, patting his hand in gratitude for the question. "Sorry, I didn't mean to get so morbid."

"That's alright," Brian murmured. The waitress returned with his drink.

"This is all very difficult for me to process," he eventually said with a nervous chuckle. "I mean, having a chat in a Connecticut bar with an honest-to-god Siren." He shook his head. "Are your sisters still around? I mean with you?"

"Oh, yes. The three of us have an estate down on the Gold Coast near Darien."

"Are they in show business, too?"

"They were. We started out as a sister act on the night club circuit. I sang lead and they did the doo-wah, doo-wahs. Then I was offered a Broadway show, and they decided to go behind the scenes. Pamela is an entertainment lawyer with a client list of top stars, and Teresa is an agent for many of the same people. They handle my career as a freebie—so it's all worked out very cozily."

"Whew!" said Brian. "You make it all sound so matter-of-fact."

Daisy laughed, then turned serious. "You ain't heard nothin' yet. Brian, I mentioned before I needed your help?"

"Yes," said Brian, sensing a momentous sea change in his life was now underway.

"Have you ever heard of New Dawn?"

Brian thought for a moment then shook his head. "No."

Daisy smiled. "Good. I'd be very distressed if you had. We're a new . . . society, very exclusive, of necessity, secret and small in number. Composed, until now, anyway, entirely of women. Women with very special talents and pedigrees."

"Uh-oh. There are more of you?"

"Yes and no. My sisters and I are the only Sirens. But there are other representative groups from the Dawn Time, as we call it—what you would call the age of classical mythology. Specifically, the Muses, the Graces, the Harpies, and the Amazons."

Brian gaped. "Of course. Just your average women's club."

Daisy giggled. "Come to think of it, more like the Five Families. We even have a Boss of Bosses—The Great Mother, we call her, in honor of the Earth Goddess, who millennia ago was the primal deity of virtually every society on earth. Then Zeus and Yahweh showed up, supplanted her, repressed her devotees, and launched four thousand years of male dominance and aggression. As the horrific events of September 11, 2001, indicate, thanks to you boys the world is now spinning dangerously close to the abyss. New Dawn was formed to try to halt the slide—to restore some female harmony and balance to the planet before it's too late—if it isn't already."

Brian asked, "Why are you telling me all this? I'm the enemy, aren't I?"

Instead of responding, she paused, then said, "It's getting late, Brian—and I'm kind of tired. I've got another show to do tomorrow night. Can we get together again afterward? Then I'll spell it all out for you. But just to keep you interested, let me tell you that we've decided that New Dawn could use a token male—of the writing persuasion. I think you'll do very nicely."

Brian made a face. "I'm not sure I have the makings of a boy-toy. But for now, I'll keep an open mind. What about the Boss Lady, this Great Mother character? Is she likely to approve of a male on the premises?"

Daisy winced. "Well, she might be a bit of a hard sell at first. But ultimately I'm sure she can be handled."

"How?"

"Well, Brian. You're a man, and when all is said and done, she's just a woman. Flowers, candy. Flattery usually works. I think she'd be very flattered, for instance, if you came to her concert tomorrow night."

Was there no end to this woman's surprises—or her enchantment?

"Sure," he said, grinning foolishly. "Uh—can I still get a ticket?"

"Thought you'd never ask!" sang Daisy perkily, plucking one from the cleavage of her blouse and slapping it down on the table in front of him.

Half an hour later, Daisy stood in her nightgown on the balcony of her penthouse suite on the Radisson Hotel's top floor. The balmy moonscape offered her a serenely breathtaking view of the entire length of boardwalk and beach below. Off to the right, the little city of Evanston sparkled with a thousand pinpricks of light piercing the velvet, ebony shroud of darkness. And to the left, the soft moonlight dappled the gentle, lapping waves of Long Island Sound. How peaceful the whole prospect was—which, all too sadly, reminded her of the hellish manner in which, forty years ago tonight in this very place, a careless, immature child had irresponsibly unleashed white, death-dealing fire from the sky. Two boys had died and the life of another had been forever blighted—all thanks to her.

Brian.

She hoped she wasn't making another terrible mistake on this night—one that might some day soon have combustible consequences that would rain down hellfire on a thousand beaches and towns and inland lakes and peaceful pastures the wide world over. Was she letting her guilt and her emotions lead her into making a fatefully wrong decision—one that could deal a deathblow to civilization?

Was Brian Ames the right man for the job? Was any man? Her sisters and the rest of the council members had fiercely denounced her proposal that a male be admitted, even in an adjunct capacity, to the society. New Dawn was HER baby, they had reminded her—a conclave of superior women who had assigned themselves the monumental task of rescuing a man-made world gone mad. They had elected her unanimously, in spite of her relative youth, to the august position of Great Mother. Surely, in return they had the right to expect the kind of wisdom and keen judgment for which she was justly renowned among them.

The Harpy contingent had been particularly harsh and critical, as she had been resigned to expect. The U.S. Senator from New York and the head of W.O.W., the World Organization of Women, were predictably strident in their insistence that men should neither be seen nor heard anywhere remotely in the vicinity of New Dawn. The Amazons, too, were militantly certain that the membership was perfectly capable of dealing with in-house matters with zero male input. On the other hand, the prim little Graces had atypically shown some spunk and backed her, as had her aunts, the Muses, always cautiously willing to indulge their favorite niece. Pamela and Teresa, too, had ruefully shaken their heads but ultimately voted yea.

And so, she had gotten her way. Now she had to make good. She hoped that Brian was the right choice, that he had the inner strength for the epic struggle facing them all. There was no question of his loyalty, of course. That had been a given ever since they were both twelve-year-olds. Still, she had just provided herself with a little insurance by inviting him to hear her sing tomorrow night. After that, there could be no escape from her while he lived—she was, after all, a Siren, "one who," according to ancient definition, "ties and binds."

While he lived. She gulped with a sudden little rush of fear. She would have to do everything in her considerable power to see that he came through this safely. Although he was undoubtedly hers to command, she felt honor bound to protect him and, when she enlisted him in her little strike force, she would have to inform him fully and openly of the appalling dangers into which he'd be drawn.

She shuddered at the prospect of what was going to unfold on the vast geopolitical stages of the planet in the months and years ahead. Her innately heightened foresight had shown her the Big Picture as long ago as early 1993, when the first bombing of the World Trade Center had occurred. Soon the most malevolent forces of East and West would be arrayed against each other, as the rabid armies of Osama bin Laden and his kind faced the equally fervid hardliners of America and her allies. In time, if sanity did not prevail, both sides would orchestrate a nuclear barbecue that would incinerate the world.

In response to what her intuition had shown her, Daisy had thus developed the concept of New Dawn and run it by Pamela and Teresa. They had agreed wholeheartedly, and so the three of them had contacted the other Dawn Time groups and proposed a loose merger for the purpose of mutually discovering some means of averting or at least postponing what, at this point, seemed like an unavoidable worldwide conflagration. The response from the other groups had been cautiously positive, and an organizational meeting had been convened at Aurora, the Beaumont estate in Fairfield County on the southern Connecticut shore—which from that point on became the new consortium's headquarters.

Immediately, one omission from the invited gathering had been duly noted and approved by all present. The outlaw group, the Maenads, had not been included in Daisy's plans. As she had dryly explained at that first meeting, to do so would be like inviting the wicked witch to Snow White's wedding. Back in the Dawn Time, the Maenads had been a large and ferocious band of priestesses devoted to the worship of the wine god, Dionysus. Their worship services were violent orgies in which the acolytes would drink themselves into a frenzy then tear through the countryside, attacking and dismembering any unfortunate male—human or animal—that wandered across their path.

Now, ironically, Daisy found that she had ample reason to congratulate herself on her instinctive decision not to involve the Maenads in New Dawn. Recent developments on the national political scene had taken an ominous turn. The President's ongoing war against terrorism had stalled, as had the economy. The enormous popularity he had enjoyed even six months ago had, as a consequence, taken a hit, and by the next election season two years hence would most likely be in sharp decline. Unfortunately, the most logical opponent the Democrats would run against him was a backbench senator with little in the way of accomplishments or charisma. Which meant that for the first time in American history, a third party candidate would most likely be elected President.

Such a candidate was already well-positioned to run as an Independent, a candidate as dangerous and unbalanced as the new century itself. His name was Donald Dillon, and he was

21

the leader of a fundamentalist TV ministry called The Blood of God—and a man who had already publicly pledged to rid the world of what he called the "Godless Armies of the Middle East." But even more frightening than Dillon was his wife, Arianna, whom Daisy and her task force recognized as one of the most violent and evil women who'd ever lived. If the Dillons couldn't somehow be stopped, America would wake up one day in the not-too-distant future to find that the new occupants of the White House were a trigger-happy, messianic preacher and a First Lady who was a homicidal maniac.

For once upon a time, Arianna Dillon had been Ariadne, Queen of the Maenads.

At the thought of the wickedness that she and Brian Ames and New Dawn were about to confront, Daisy found that in spite of the warm night, she was shivering. Glancing upward at the nearly full moon—from the Dawn Time on one of the most visible manifestations of the Great Mother—she stepped back inside her hotel room and slid shut the balcony window.

Three

Arianna Dillon was seething, and not even the two tablets of Ecstasy she'd downed half-an-hour ago had been of any help. And certainly the fact that the ground floor of her Long Island mansion was currently jammed with raving teenagers spacing out on designer drugs and gyrating to migraine-inducing techno music—whatever the hell THAT was—amidst flashing crimson and blue strobe lights only made matters worse. Of course, she only had herself to blame—she'd invited the wealthy little bastards.

But the real reason for her foul mood was that she'd just answered another harassing phone call in the soundproofed master bedroom upstairs. She'd been getting them at unpredictable intervals for the past two months—seven or eight of them so far. Always they were the same—and not recordings, either. The message was delivered in a liltingly musical female voice that was girlish yet somehow stunningly sensual. What the voice said was, "The Great Mother is watching you, Ariadne, and a new dawn is coming." Then the caller would hang up.

Someone was on to her. Someone knew her—obviously another Dawn Timer like herself. *But who?* Damn it! This was her fault, too. If she hadn't spent the last thirty-five years totally frying, scrambling, and poaching her brains on every drug known to men, women, and gods, her naturally heightened psychic powers would be focused enough to identify her tormentor or at least narrow the range of suspects. As it was, she had to make do with more prosaic means. She certainly wasn't in a position to hire a private investigator—so that meant relying heavily on her friend and assistant, Rhonda Raveneaux. Well, maybe "friend" was a bit strong. Rhonda was useful and had a crush on her. That insured her loyalty.

Rhonda was a tall, muscular, somewhat butch TV actress who had a supporting role as Maid Marian in a syndicated Robin Hood series. She wasn't in every episode so she had plenty of time to devote to the cause of getting Donald Dillon and his wife eventually installed at 1600 Pennsylvania Avenue in our nation's fair capitol.

Jesus! That music!

Just then she spotted Rhonda in her tux coming down the stairs. She met her at the bottom.

She shouted above the din, "You know about the latest call?"

"WHAT?"

"I GOT ANOTHER ONE OF THOSE CREEPY NEW DAWN CALLS! ANY LEADS?"

"NOT YET!"

"DAMMIT! RHONDA, GET ON IT! WE'RE SIX MONTHS AWAY FROM EVEN ANNOUNCING DON-ALD'S CANDIDACY, AND SOMEBODY EVIDENTLY FEELS THEY'RE IN A POSITION TO BLOW SEVERAL SERIOUS WHISTLES!"

"I'LL DO MY BEST. YOU DON'T HAVE ANY IDEA WHY SHE KEEPS CALLING YOU ARIADNE?"

"NOT A CLUE!"

Rhonda raised her hands helplessly and walked away.

Christ! These idiotic kids! She knew now what the mad Roman emperor Caligula meant when he told his fawning sena-tors he wished they all had one neck so he could simultaneously cut all their heads off. The guy wasn't so crazy! The trouble was she needed the little jerks. She was holding a rave every Friday night at her mansion, the Labyrinth, in the isolated midsection of Long Island, where she wouldn't disturb any neighbors. With her central location, she was able to draw dissolute rich kids from both Manhattan to the west and the Hamptons to the east. She charged them a hundred bucks a head, and since they brought their own drugs, it was pure profit. There must be sixty of them here tonight—at least.

The orgy was invented two thousand years before Arianna herself was born the first time as the Cretan princess Ariadne, three-and-a-quarter millennia ago. The political fundraiser, as far as she could tell, was a modern American invention. It was Arianna's genius to have combined the two. She knew that Congress in a recent, illusory display of Doing The Right Thing had gotten around to banning "soft money"—large, unregulated contributions by corporate entities to political candidates and parties. To counteract that inconvenience, Arianna had developed and implemented a plan that every Friday night turned her home into a combination rave club and whorehouse. For the past year, the cash flow had steadily increased until it was now a merrily raging torrent.

Now beckoning to a young black man with a camera, she led him upstairs to do some SERIOUS fund-raising. The second floor was where the grown-ups and the more enterprising teens spent their Friday nights. Arianna had done much renovating of the top two floors of her house, partitioning them off into warrens of mazelike corridors that shot off in all directions and were lined with identical little cubbyhole bedrooms. Each room was equipped with a round water bed, a mirrored ceiling, and erotic toys. Also, of course, hidden video cameras.

Arianna barged into the first room she came to and stood aside while the photographer snapped off a shot and the room exploded in the camera's flash. Too late she recognized the darkly handsome, bearded man who somewhat resembled the comedian Dennis Miller. It was her husband.

"Oh, Christ, Donald! We wasted a shot!"

Then she noticed the frumpy-looking woman in the bed with Donald. She was a has-been now—but back fifteen years or so she had achieved massive tabloid notoriety for having emphatically down-sized her husband. Arianna kind of admired her for that.

The woman cringed and whined, "I'm sorry, Arianna! Honest!"

"No problem, Lorena. But go easy on him, huh? We want him intact inauguration day."

She shut the door on them and moved with her companion on to the next room. Again, she unceremoniously threw the door open, and the photographer got his shot.

"Say 'soft money!' " cooed Arianna to the frolicsome threesome on the waterbed.

There, blinking away the blinding light of the flashbulb and yelping with embarrassment, fear, and outrage were a prominent Wall Street investment banker and two teen stars of a wholesome family sitcom, one female and one male.

Paydirt!

"See you kids, later. Your picture will be ready in a half-hour or so. We can discuss price then. We have a special going on a wallet-size six-pack this week."

So saying, she shut the door on howls and whines of protest. She sent the photographer upstairs to the little darkroom she'd installed there. The three playmates would pay handsomely, she knew, for the picture and the negative. No need to tell them about the video camera, of course, She might require a videotape for the media blitz that would be needed in the final weeks before the election—when the campaign coffers would be scraping bottom.

Now for the special treat she had promised herself. She descended into the musical maelstrom below and, cringing from the noise and the blinding, rapid-fire light flashes, made her way to the back of the house. On the way, she stepped into the downstairs bathroom for a moment, found her stash of OxyContin in a little hidden panel behind the medicine cabinet, crushed a tablet and snorted the powder through a straw.

Okay, let's roll.

Glancing furtively toward the front of the house where the rave soared on unabated, Arianna saw that she was unobserved and walked quickly to the door leading to the basement. Opening it with a key, she passed through and locked it behind her. Then she descended rough-hewn stone steps to the cavernous cellarage below. The room she found herself in, she had to admit grimly, looked like the set of a cheesy Vincent Price movie. No matter. As far as she was concerned, its design was purely functional—and hugely entertaining.

The cellar was a large rectangle with original stone walls and a dirt floor. At set intervals around three sides of the room were a dozen lit torches in bronze sconces bracketed to the wall. In the center of the fourth wall, the one to the left of the stairs, was a huge, barred double door of formidable looking oak.

Directly across from the stairwell was the dramatic centerpiece of the room. This took the form of a low table constructed of the same rough stone as the walls and the stairs. It had the look of an ancient sacrificial altar, a likeness heightened by the fact that a handsome, naked young man was stretched upon it, his hands and ankles chained to four rusted fittings bolted to the corners. His mouth was gagged with duct tape, his eyes glazed with fear. He had been there for quite a few hours.

On the wall above and behind the table and directly within his line of vision was a curious but formidable looking weapon held in place by a vertical pair of heavy iron brackets. The implement was a two-headed ax made of bronze. Its twin heads flared out from the central wooden hasp to end in blades that were rounded and razor sharp. This weapon was actually a replica of the sacrificial instrument of choice used by priests on

27

the island of Crete back in the Dawn Time around 1300 B.C. The royal princess Ariadne, daughter of the universally feared King Minos, had seen it used many times on bulls dedicated to Poseidon and had concluded even then that it could be applied just as effectively to men.

As Arianna crossed the room toward the altar, she briskly stripped off her clothes. By the time she'd circled around to its rear and taken her place below the ax, she was fully naked.

"Hello, Derek," she crooned. "Sorry for the long wait."

She found the look of sheer terror in the boy's eyes highly erotic. Knowing suddenly that she couldn't wait, she climbed up on the table and aboard her captive. In spite of his intense fright, she quickly brought him up to speed as well. The end of their exertions was highly satisfactory—certainly, at least, from her point of view.

Climbing back down from the table, she turned and lifted the big ax down from its fastenings. Holding it aloft by its two-foot-long handle, she spent a moment admiring its glittering wickedness.

"The double-ax," she breathed reverentially. "The labrys, from which the palace of Minos, my royal father, took its name—the Labyrinth."

Having shared this information with Derek, she seized the ax in both hands, raised it above her, and slashing it mightily downward, cut off his head.

Then she took several more savage swipes with the weapon, probably quite a few more than were strictly necessary. Bits of the boy flew hither and yon, and blood splattered Arianna's nakedness and poured over the altar and down its side to soak into the earthen floor of the cellar. Gazing at the runoff, she felt that Dionysus would be well pleased. As a result the world's vineyards should have a banner year coming up.

Surveying the carnage, it did occur to her that the last minute OxyContin tablet might have been a tad too much.

Four

In a single evening, Brian Ames' musical appreciation had taken a quantum leap forward. Up till that night, music, to the extent that it had permeated his consciousness at all, had done so merely as white noise—aural background on a par with automobile traffic and other people's overheard conversations. He had always, even as a child, been a bookworm and a loner. After the death of his brother and with the introspective years of psychoanalysis it led to, his solitariness deepened. His parents sadly deferred to it. His whole life then devolved upon his reading, his writing, and his never-ending search for Beatrice. Whenever he heard acquaintances—he had no close friends—blathering on about the Beatles and the Stones, Jimi and Janis, Led Zeppelin and Jefferson Airplane, Pearl Jam and U2, he was always mildly astonished at both the degree of their enthusiasm and the extent of his own indifference.

Now, Daisy Crandall had single-handedly changed all that. By handing him a tiny piece of cardboard that had assigned him to the center aisle seat in the second row of the Samantha Eckland Memorial Theater in Evanston, Connecticut, on Saturday evening, August 25, 2002, she had contrived to open up to him inner landscapes and vistas of unimagined and almost unendurable beauty. Last night, when she had revealed herself to be Beatrice, she had returned him his soul; tonight, when she sang for him and him alone—just as she did for every other man in the audience—she had irrevocably stolen it back. He knew that he could never reclaim himself after her performance this evening, and he was drowning in happiness at the thought.

With a flash of insight, he recognized what wily Odysseus, the mighty warrior of legendary antiquity, had been up against. The great hero had conquered Troy, defeated a one-eyed giant, outwitted Circe the witch, and survived a journey to the Land of the Dead. Yet if he hadn't had the wit to have himself lashed to his ship's mast while he sailed past Daisy's little seaside home, she would have nailed him. At the sound of that lilting, beguiling soprano voice, he would have had no choice but to leap overboard in a doomed attempt to attain paradise.

For as long as she sang her songs this evening—whether they were operatic arias, show tunes, pop songs, or comic ditties—it became obvious to Brian in another moment of clarity that beautiful, blue-gowned Daisy, glowing ethereally in the soft-hued stage lighting, was the essence of Eternal Woman revealed in Music. She WAS her song. She was Beauty, she was Grace, she was Irresistible Mystery. And when at the end of the performance, she stepped closer for an instant to the edge of the stage, winked at him, and blew him a little kiss, he knew what he was, too.

He was going, going, gone.

❋   ❋   ❋

"How did you like me?" asked Daisy. She and Brian were sitting on the little balcony of her hotel room snacking on chicken salad sandwiches ordered from room service and sipping Chardonnay from the suite's mini-bar. Daisy had changed into a sea-green top with white slacks. It was another warm, velvet night illuminated by a resplendent moon and a radiant panoply of starlight. Daisy had suggested that the seriousness of what she wanted to discuss with him called for a more private venue than a late night restaurant or lounge. Brian didn't have the strength of character, or for that matter, any earthly reason to disagree.

"You were and are the most beautiful creature I've ever seen or heard," he said now, speaking the stark and literal truth.

Daisy's grin held for a moment, then was replaced by a gentle, sad smile.

"I know, Brian. I've stacked the deck against you horribly, haven't I? It isn't enough that you've devoted your entire life, in one way or another, to me. Now I've assured that you can never erase me from your consciousness or heart. You are technically free to leave me, of course. You can, if you wish, spend a pleasant hour or two here with me talking and watching the stars—then go. But you will never rid yourself of me now, and regarding me there will continue to be a gnawing ache in you that will consume you till you die."

"As you say, you've stacked the deck."

Daisy nodded, then fell silent for a moment.

"All right, then. Let me try to make your captivity pleasant and comfortable. You may ask me anything you like about my nature . . . my place in the scheme of things, my apparent subversion of the familiar world you thought until yesterday you knew and understood. It's important to me that you're at ease in your mind about me—that you feel comfortable with me as a fellow being. That's very important to me, Brian. YOU'RE very important to me."

"Very well, address precisely that point, if you will. How is it possible that I'm sitting here conversing with—for lack of a better phrase—a supernatural being, a creature who, according to ordinary human experience, has no business sharing this point in time and space with me?"

Daisy was silent for a moment, as if marshalling her thoughts.

"Well, Brian," she said eventually, "it seems to me that you have at least partially answered your own question with the title of your first and best book—*More Things in Heaven and Earth*. The complete comment attributed to Prince Hamlet, of course, is, 'There are more things in Heaven and Earth, Horatio, than are dreamt of in your philosophy.' Place me in that context, and what do you come up with?"

Brian spoke slowly. "That you ARE a natural being—but so far science hasn't been able to place you or account for you. Science most likely isn't even aware of you."

Daisy looked pleased. "Exactly, Brian. I'm hidden in plain sight. I am, in fact, a human being. But I'm a different KIND of human being. Take an X-ray of me or a DNA sample, and you'll find my biological structure and design duplicate exactly those of any . . . normal woman. The main difference as nearly as I can determine is that I and my nearly extinct kind have developed over several thousand years concentrated mental and spiritual gifts that so far have eluded MOST of the rest of you."

Brian asked, fascinated "Most?"

"Yes. I believe, all conceit aside, that we have much in common with the acknowledged geniuses in human history—Shakespeare, Mozart, Einstein, Jesus, for example. It seems to me that what constituted their greatness—their supreme DIFFERENTNESS—was their ability to tap into—I don't know—the infinite, I guess. I've read that scientists estimate that the average human goes through life functioning at only ten percent of his or her brainpower. Obviously, that depressingly lowball figure did not apply to THOSE boys! Imagine an English country lad with a fourth-grade education effortlessly spinning out poetic lines of unfathomable sublimity. Scholars are so frantic to 'explain' Shakespeare that they twist themselves into idiotic knots trying to prove he was really one of his famous contemporaries with a better education—Francis Bacon or Christopher Marlowe—using 'Shakespeare' as a pen name.

"Or consider the case of Mozart, who composed entire operas in his head from early childhood on—yet was a social idiot. Or another boy, Einstein, written off by his grade school teacher as academically slow, ending up by standing the known universe on its mathematical ear.

"Then there was Jesus, a simple Galilean carpenter who accidentally got his superstitious, ill-educated, peasant followers to believe that he was God—when all he was really trying to do was show them that he was what they ALL were—a Son of Man, as he called himself. He told them that if they believed unreservedly in THEMSELVES—identified with the god WITHIN them, as he had—why then they, too, could 'move mountains.' He TOLD them that!"

"Or summon thunder and lightning with a song," Brian interjected.

Daisy lowered her head. "Yes," she said quietly. "Exactly."

"But instead of the Judeo-Christian God, you believe you have internalized the Great Mother."

"Yes."

"One primal deity for each sex, is that it?"

"No," Daisy smiled impishly. "We accept men and most major credit cards. Remember, Brian, that She came first. Call the Father Uranus, Cronos, Zeus, Woden, Yahweh, or God. Call the perpetually dying and reborn Son Osiris, Adonis, Dionysus, or Jesus. They all came from Her womb, whether you call Her Gaea, Rhea, Hera, Demeter, or Mary."

Brian, feeling as if he were having his ears boxed by Tinkerbell, got up and moved to the balcony railing.

"Well, I'm glad you straightened me out on all THAT!" he said peevishly. "But, you know, Daisy, all this homage to the Great Mother sounds suspiciously akin to the New Age Wiccan beliefs."

"Oh, yes, witchcraft." Making a disapproving face, she joined him at the railing.

Ah! He'd gotten to her—maybe.

"Do you deny the similarity?" he needled.

"Not the surface similarity, no. But there's a profound difference in approach."

"Which would be?"

She gazed up at him, making his head swim deliciously.

Then she said, "The Wiccans make the same fundamental error all the traditional organized religions make. They all substitute form for substance, hocus pocus for Truth. They invoke, they cast spells, they sacrifice sheep, bulls, and each other, they pray for gifts and acknowledgment—like children firing off Christmas lists to Santa. They yell, 'Double double toil and trouble,' 'Hallelujia,' and 'Hail, Mary.' Now THINK of this, Brian! All of these invocations, chants, and lit candles imply that their target, their God of Gods or their Mother of Mothers, has the IQ of a squid and is so bereft of meaningful activity that He or She sits around—WHERE, by the way?—throughout the ages preening and DEMANDING an unceasing hurricane of praying, braying self-interest from all quarters of the globe."

"And just how do you worship the Great Mother?" he said somewhat lamely, certain that she had a comeback.

"I don't worship her. I USE her."

He had to admit, he didn't expect THAT comeback.

She went on, as if thinking the thing out as she went on, but knowing where she'd end up anyway. She was really enjoying herself, enjoying the exercise of what was obviously a natural and formidable intellect.

"Don't you see the error, Brian? Worship is ultimately nothing more than narcissism. Whatever deity you choose to pray to—you're praying to YOURSELF, to the god in YOU! Jesus had it right—though he may have overstated the physical possibilities—we can move mountains, so to speak. We all have direct access to our inner selves, and at the core of our beings we are one with the Eternal, the collective spirit that animates the universe. No sacrifices, no spells, no prayers, no chants necessary. THY will be done, Brian Ames! Go for it!"

Brian thought he saw a chink in her argument.

"No chants, no spells? Then what's that humming thing you do while calling an airstrike?"

She laughed. "Oh, that! Just limbering up exercises—like an athlete doing some preliminary knee bends. The tune I hum could be Verdi's *Requiem* or 'Strangers in the Night.' It's not needed."

"No?"

Daisy waved her hands languidly, as if swatting away a mosquito. Instantly, there was a lurid flash of blinding white light over Long Island Sound and a bang of thunder that must have jolted the whole town awake.

"No."

Brian's heart bounded in his chest. "Jesus! Daisy, if we're going to hang out together, that's going to take a lot of getting used to!"

For a moment they both looked at each other then burst out laughing. When they'd finished with that, they did some more looking at each other. Then Brian saw it—a change had come over the woman before him. Was he imagining it? All of a sudden, Daisy Crandall, Queen of the Sirens and cocky little Mistress of the Universe, looked like a fourteen-year-old being brought home by her date and wondering if he were going to try to kiss her—and how she should react if he did.

Abruptly, she turned from him and cleared her throat.

"So, uh, Brian, are you satisfied that, when all is said and done, I'm just one of the girls?"

"Yeah," said Brain, "that thunder clap cinched it for me. No doubt about it—you're the girl next door, all right."

Daisy giggled uncertainly. Suddenly, he realized that he not only was thoroughly comfortable in her company but that he felt sorry for her. Gently, he asked. "What is it you want from me, Daisy?"

She looked up at him, grateful and relieved, and smiled.

35

"Wait here a minute," she said and stepped back into the hotel room. When she re-emerged, she wore a troubled expression and held in her hand three manila file folders. She set these down on the little patio table between their chairs and walked back to the railing and stood looking out at the night for a moment. Then she turned back to face him.

"Where to begin?" she sighed. "Well, let's try the literary route. Brian, I assume that since you were an English major you're familiar with William Butler Yeats' poem, 'The Second Coming'?"

Leaving aside the question of how she knew his academic background, he answered, "Yes, quite vividly."

"No wonder. It's brilliant—and the most chilling little piece ever committed to paper. In twenty-two lines, Yeats totally trumps the rambling, hallucinatory ravings of The Book of Revelations and the similarly opaque prophecies of Nostradamus."

Brian began to recite:

"Things fall apart; the centre cannot hold;
Mere anarchy is loosed upon the world . . ."

Daisy took over and finished it for him:

"And what rough beast, its hour came round at last,
Slouches towards Bethlehem to be born?"

They were both silent for a moment, each privately envisioning the apocalyptic darkness the poet had foreseen occurring at the dawn of the new millennium—certainly not the New Dawn Daisy was desperately trying to engender.

"It's almost as if Yeats had seen the blueprint of our time back in 1924, isn't it?" she finally said.

"Yes, right down to the desert locale, Saddam Hussein, and Osama bin Laden," agreed Brian.

"I concur about the desert imagery," said Daisy. "No one can deny that much of the horrific upheaval of recent decades has been spawned in the cauldron of the Middle East. But Saddam and bin Laden are relative pipsqueaks, bit players, mere heralds of the Anti-Christ. If you want to check out the real 'rough beast,' Brian, take a look in that top folder."

Brian sat down again and opened the folder as directed. Inside, he found two large, glossy, black and white photographs. The picture on top was a glamorous portrait of a gorgeous, sleek-looking lioness of a woman who reminded him of the sixties sex goddess, Raquel Welch. The other photo was of a man with dark hair and a neatly trimmed beard. Except for his hard, penetrating, almost lunatic eyes, he looked a lot like a TV comic he'd seen from time to time whose name eluded him.

"Who are they?" he asked.

"If all goes horribly wrong, as I fear it might," replied Daisy, "quite probably the next President of the United States and his First Lady. HIS name is Donald Dillon, and even this far in advance of the election, he pretty much has a lock on the Independent Party nomination. The incumbent's still fairly high poll numbers are already in steady decline and are likely to be in the low thirties two years from now. The Democrats don't have anybody credible remotely ready to mount an effective challenge. That means that Dillon, a TV evangelist who calls his ministry—get this—The Blood of God—and who has sworn to scour the heathen Muslim forces from the earth by ANY means—will most likely end up in the White House."

"But surely the voting public has more sense than to elect such a man President."

"Are you kidding? A good-looking, polished, mesmerizing speaker who wraps himself in God and the flag and promises to take on the architects of 9-11 in mortal combat? How can he miss?"

Brian looked at the man in the photo again. "Oh, I place him now. He's one of those late night, obscure channel guys who just sits there yakking about your sending him money so he can save your soul."

Daisy nodded. "That's the one, but he's not the real problem. You'll notice, Brian, that I put the lady's picture on top—and, believe me, that's no lady, that's his wife."

"Bad news? She looks harmless enough. Certainly not hard on the eyes."

"So votes the American male," observed Daisy wryly. "Which means we're dead. Brian, you're looking at the 'rough beast' and she's slouching not toward Bethlehem but toward Washington, D.C. You're looking at Madame Anti-Christ, herself—Arianna Dillon."

"What makes her so fearsome? How do you know . . . oh, she's another one of your early bird specials?"

Daisy chuckled in spite of herself. "Not bad. Yes, Brian. When I set up New Dawn, I deliberately dis-invited one particular group—the Maenads. Do you remember them from your high school mythology?"

Brian pursed his lips and thought a moment. "I think so. Weren't they madwomen who worshipped the wine god, Dionysus?"

"His priestesses, yes. At one point their leader was the Cretan princess Ariadne—a.k.a. Arianna Dillon."

"Time out," said Brian. "I thought Adriadne was one of mythology's good girls. Didn't she help Theseus defeat the bull-man, the Minotaur? Gave him a ball of string or something so he could find his way out of the monster's lair—the maze, the, uh, Labyrinth?"

"True enough, Brian, up to a point—and 'The Labyrinth,' by the way, is the name of the Dillons' Long Island mansion. The myth then goes on to say that Theseus headed back to Athens with her, intending to make her his queen. But then he mysteriously and abruptly dumped her when his ship put in at Naxos, an island in the Aegean Sea—an island that was infested with Dionysus worshippers. It seems Ariadne went partying while she was there, and in the wee hours Theseus discovered her dispensing her favors at an orgy as the focal point of what is crudely known as a gangbang. He left her there in disgust, and Ariadne signed on full time with the Maenads. In no time, she became their leader."

"The mythology books don't include any of that, do they?"

"No, but it's there if you read between the lines. Mary Renault, the novelist, brilliantly did so in *The King Must Die*. In that book, you get the REAL Ariadne. Anyway, let's move on. Take a look at what's inside the next folder—for which I apologize in advance. It's highly unsavory."

Opening the folder, Brian saw instantly what Daisy meant. He found himself looking at a photograph of three people—an adult male and a teenage couple. All three were lying naked on a waterbed.

"What's the context of this?" he said, not sure he was ready for the answer.

Daisy said, "That was taken just last night at the Dillon mansion. It's a prime example of Arianna's remarkable approach to fund-raising. Every Friday night for the past year or so, she has secretly sponsored a rave—a drug party at her home. Her 'guests' pay at the door to get in—and the money goes into a secret account earmarked for the 'Dillon for President' campaign. As a bonus, the hostess at some point in the evening catches several unlucky guests disporting themselves as you see there. They pay thousands to get back the picture and the negative. They don't know they've also been videotaped, as well, so Arianna can do some double-dipping when money gets tight, as it inevitably will just before the election. Then she can hit the same victims again. The people in that picture, by the way, are a prominent Wall Street banker and two teenage television stars."

"So how did YOU get hold of it?" Brian asked.

"We've managed to get someone on the inside, as they say. One of our own—a Dawn Timer. She relays pictures and other pertinent information to us and occasionally is able to get away and make an in-person report. She's excellent, but she's doing a real high wire act. If Arianna ever discovers her, she'll be in terrible danger."

"Then why not pull her out now? Expose the Dillons and abort their campaign before it's even announced?"

Daisy sighed and sank down into the chair opposite him. "Because the raves and the blackmail are just the tip of the iceberg, Brian—or so I firmly believe. I have solid reason to believe that the Dillons are involved in something far worse. I think they're a pair of serial murderers. Which brings us to folder number three."

Speechless, Brian opened the last folder, feeling his finger fumbling nervously as he did so. Inside were three more glossy photos, like the two in the first folder. Each showed a ruggedly handsome young man. They looked like publicity photos made to advance the careers of aspiring actors and models—which, as Daisy now explained, was exactly the case.

"Bachelor number one," she said. "Gerald Anson, an off-Broadway actor, who became Arianna Dillon's lover three years ago. According to our source, he disappeared a year to the day after their involvement began. The same with the next young man, Jeffrey Mallon, a male fashion model. Arianna took up with him the day after Anson disappeared, and the same thing happened. A year later, he vanished—to be replaced by the third man, Derek Dunne, another minor actor, a year ago yesterday. Now it's Derek's turn. He hasn't been seen in the last thirty-six hours. I doubt that he will ever be seen again."

40

Brian heard the horrified awe in his own voice. "What do you make of it? What do you think's going on?"

"Honestly?" replied Daisy. "I think Arianna/Ariadne's sacrificing them to her favorite god, Dionysus. I think she's butchering them according to ancient Cretan custom. If I'm correct, she's slaying them somewhere on her estate, probably with a copy of an ancient weapon called the labrys—a double-headed ax. So far, I'm going on only circumstantial hunch—but I'll bet that what's left of those poor boys is buried somewhere on the premises."

"But why would she DO such a monstrous thing—particularly given her political ambitions—and with the modern media's voracious appetite for digging up celebrity dirt? Is she totally crazy?"

"You have to ask? 'Totally' doesn't begin to do Arianna justice."

Brian pondered all he'd been told for a couple of minutes. Daisy left him to his thoughts and kept silent.

Finally, he spoke. "What about Dillon himself. What's HIS level of involvement?"

"I can't be sure, yet. Remember, even my fears about his wife are only informed supposition. I think she's acting out the darker aspects of the ancient beliefs—enacting the role of the Great Mother herself, taking a year-king consort who stands in for Dionysus, copulating with him one final time, then killing and dismembering him, so that his blood will fertilize the Mother, who will then reproduce the vines and other crops. As far as Dillon himself goes, he's surely in on the drugs-and-blackmail business—but I don't know if he's involved with these disappearances, or even aware of his wife's activities. However, our informant has recently stumbled onto an ominous coincidence. Dillon has employed a series of female co-hosts, at least a dozen of them, on his TV show. All apparently have been rootless show business hopefuls with no known family ties; many have been provided, like the three young men, with a roof over their heads at the Dillon estate, and all have then abruptly vanished both from the TV screen and the Labyrinth. Yet Dillon himself is no Dawn Timer—which means he may be into his own private, entirely separate dementia. We need more proof, obviously."

"Ah! And that's where I come in?"

Daisy nodded.

In spite of the warm night, Brian felt a harrowing chill.

"What kind of assignment do you have in mind for me?"

"An appropriate one that draws on your writing and investigative skills. My plan involves spending the next few months providing you with a mountain of background information on our dynamic duo—then we sic you on Arianna."

"How do 'we' manage that?"

"One of my aunts on the council—who originally was Clio, the Muse of History—is the editor-in-chief of *Trendsetter,* the big, glossy arts and fashion monthly. I picture her shortly 'hiring' you as an ace investigative reporter assigned to the political beat. And as such, once Dillon makes his presidential quest official, we send you in for a major interview/profile of the candidate and the little woman. You get to ask pointed questions and request a tour of the grounds. Besides, how can Arianna help 'opening up,' shall we say, for a man who looks a little bit like Mel Gibson?"

"Now wait a minute, Daisy! This sounds like it could be very—*Mel Gibson?* You really think so?"

"Just a bit. Very similar ears, it seems to me."

"But what if she's INTO ears—and starts sizing me up as her next-year-king?"

Daisy turned somber. "Brian, I have to level with you. That IS the plan. Our agent inside is currently stymied. We need an attractive male who will appeal to this monster and be clever enough over time to gain her confidence. On the other hand,

I can't deny that there's enormous danger involved. I have the . . . means, I think you know by now, to look after you, up to a point. The question is—can you accept that kind of help from a woman? I happen to think that you can—that you're not a man subsumed by your male ego."

Brian lowered his head, then looking up, said, "Daisy, assuming you're right—and I think you have to admit that a lot of what you claim sounds a little over the top—why not turn these photographs over to the police and let them take it from there? This all sounds like it could get way out of hand."

"Brian, do you feel comfortable entrusting the future of the planet to the Long Island police? Because, while I don't claim that my instincts are infallible, I have a gut feeling about this situation that makes extreme measures, in my view, vital. With or without you, I will do everything I can to stop Donald Dillon from assuming the highest office in the land."

What could he do? She was so pretty and so tiny and so ferocious that, finally, he could only say yes.

"Thank you, Brian," she said simply, reaching forward and clasping his hands. She stood up. "Well, I think this has been a productive little conference, but I know you have a lot of concerns that need to be addressed if you're going to feel at all comfortable with the task ahead. Why don't we get together yet again after my final performance here tomorrow night? Maybe if it's nice out, we could take a moonlit stroll on the beach and iron things out? What do you say?"

They both stood up, and Brian gathered the picture folders up and handed them to her.

"A midnight walk on the beach alone with Daisy Crandall? At long last, woman, have you no mercy?"

Daisy laughed, well pleased, and taking his hand, walked with him inside and toward the door of her suite, setting the folders on the sofa on the way. At the doorway, Brian turned and, wondering if lightning could strike indoors, impulsively bent down and kissed her.

Daisy looked up full of apparent delight.

"Well, Daisy, you did tell me earlier to 'go for it.' My will be done, you said."

Her eyes sparkled. "I did say that, didn't I?" Then she reached up in turn, drew his face down to hers, and kissed him sweetly and for a very long time.

Withdrawing her lips, she said, "Don't let that go to your head."

"Don't worry," Brian replied. "That didn't go anywhere NEAR my head!"

"Good NIGHT, Brian!" Daisy laughed with mock outrage, shoving him playfully out the door and closing it behind him.

A moment later, Daisy still stood with her back to the door, barricading it, as if she expected Brian to force his way back in. She closed her eyes and felt a smile spreading across her face.

"Goodnight, my love," she said softly.

Her eyes popped open in shock.

WHAT?!!?

Oh, Dear Mother, what had she just heard herself say?

Then she realized she was tremulous, that her stomach was aflutter with excitement—and that she had never felt quite so happy in her entire life.

Sighing and feeling delightfully shaky, she began to walk toward the bedroom, undressing as she went. Heading into the bathroom, she caught sight of her naked body in the full-length mirror on the back of the door. She stopped and backed up and made a highly satisfactory appraisal of her attributes. She pictured Brian's eyes wandering appreciatively over her body, and then his hands, . . . and then perhaps . . .

She snapped out of it suddenly and wrinkled her nose at her image.

"Good NIGHT, Daisy!" she said and went in to take her shower.

Five

Arianna would have to go next, Donald Dillon thought angrily—the woman was out of control, totally gonzo. He straightened up, perspiring with his exertions, and stretched his aching back. He looked down and surveyed with some satisfaction his handiwork—the tamped-down earth that covered the head, limbs, bones, organs, and entrails of a human entity recognizable only a few, short hours before as a young, out-of-work actor named Derek Dunne. Next to the shallow-covered grave were the now faded outlines of two similar holes, the final abodes of Arianna's two previous year-kings, as she called them.

Dillon stood in a twelve-foot-wide tunnel originally constructed in the nineteenth century for the temporary concealment of escaped southern slaves. It was walled with original granite rocks of various sizes and shapes but, unlike the large subterranean cavern through the wide double door to his left, it was lit by electricity. A hundred yards to his right, Dillon knew, the winding tunnel ended in a short wooden ramp that led up to the wide sliding door of the large barn that was the headquarters of the entirely fraudulent Blood of God compound. When he was finished here, he would exit in that direction—stopping enroute to harvest his mad wife's next year-king. *Kyle,* he thought—*Kyle Webber would serve and service her nicely.*

He stepped now into the wider chamber, his wife's infernal rec room. He thought back to the moment a few hours earlier when he had awakened alone in bed and wondered where Arianna was. Then he'd remembered through the haze of a hangover what night it was. Sighing he'd gotten up, dressed again,

46

found the spare key to the cellar, and headed downstairs. Sure enough, he could see dim, wavering torchlight edging the door as he'd unlocked it.

As he descended the cellar stairs, he'd known pretty much what he would see—his own private Lady Macbeth, naked, dripping in blood and caked in dirt, briskly carrying bits of Derek Dunne like chopped firewood from the altar to the tunnel, where she threw them down for him to dispose of. When she became aware of her husband's presence, she stopped whistling.

"About time!" she snapped. "Take over, will you? I've got to get cleaned up and grab a couple of hours sleep. I wish you'd be a little more considerate."

So saying, she tossed a forearm in the general direction of the tunnel opening, glared at him and, sweeping by him, climbed the stairs and pushed through into the darkened house above.

Now Dillon felt another surge of anger. Why couldn't she be more discreet? He didn't really mind her little pastimes and excesses, but perpetrating them at home was really pushing her luck—and, much more importantly, his. Now that national celebrity was only a few months away, and the White House within a couple of years' striking distance, they couldn't risk exposure as serial murderers.

Why in hell couldn't she follow his example? HIS kills were quick, clean, and, most significantly, carried out far from this place in the anonymous depths of midtown Manhattan. His own tastes ran to petite blondes, would-be actresses and models who haunted the "cattle calls"—mass auditions for roles in upcoming plays or for commercials at the major ad agencies. Once a month, Dillon would "raid" an audition, cull out a likely-looking prospect, and offer her a lucrative assignment as the new co-host of his syndicated TV program that aired five nights a week in the early morning hours throughout the country to ever-growing audiences of evangelical Christians.

The girl's on-camera assignment would be to sit opposite Dillon and read anecdotal "letters" from viewers testifying to the efficacy of The Blood Of God ministry in shoring up their lives in moments of desperate personal crisis, usually involving bank foreclosures on homes or terminal illness. After each letter, Dillon and his partner would alternate in petitioning for further financial backing from the vast TV audience of hinterland rubes so that the sacred work of the ministry could proceed apace—concluding the appeal by fervently murmuring in unison, "Thank you, Jesus." Once out of camera range, they would then head by separate routes to Dillon's room in a Times Square family hotel and fornicate like minks.

To make his initial tender of employment even more attractive, Dillon would offer his new co-host free weekend room and board on the grounds of the Long Island estate he and his wife owned. During the workweek, of course, when Dillon stayed in town and taped his show, she spent the nights with him. When audience enthusiasm for the new girl waned or his own interest in her flagged, he would strangle her in a deserted section of parking garage before their Friday drive back to Long Island, pop her into his trunk, and finally, at a dark and solitary hour, dump her over the side of a backwoods bridge into a deep, sluggish estuary. So far, the by now routine procedure had worked flawlessly.

If there were times when he questioned his own behavior and wondered if he did indeed possess a dark side, he simply reasoned that he was, at bottom, a human being—with certain urges. After all, holier-than-thou's such as Martin Luther King, Jim Bakker, Jimmy Swaggart, and Jesse Jackson had all succumbed to fleshly lust now and again—yet after an initial flurry of bad press, most had come sailing through and retained the only slightly stained admiration of their respective flocks. Then how much more worthy was he, who, with skill and foresight, summarily eliminated any problem areas in his past? He consistently saw to it that no woman would ever surface—literally—to file against him a rape charge or paternity suit.

The military analogy he occasionally invoked to himself when an irritating smidgeon of conscience fleetingly engaged his thought processes was extremely helpful. Just as any military general worthy of the name thought nothing of sending hundreds, possibly thousands of ordinary foot soldiers to their deaths in the service of a larger cause, so a prominent commander in God's army was certainly justified in sacrificing the occasional grunt for the good of a grand and cosmic vision, even one as largely undefined as his own. After all, who were Arianna's young stallions or his little fillies but starry-eyed, blank-brained waifs, flocking from distant farms and villages to the big town, deserting family and friends, changing their names, selling their bodies and souls merely in the shabby hope of securing personal fame, fortune, and self-aggrandizement? At the end of the day, he provided their trivial little lives with a larger purpose before snuffing them out.

Returning to the tunnel, Dillon retrieved his pick and shovel and headed for its far terminus. Here he slid back a wide door on its track and entered a huge barn that had been converted into a dormitory with half-a-dozen small bedrooms, three on each side of a central hallway. Toward the rear of the structure were a communal kitchen, a shower, and men's and women's lavatories. The open front section of the barn still retained its original, wide-planked flooring and a couple of empty stalls that had once accommodated more conventional livestock.

Dillon securely padlocked the door by which he'd entered and stepped into one of the little rooms where a vacuously good-looking giant reclined on his bunk bed, furrowing his brow over a crossword puzzle. His name was Kyle Webber, and until recently, he'd been a weight trainer at the Manhattan gym that Arianna attended twice a week. For the past month he'd served as the Dillons' groundskeeper and handyman.

"Good morning, Kyle," said Dillon. "Interested in moving up in the world?"

"Well, yeah, sure, I guess," observed Kyle.

"Good! That's the spirit! It turns out Derek Dunne handed in his notice yesterday morning. Said he had to return to Iowa to look after his sick, elderly mother. So we're short a chauffeur. What do you say? Want the job?"

"Yeah, sure, I guess. So Derek split, huh? Bambi June and I have been wondering where he was."

Speaking of Bambi June, a pretty little blonde who seemed no more cerebral than Kyle emerged from the kitchen dressed in a halter top and short shorts.

"Oh, hi, Bambi June," said Dillon pleasantly. "Don't forget we've got a date bright and early Monday morning. Got to get in to the studio by nine."

"Sure thing, Reverend. I'll be ready," smiled the girl. Dillon winked at his current co-host, but, obviously, made no mention of the fact that she wouldn't be coming back there—or anywhere else after next Friday. Her option wasn't being picked up—except, perhaps, by the Almighty.

Turning his attention back to Kyle, he said, "So, why don't you report to Mrs. Dillon up at the house in an hour or so? I suspect she may want you to give her a lift."

Kyle said that he'd be there, and Dillon, feeling that he'd already done a good morning's work, headed for the house himself.

In the meantime, Arianna, looking relaxed and drop-dead gorgeous after a mere two hours sleep, was huddled in her kitchen with her special assistant, Rhonda Raveneaux. Both

women were seated having their second cup of coffee and por-
ing studiously over a single page computer printout.

"This never showed up before?" asked Arianna, seeming
concerned but also intrigued.

"I swear," responded Rhonda. "I've been all over the Web
for the past two months searching for any references to New
Dawn and have barely even seen the two words together before.
Now, all of a sudden, this very specific-seeming site."

"Meaning?"

"Well, here you are getting all these harassing calls from
someone calling you by the Greek name 'Ariadne' and warning
you about The Great Mother. It's almost as if this is aimed
directly at you and you alone."

"You make a valid point," Arianna finally conceded. "Well,
thanks, Rhonda. Let me puzzle over this on my own for a
while—then we'll take it from there."

Rhonda saw that she was being dismissed and left the
room. The moment she was out of sight, Arianna visibly sagged
in her chair. *What the HELL was this?* She stared again at the
sheet that consisted of nothing but a title followed by a vertical
list of names.

New Dawn

The Great Mother and Her Council

Aellopos
Aglaia
Aglaophone
Antiope
Calliope
Clio
Euphrosyne

Euterpe
Hippolyta
Kelaino
Okypete
Peisinoe
Penthesilia
Thalia
Thelxepeia

A shudder went through Arianna. If she were right about the list—that, as Rhonda had suggested (known?), it was an Internet message directly targeting her—then she and Donald were in very serious trouble. For this appeared to be nothing less than a powerful coalition of Dawn Timers like herself formed for the express purpose of derailing the Dillon presidential campaign.

Grabbing a pen from the counter behind her, Arianna began unscrambling and decoding the strange list of alphabetized names.

Aellopos—Harpy—Swift storm
Aglaia—Grace—Splendor
Aglaophone—Siren—Beautiful voice
Antiope—Amazon queen
Calliope—Muse of Epic Poetry
Clio—Muse of History
Euphrosyne—Grace—Happiness
Euterpe—Muse of Music
Hippolyta—Amazon queen, her sister Antiope's successor
Kelaino—Harpy—Howling dark
Okypete—Harpy—Swift wing
Peisinoe—Siren—Persuader
Penthesilia—Amazon general—fought at Troy
Thalia—Grace—Comedy
Thelxepeia—Siren—Soothing voice

Having finished, Arianna sat back and sighed. So what did she have here? Then almost instantly she saw it—the pattern. The council was formed of fifteen women evenly representing five separate Dawn Time groups—the Harpies, the Graces, the Sirens, the Amazons, and the Muses. No Maenads, though. *Hmmm.* A nearly perfect blend of light and dark, sweet and menacing forces. And if the web site's subheading were to be taken literally, then one of these little darlings was The Great Mother herself, either the guiding force behind the coalition's formation or elected from its membership.

Okay, let's go with that. Which group would most likely provide a capable leader? Obviously not the Harpies—too strident and polarizing. Ditto the Amazons—too militant. They would already have lobbed a SCUD missile into the middle of Long Island. On the other hand, the sweet little cookie pie Graces lacked the stern discipline needed even to run a meeting. Similarly, the Muses would be too sedate, matronly—nonconfrontational.

Ah, of course. The Sirens. Mythology's good-bad girls. Lovely to look at, deadly to hold. Sweet, seductive, promising, withholding—Multifaceted Femininity Incarnate. They were neatly central to the coalition. They could both sweet-talk the Muses and Graces and promise the thrill of battle, of red meat, to the Harpies and Amazons.

Arianna, you ARE good! Now which of the three Sirens would most likely be Big Bad Mama? Her best guess, once she zeroed in on the A-list, would have to be Peisinoe—the Persuader—most likely a sharp corporate lawyer who could hammer her points home to the others with force and logic. On the other hand, her smoother talking sister—Thelxepeia—a psychoanalyst, maybe?—might combine the requisite leadership skills with the ability to calm and smooth the Harpies' easily ruffled feathers.

Just then, Dillon entered the kitchen, having showered, shaved and cleaned up.

"Good morning, sweetmeats! I trust you're well rested. I've tidied up the cellar for you."

Arianna got up to pour herself a third cup of coffee. She nodded at the sheet of paper on the table. "Take a look at that. What do you think?"

Dillon gave it a glance. "Looks like Greek to me."

Arianna groaned. "Don't try to be clever, Donald. It gives me a migraine. God KNOWS what it must do to you."

Unperturbed by her sneering, Dillon went to the refrigerator. Whistling, he withdrew a cardboard container of orange juice and poured himself a glass.

"So educate me. What do YOU think it means?"

"I THINK, Donald, that we could be in the soup. Unless I'm seriously off base, a consortium of my colleagues from the Dawn Time have your little presidential run right in their crosshairs."

"Oh for God's sake, Arianna! Are you still pushing that demented Shirley MacLaine mythological twaddle about being the reincarnation of the princess Ari—whoever? Get a grip!"

"Oh, yeah, right! This from a man who yells, 'Thank you, Jesus!' every time he has a bowel movement!"

"Fine, darling, you worry your wacko little head about it. I'll be in my study." He headed out of the room. Then he paused in the doorway. "Oh, better gird—or ungird—your Dawn Time loins. Your next year-king will be along in about fifteen minutes. Toodles!"

Arianna glared after him then refocused on her puzzle. Which of the two Sirens . . . Jesus and Dionysus!! With a startled yelp, she nearly spilled her coffee. She stared fixedly at the list. There it was hitting her right smack in the eyes!

Aglaophone! Beautiful voice!

Aglaophone! The obscure little princess from some postage stamp-sized Greek river kingdom, whose underground fame had spread like wildfire throughout the ancient Mediterranean world. Virgin-priestess to the raped grain goddess, Persephone, Queen of the Dead. A girl who'd wedded her mother Terpsichore's balletic grace to the craft and wiry strength of her father Achelous, a bull-king, like Ariadne's own father, Minos of Crete. A girl who could sing like a goddess and dance and leap with the bulls. The exiled princess who single-handedly had nearly saved the gentle Sicilian shore folk, the Cyclopes, from the vicious and predatory pirate, Odysseus. A girl, it was rumored, who could summon lightning and thunder at will—as if she'd been The Great Mother herself.

Aglaohone—who, if Homer had been a woman—might well have become Legend's greatest heroine. But the humiliated Odysseus had successfully spread his lies and tall tales throughout an aggressive and gullible world of barbaric and ignorant men—and the princess and her twin sisters had instead come down through the ages as malevolent seductresses.

Arianna pulled herself up short. That was quite enough praise for a woman who was obviously out to undo her!

Alright, Great Mother. I know now who you were.

Now—who ARE you?

Six

The cool sand squished deliciously between their naked toes as Daisy and Brian walked hand-in-hand down Evanston's Crown Point Beach under the benevolent glimmer of a full moon. Brian wore a polo shirt and slacks, Daisy a light summer dress of green and gold. They had left their shoes behind them on a secluded bench on the lower boardwalk that bordered the sand.

Daisy was exhilarated. Brian had delighted and surprised her by coming to her final performance at the Civic Center. She had responded by singing all evening for him and him alone—while, of course, managing to give every other male in her audience the identical impression about himself. As a chanteuse that was her job—as a Siren it was infallibly her nature.

As they walked, they finalized arrangements for their up-coming venture. It was agreed that Brian would spend the next week or so winding up his affairs in Evanston, which mainly involved subletting his apartment. As an independently wealthy writer sporting a long-term book contract with a major publishing house—and no local emotional ties—he felt he'd have no problem making any adjustment to the new lifestyle which Daisy was presenting to him.

Brian was to come and live at the shoreline estate that Daisy shared with her sisters Pamela and Teresa an hour or so down the Connecticut coast from Evanston. There was a small, fully furnished guest bungalow down by the private beach fronting the property that would serve as both his home and his office. He would be placed on the payroll of Teresa's talent agency as Daisy's "publicist" and paid a handsome retainer for maintaining computerized archives of her engagements and critical notices, as well as occasionally updating her official biography for publication in theater programs. Unofficially, his job would be to join forces with Daisy in doing everything humanly possible to deep-six the presidential ambitions of Donald and Arianna Dillon.

As their discussion of these arrangements drew to a close, Daisy stopped abruptly and pulled him up short.

"Oh, Brian, I'm sorry," she said softly.

"What?" he asked, puzzled.

"Look where we are," she said, holding her head down. Then he realized she was alluding to the fact that they were standing where his brother had died all those years before.

Tightening his grip on her hand, Brian said, "Daisy, I must have visited this spot a thousand times on my own. It's all right."

"Then say it!" she said with startling fervor and deep anguish in her voice. In the refracted moonlight he saw her soft eyes brimming with tears.

"Say what?" he asked, genuinely perplexed.

"Say that you grant me absolution. You haven't said it."

"Daisy, I'm not a priest. But, of course, I'll say it—and mean it. You've already made mincemeat of my heart and soul. How can I deny you forgiveness for something I don't really blame you for? You only meant to save your sisters—not to kill my brother. Besides, you did save MY life, in the process. You were a frightened child, trying to marshal uncanny gifts you knew you possessed but couldn't yet control."

"What you say is true," Daisy said sadly. "But that makes it all the more horrible. Because I panicked, I wasn't thinking. If I had been, I would have realized that my sisters were in no danger at all. It's just that with the suddenness of the two boys' attack, they were momentarily caught off guard."

"I guess I'm not following you. I don't know how far things would have gone, but as I recall, they were pretty helplessly pinned down, and . . ."

He saw that Daisy was emphatically shaking her head.

"No, Brian. You see, when we access the Mother—to use the modern term—we tap into not only enormous psychic energy but exceptional physical strength as well."

Brian felt himself smiling skeptically. "You mean, you all start bursting at the seams and turn green? The Incredible Hulkettes?"

That seemed to snap Daisy out of her guilt trip. "No, you sexist swine! What it MEANS is that if I hadn't shown up when I did, the BEST scenario your brother and his friend could have hoped for was to spend one week in traction instead of three."

Then she instantly became subdued again. "That was a sick thing to say—considering what DID happen to them. I'm sorry."

"Daisy, don't go punishing yourself anymore over this. It's long since done with and can never be reversed. Besides, you've pretty much convinced me in the last two days that in a sense—given the very special circumstances of your existence—it was an extraordinary but 'natural' event." He lifted her chin up so that he could see her eyes. "So forget it, please. You stand absolved."

"Thank you, Brian," she whispered.

They turned around at this point and began to walk back up the beach.

"One thing you haven't mentioned is how the three of you happened to be here that day. When I gave my hysterical account to the police and mentioned three young girls, they checked around the entire beach community. No children were ever reported missing in the wake of the freak storm. Nobody had a daughter named Beatrice."

"No," answered Daisy. "We lived then where we live now. Our mother, who sang opera professionally around Connecticut, was just making a day trip up here to visit her elderly voice coach in a nursing home. She knew about the beach and decided to bring us along and drop us off here for a treat. That was considered safe back in those days—leaving three young girls alone in a big public place." Daisy gave a humorless little laugh. "It never occurred to Mom that it was everyone ELSE who was in danger."

Brian drew them both to a halt. "Whoa. Are you saying that your mother was unaware of your nature? Your abilities? Then she wasn't one of you?"

"No, Mom was a civilian. Dad was a Dawn Timer, though. Did you ever hear of the Aurora Cruise Line? It specializes in Mediterranean island-hopping cruises. Dad—his name was Arthur Beaumont—founded and operated it. He had a dozen ships sailing out of New York and several European ports, so we were all financially set for life."

"And who was he . . . originally?"

"Achelous, king of the land surrounding the largest river in Greece—which bears his name. Our original mother was the Muse of Dance, Terpsichore. She's not currently incarnated, though three of her sisters are on my council."

"Of course," said Brian, feeling, as he had so often in the last two days, not a little surreal. After a moment, he asked, "So what happened afterward? That day, I mean. Did you tell your parents?"

"Not Mom, since she would have just thought we were raving. However, we were all crying hysterically when she came to pick us up. Of course, the whole beach was a madhouse, with police and ambulances all over the place. We tearfully told her about the storm—how we'd seen two boys get killed by lightning. She was quite shaken up herself, naturally, but spent the drive home trying to calm us down.

"Facing Dad was another story. By the time we got home, the story was all over the TV news. He asked Mom to excuse the rest of us, then took us into his study. He knew where we'd been and guessed at our involvement. I told him everything truthfully. He sent Pamela and Teresa to go get their supper—then he lit into me. He shouted at me that I had been very irresponsible with my special gifts—that I had caused a terrible tragedy and great suffering to the families of those two boys. I sobbed throughout his tirade and when he was finished, I asked if he were going to call the police and have me put in jail.

"Then do you know what he did, Brian?" Daisy turned to face him, and in the moonlight, he could see the dreamy smile on her face. "He sat down in his favorite armchair and sat me on his lap. He told me that would do no good since no one would ever believe a little girl could cause what had happened—and besides, he said, he would never let anyone put me in jail or harm me in any way. It would remain our secret—ours and Pamela's and Teresa's. Then he hugged me so hard I could hardly breathe and told me he had another secret for me—one that I must never tell my sisters because it would hurt their feelings. Did I promise? I solemnly did so between sniffles—and then he told me that I had always been his favorite daughter, both then and in the Dawn Time—and that I always would be for as long as the world survived. When he said it, he was crying, too."

"You sound like you love him very much. Is he still alive?"

"No. Both my parents are gone now."

Brian and Daisy resumed walking in silence, their hands tightly clasped. Then as if on cue, they stopped in their tracks. Turning again toward each other, they suddenly fell into an abandoned embrace. Brian began pulling them both down to the sand; but Daisy gave a muffled protest and pulled away.

"What's the matter?" Had he offended her?

"Not here, alright? Let's . . . let's go back to the hotel."
Daisy looked nervous. More than nervous—frightened.

"Sure, Daisy. Look, I didn't mean to alarm you. If I misunderstood your signals, I'm . . ."

"No!" Daisy laughed skittishly. "You've picked up my signals, just fine. I know I'm behaving oddly—but, please, Brian, could we go back to my room now?"

"Of course," said Brian, taking her hand again. They retrieved their shoes and put them on, then returned to the hotel. All the way back and up in the elevator, Daisy remained silent, oddly distant. Brian couldn't shake the feeling that she was very afraid of something—that this extraordinary woman had yet one more surprise in store for him, one she was extremely reluctant to reveal.

Inside the room, she turned to him and kissed him sweetly at first; then more aggressively, till they were both loudly panting and pawing at each other. Then again, Daisy broke away, but the strangeness and the fear had vanished.

She smiled. "Okay, I can do this now!"

The odd statement took them both by surprise, and they laughed. Then Brian swept her up in his arms and headed for the bedroom. The door was partially shut, and Brian had to shift her weight a little in order to give it a playfully dramatic kick.

"I guess this is Rhett and Scarlett time," Daisy observed.

"Frankly, my dear," said Brian, unintentionally sounding more like W.C. Fields than Clark Gable, "YES!"

Five minutes later, when they lay side by side in the bed as man and woman had since the Dawn Time itself was still ages in the future, Brian did indeed discover that Daisy had been holding one last surprise about herself in reserve, a surprise meant for him alone, a surprise that was wondrous yet somehow heartbreaking.

Daisy Crandall was a virgin.

Later, as she lay in his arms—after her great awakening, and after the sublime ecstasy she had put both of them through, and after her tears had all dried—Brian had a question for her.

"Why?"

"I honestly don't know," she whispered. "It must have been wired into me, programmed into my brain, ever since my original life. The same for my sisters, I suppose. From girlhood on, we were all dedicated to the Mother. Just as Christians speak of the Trinity—God the Father, the Son, and the Holy Ghost—so the Mother was often thought of in three guises. She was Demeter, the Grain Goddess, responsible for all things that grow on Earth; She was the daughter, the Corn Maiden, known as Kore; and She was Hecate, the Crone, the wise but fearsome grandam spoken of by MEN as the queen of witches.

"So anyway, my sisters and I were the virgin priestesses of Kore, the Maiden—and as such, we happened to be on hand for one of the biggest of all Dawn Time events. One day, while the three of us were at the shrine, a troop of soldiers led by Odysseus, the young king of the nearby island of Ithaca, stormed in, bronze swords unsheathed. Under orders of the High King Agamemnon, we were informed, the Maiden Kore was no longer to be worshipped. Her shrine was to be demolished and her image removed and taken away so that She could become the bride and therefore the servant of the Lord of the Dead, Hades. Henceforth, we were told, She would be known as Persephone.

"We were terrified—we were only children! A couple of the soldiers were leering at us. Thankfully, Odysseus seemed to take pity on us and warned them off. Then they rode away. But the rape of Persephone soon became a scandal that spread throughout Greece—and as young as we were, my sisters and I were widely condemned for standing by and letting it happen.

The fact that our father was the local king couldn't save us. We were perceived, like Jonah in the Bible, as cursed. As long as we were around, it was rumored, no crops could grow. Demeter the Mother would blight the land. To save our lives, our parents had us spirited away on a ship one dark night under the protection of a trusted palace guard. We sailed into exile far to the west and were finally set ashore with a few food and clothing supplies somewhere on the eastern coast of Sicily. The ship departed and there we were."

Brian listened to all this in awe. The woman in his arms had actually experienced the events that, transformed millennia ago into fable, were central to the way western civilization viewed itself. Demeter, Persephone, Hades, Odysseus—immortal names that rang down the corridors of the ages—these had once been the everyday coin of Daisy Crandall's existence.

Suddenly, something occurred to him. "Who were YOU?" he asked.

He felt Daisy stiffen slightly beside him, then heard her nervously clear her throat.

"You'll laugh," she said.

"No, I won't, Come on, tell me."

"My name was Aglaophone."

"WHAT?"

"Aglaophone."

Then, despite his best intentions, Brian started to snort and snuffle then shake the bed. Daisy socked him in the ribs.

"I TOLD you you'd laugh," she cried. Then she caught the bug herself, and it was several moments before either of them could get it together.

When they were serious again, Brian pursued his original thought. "But surely you're not claiming that an incident or a lifestyle experienced thousands of years ago could still affect you throughout so many . . . incarnations, is it?"

Daisy appeared to ponder this for quite a while. Then she acknowledged that Brian was right.

"Obviously," she finally said. "For this lifetime, anyway, I've been in deep denial. *Eerrrggghh!* I HATE it when I hear myself using such an asinine catch phrase. But that's the word that fits. All this time, I've somehow managed to persuade myself that MEN were second class citizens, as if I were single-handedly paying your sex back for four thousand years of male domination and chauvinism. My deity's shrine had been defiled—but my body, I assured myself, was an inviolate temple that CONTAINED Her and my voice a sacred gift that I couldn't allow to be diluted by the physical possession of my person by another. How idiotic! Here I've always prided myself on my intellect and my logic—and all the while I was blind to the central fact of the Mother. She is the fertility principle incarnate. She has brought forth all life, and Her aim is to resolve all conflict into final universal harmony—of which the male is as vital a part as the female."

Now she turned to face him, her eyes shining with love. "Think of what you've done for me here tonight, Brian! You've made me a whole being for the first time ever."

Brian was deeply moved by her words but felt a need to lighten the moment.

"Well," he said, "I have to admit that it was an out-of-body experience for me, too."

Daisy looked at him, startled, then hooted with laughter.

"Only a man could define sex THAT way," she said. "So much for a universal, holistic view of gender relations!"

They snuggled together for a while quietly. Then Daisy said, "Remember the other night when I so smugly laid claim to you, body and soul? Well, the opposite is just as true, Brian. You have haunted me and possessed me for forty years. I HAD to save you that day on the beach. From the moment I saw you, I loved you. From the moment I saw you, I KNEW you, somehow! Now I know why.

"Brian, you're a Dawn Timer, too."

He slept and he dreamed. . . .

HE was Brian-but-not-Brian, and the baking noonday sun poured down on him and a roaring, clamorous crowd of several thousand others. He was seated in the royal box of a rectangular amphitheater/courtyard. Around him stretched the luxurious three-tiered gallery of a grand palace. He was twelve years old.

He glanced immediately to his left and saw the beauteous young queen seated gazing down at the games taking place in the sand before her. She was flanked by her stunningly lovely, titian-haired twin daughters of fourteen years. His own father, the head of the palace guard, stood behind her with his six most trusted warriors, all ready to give up their lives if need be to save the king's family.

As he thought of the king, young Brian-but-not-Brian craned his head further to the left and gazed in awe at the ominous looking, giant figure who stood alone upon a stone platform at the far end of the courtyard. The huge man wore the mask and horns of a bull and leaned upon the long hasp of the fearful, double-headed ceremonial ax known as the labrys. This was the king, holding himself in readiness for the sacred act he must perform when the dedicatory games being played out before him and the excited crowd were concluded, only moments from now.

Which brought Brian-but-not- . . . *Aganus!* That was his name! He was Aganus, son of Diomedes, and his attention now focused on the bull-dancers. These comprised a team of six youthful slaves in middle adolescence—three boys and three girls who were in the center of the amphitheater. All six were naked except for their green linen loin cloths. They were concluding their exciting acrobatic routine with the fifteen-hundred-pound bull around which they capered, executing elaborate vaults and somersaults over the confused, bellowing beast. Their act successfully concluded, the young performers accepted the appreciative shouts and plaudits and coins of the amassed audience and disappeared through a door immediately below the royal box.

Next, six muscular animal trainers emerged from the subterranean bullpen to Aganus' far right and began to subdue the gigantic black bull. Two of the men deftly threw loops of ropes over the lethal, foot-long, gold-gilt horns of the animal and pulled back, their corded biceps visibly strained to the uttermost. The four other men remained at the ready, each twosome holding a net. Meanwhile, an expectant hush had descended over the crowd.

Then began a muttered roar that quickly swelled to deafening proportions as from beneath the stands a golden-haired little girl dressed in a short white linen tunic sprinted barefoot out onto the sand, a girl no older than Aganus himself.

The dreamer saw that it was Beatrice-but-not-Beatrice. It was the youngest of the three royal princesses. Turning around, back-pedaling, and circling, she acknowledged the cheers on all sides. Then she ran down to where her father stood and formally bowed before him. After he had inclined his masked head to her in turn, she turned back and approached the center of the courtyard, stopping sixty feet out from the bull. The crowd noise rose to a seismic tumult as the girl stood erect and waited.

When she had satisfied herself that the two men who had tethered the bull's horns were holding his head steady at the proper angle, she gave a slight nod. Then, as the crowd noise increased still further to an impossible crescendo, she began her run at the bull. Seven feet out, then six, then five; she sprang forward once, landed briefly on her toes and vaulted aloft into a forward somersault, soaring deftly between the wicked horns and landing squarely on the animal's shoulders for the barest instant before pushing herself upward again, executing a second flawless flip, descending onto the beast's hindquarters, then, impossibly, lifting off into a third airborne roll before hitting the sand on both feet, her arms extended in triumph symmetrically above her head. A perfect triple!

The sound from the audience reached such an insane volume that it was some time before the dreamer-who-recognized-himself-as-young-Aganus could decipher the relentless chant that must surely be reaching the new sky gods on the high peaks of Mount Olympus. The crowd was deliriously shouting the name of the darling child who had long ago claimed its collective heart.

"Aglaophone!" they cried again and again—and yet again!

Now the girl trotted over to the stands and bowed before her mother and sisters. Then, before disappearing through the door directly below, she turned full circle, waving to the hoarsely cheering throng—and finally, looking straight at Aganus, grinned and winked and waved to him alone.

The boy's heart leaped far higher than the little princess had.

Meanwhile, the bull handlers had netted and wrestled the madly lowing beast down to the platform at the far end of the yard. There, after the priest-king declared the bull an offering to the Great Mother and her son-consort Dionysus, he raised the mighty double-ax and brought it flashing down. . . .

And the dreamer found himself now in the torchlit royal hall. He saw the king and queen surrounded by their three surpassingly lovely daughters, all dressed like their dainty mother in full, diaphanous gowns, their foreheads encased in golden circlets, and their ringletted hair descending in three separate tresses on each side of their heads. Now the dreamer-who-was-Aganus found that he could easily match faces and names. The giant, bearded king was Achelous, ruler of the western Greek kingdom of Aetolia, a man so formidable that only Heracles, the mightiest of champions, had ever bested him in wrestling. His queen, as tiny as her husband was huge, was Terpsichore, whose graceful dancing skills had won her far-flung fame as a demi-goddess whose father was reputedly Zeus himself.

Now the dreamer turned his attention to the three young princesses, who were entertaining their parents and the royal guests with their spellbinding music. This was their habit every evening after the supper hour, while the adults and older children of the court digested their meals and listened entranced to the melodic tales chanted by the girls. One of the twins, Peisinoe, coaxed persuasive music from a fluted pipe she played, music that could turn bouncing and merry or poignant and sorrowful as the narrative of the sung story demanded. Her lyre-strumming sister, Thelxepeia, meanwhile provided alternatively soothing, limpid notes or dramatic string accompaniment, again, according to the dictates of the story.

Although both girls occasionally chimed in with their singing as well, for the most part this was left to the youngest daughter, Aglaophone, the heroine of the bull ring. Tonight she was melting the hearts of her listeners as she sang in her soft and high and bewitching voice the sad story of the lovely Cretan princess Ariadne, who a number of years back, had helped her lover, the Athenian prince Theseus, achieve a life-saving victory over the evil bull-man called the Minotaur—only to find herself betrayed and deserted by him after they'd made their planned escape together.

Aganus felt his eyes watering as Aglaophone brought her song to a close. Looking around the room furtively, he was relieved to see that many of the grown men, including his father and the king himself, were taking hasty, secret swipes at their eyes.

This was not unusual, Aganus knew. Many a visiting foreign king or dignitary had in the past tried to cloak his weeping by jesting with Achelous about how he saved himself the expense of a professional bard by having his beautiful daughters double as court entertainers. In fact, so far flung had their fame as musical seductresses grown in only a few short years that they had begun to be known by the strange foreign word, the SEIRA-ZEIN—meaning "those who tie or bind." Locally, this was shortened to the Sirens.

Now, as if to relieve the melancholy mood, Queen Terpsichore signaled to Peisinoe to strike up a merry ditty on her flute and, leaping to her feet, dragged her husband to his as well. In a moment, everyone in the room was wiping his or her eyes for a different reason, roaring with laughter as the ungainly bull of a man tried to match the dancing, light-footed grace of his tiny partner. Finally, taking pity on him, the smiling queen pushed the grinning, puffing king back into his seat and turned to Aglaophone. Seizing the girl by the hand, she led her without warning across the floor to Aganus and then retreated to her husband's side. Tongue-tied, the two children regarded each other with red faces for a moment before Aglaophone recovered herself and, with a grin, grabbed both his hands and led him to the center of the floor. Aganus' heart was so full, he thought he would burst. . . .

Then in a flash, the golden moment vanished—to be replaced by the blackest pit of nightmare. A dark and gusty night down by the river . . . torches guttering in the wind . . . the lovely queen kneeling on the dock, her head bowed to the ground as she shrieked her grief . . . the king leaning over her, trying desperately to comfort her, to raise her to her feet . . . the royal vessel being cast free of its moorings . . . and on its wind-swept deck, the most pitiless sight of all . . . the three cloaked princesses, their faces open-mouthed and distorted with hysterical crying . . . Aganus' own father hovering protectively behind them, as he prepared, grim-faced, to escort them into exile in the far, unknown, western reaches of the Great Sea—before their father was forced to sacrifice them to the double-ax in order to appease the angry Mother, who had afflicted the land with drought ever since the theft of Her Daughter from Her shrine, the shrine the princesses had failed to protect.

As the ship drifted away into the fathomless dark. Aganus watched in utter despair as the blond little princess he loved disappeared forever from her homeland and his life. Then his heart shut down for good, as he understood that it would never know another moment of light if he lived a thousand years. . . .

Brian awoke with tears streaming down his face, only to see Daisy gazing down at him with a misty-eyed smile.

Tracing one of his tears with her finger, she murmured, "Did you see, gentle Aganus? Did you see?"

Brian could only nod mutely. Then grasping her feverishly, he pushed her back on the bed and rolled atop her. From then until the new dawn arrived, the lyrical and enraptured love they made to each other had never before been dreamt of in ANYONE'S philosophy.

Seven

By rights, the night they'd just spent together should have left them both exhausted, but before sun-up Daisy cried, "Come on, Brian. Let's go!"

"Again?" Brian asked plaintively.

"No, silly! Get dressed! This is a real New Dawn for both of us, and I want to enjoy it to the fullest! Let's go down to the beach!"

He groaned, but Daisy's excitement was infectious, and he climbed somewhat stiffly out of bed. The two hastily threw on the clothes they'd discarded on the floor the previous night and, laughing like teenagers, headed out the door of the suite.

Within five minutes, they were walking arm-in-arm down a boardwalk still pale with just the glimmer of approaching daylight. They were halfway down its length when suddenly Daisy gleefully yelled "Eeeeyyowww!" She broke loose from Brian's grasp, and raced ahead of him. Then, to his astonishment, she executed a pair of cartwheels, providing both him and a strutting seagull with a saucily immodest display of leg and underwear. The first of the acrobatics went according to plan, but the second ended disastrously, as Daisy hit the wooden deck on her backside with a *whump*.

"Ooooff!" she cried.

Brian winced and hurried to her side. "You okay?" he asked.

Daisy laughed as he helped her up. "Yep! But I guess I won't be adding any bull-leaping to my concert appearances!"

When she had set herself and her dress to rights again, they continued their stroll. It wasn't till they got to the pavilion where they'd first met three days earlier that Daisy seemed to take notice of how quiet and pensive Brian was. They stood for a moment leaning their arms on the broad red balustrade of the railing.

"What's wrong?" she finally asked.

"I don't know exactly," Brian responded quietly. "Except that I'm feeling awfully discombobulated. Daisy, what in the world happened last night?"

"Heaven on earth!" she sighed with a little laugh, but Brian refused to be put off.

"Seriously," he said.

"I know," Daisy said, placing her hand over his and clutching it. "In a way, it must be an awful shock to you. Maybe I shouldn't have sprung it on you so abruptly—or in the way that I did."

"What do you mean? Have you known about it long? That I'm . . . one of your kind?"

"One of my kind? We're not vampires, darling! No, seriously, I've probably known subconsciously for a long, long time. On the other hand, the pure fact of it—the sudden insight—didn't hit me till the words were almost out of my mouth."

"Wow!" was all Brian could come up with.

"Exactly," Daisy agreed.

"Then what?"

"What do you mean?"

"I mean, how did we go from your sudden little epiphany to my dreaming BEN-HUR in technicolor and Surround Sound?"

Daisy looked out at the still dark waters of Long Island Sound for a little while. She sighed. "Oh, that. I'm afraid I cheated a little, Brian. I hummed a bit of a tune—'How Much Is That Doggie In The Window?,' I think—and put you . . . to sleep."

"Oh, great!" Brian said quietly. "I suppose I should be grateful you didn't have me put down."

"Do you want me to attempt a serious answer or not?"

"Go ahead."

"Okay, then. I induced you to sleep, and then I . . . downloaded a series of images from my past. From my conscious mind into your subconscious one."

"Just like that?" Brian frowned. "It's discouraging to think that I'm that malleable. Or do I have similar abilities?"

"We ALL do—all men and women—both normal people and 'our kind'."

"Then why aren't we invading each other's interior space all the time? The ultimate Orwellian horror show. Zero privacy—the absolute end of Free Thought."

"Obviously, that would be an intolerable world to live in. But as I tried to explain the other night, ninety-nine percent of humanity lack the mental focus to utilize their unknown natural abilities."

"Thanks, but no thanks. Manipulating other people's minds—arranging their dreams—if I DO have that innate ability, I think I'll take a pass."

Daisy looked hurt. "I'm sorry this is so upsetting to you, Brian. I swear to you I'll never do it again. I guess I was just over-anxious to persuade you that we belonged together—that back in the Dawn Time we'd been very close. I purposely chose mutual memories—vivid moments we'd actually shared."

"Some of your Golden Oldies, I take it."

"If that's how you choose to describe being torn away forever one dark night from your parents and your home—and the boy you loved to distraction—well, yes," Daisy said quietly.

Suddenly, Brian crushed her in his arms. "I'm sorry. Just remembering MY agony at watching you slip way from me into the darkness. . . . I can't begin to imagine the horror you were facing."

"If there is Hell on earth, my sisters and I were there that night," Daisy admitted.

A soft, diffuse pink began to define the horizon to the east.

Eventually, Brian said, "So if I've lived all these past lives—does that mean I'm going to begin remembering them all now?"

"No, most likely not," replied Daisy. "I don't mean this to sound snotty, Brian, but you're not cut out for it. With the exception of Merlin and one or two others, few men I can think of ever have been. Your sex has always been too outer-directed, too aggressive, too involved with getting and spending and conquering and raping and beating up to smell the roses, to reflect, to nurture, and to remember. Name me a schoolboy who doesn't hate history and, thus, refuses to learn from it. Name me a young girl who doesn't, at least in the dewy dawn of her childhood, think she's Snow White. We women were made to carry forward the dreams of our species; you men were made to bend them to your perception and your will—or to destroy them for the rest of us. Thus, the everlasting murders and executions. Thus the Crusades, the Holocaust, and Hiroshima. Thus, the destruction of me and my sisters—so MEN'S religious and political views could prevail. Your way or no way."

"So men bad, women good? Always and forever?" Brian sniped.

"No. It's just that women intuitively see or guess at the eternal connective tissue of the world and want to perpetuate it—men see only their particular time and place in it. Don't know much about History."

Daisy saw that he was sulking.

"Brian, if what I say is false," she said gently, "why'd it take you till last night to even ENVISION a past life? And you're an introspective man—an author who's gotten rich speculating upon the unknown."

74

"And if you're so wrapped up in 'perpetuating the connective tissue of the world,' why'd it take you over three thousand years to spread your legs?"

Daisy blushed and turned away "What a terrible thing to say!" she whispered. Then she gave him a sharp elbow in the ribs. "Good shot, though!" she said with a grin, "and well deserved. I've really gotten on my moral high horse this morning, haven't I? When all I really want is to get you back to bed and have at it again."

Now she really did blush.

"Oops!" she said.

Then suddenly she fell against him and burst into quiet tears. "Oh, Brian, that was wonderful last night!"

He drew her down on a nearby bench and held her. When she grew calm again, they sat and watched as the sky before them turned from pale pink to a deeper, richer hue.

"Well, at least that's ONE thing old Homer got right in *The Odyssey*," remarked Daisy.

"What?"

" 'Rosy-fingered dawn'! Can you think of a more sublime way to describe it?"

Brian silently agreed. Then a moment later, he said, "So tell me all the stuff Homer got wrong."

And so, for the next hour, Daisy did.

The Dawn Time—1250 B.C.

As the hot summer wind called the sirocco buffeted them, the three girls shielded their eyes from the gritty dust swirling up from the dirt road they traveled. Dust and grime caked every inch of them from the crown of their stringy hair to their swollen feet being chafed by their worn sandals. Their meager food supply was running dangerously low, and they had less than half a wineskin of water left among them. The worst thing of all was that they had no idea where they were and only the vaguest of destinations in mind.

The day before, the ship that had carried them westward across the Ionian Sea had finally reached southeastern Sicily. Turning northward along the coast, the vessel had put in at a substantial-looking settlement, lining a natural harbor. The royal emblem of a bull that decorated its single sail had caused a stir on shore, and by the time the ship had pulled up alongside an empty quay, a crowd had gathered. Very shortly thereafter, a self-important man of considerable girth had approached, surrounded by a small retinue of slaves. Diomedes, the head of King Achelous's palace guard, and three of his men had marched down the gangplank to accost him.

The man, who fortunately spoke a Minoan dialect that was at least partially decipherable to Greeks, said his name was Lysander and claimed to be the personal emissary of the local king. Diomedes, in turn, announced his own identity and his mission. A naturally honest man, he told the truth—that it had fallen to him to escort the three young princesses of Aetolia into exile and that Sicily had been decided upon as being far enough away to afford them a safe haven from those who might wish to track them down and harm them.

At this point in Diomedes' recital, Lysander's face darkened and he demanded to know what the offense of the young women had been. When told that they had inadvertently run afoul of the Great Mother and had been condemned to death in their own land, he grew decidedly hostile and, in his master's name, forbade the party permission to disembark. It was obvious that the young women were guilty wretches, and to let them inside the settlement would mean that the curse upon them would be transferred to the local inhabitants.

As if on a pre-arranged signal, Diomedes and his three henchmen unsheathed their bronze swords. While the others held Lysander's retinue and the rest of the crowd at bay, Diomedes quickly stepped behind the portly official and with one arm around his chest held the sword edge to the man's throat. He bade Lysander look at the three princesses as they stood clustered forlornly amidships. The man did so and then coolly brushed Diomedes' sword aside with his hand. His face softened.

"They are very young," he said.

"True," said Diomedes. "And right now, you and I are the only friends they have in this part of the world. In the week we've been at sea, the crew tried twice to throw them overboard when my men and I couldn't keep our eyes open any longer. Do you have anything to suggest?"

Lysander sighed. "Sail north for roughly two hours, and you'll find an isolated harbor along the shore road. You can put in and leave them off there. About a day's walk further along, they will come to a villa owned by a mysterious Cretan lady, something of an exile herself, as I understand it. She is known by the name of Circe. She is said to be very beautiful—but I can't say much for her morals. Rumor has it that she keeps her home well-stocked with handsome, indolent young men. Hardly the place I would normally recommend for the young ladies—but it's the best I can do. As I indicated before, it would be taboo to admit them here—and risk the Mother's wrath."

It was Diomedes' turn to sigh. "Well, maybe they can at least get a decent meal there and some directions that will do them some good. Thanks, friend. Sorry I misjudged you."

He nodded to his men to sheathe their swords and get back on board. As he began to follow them up the gangplank, Lysander called to him. As Diomedes turned, the man untied the bulging purse he wore at his waist and tossed it to him.

"That should help a little," he said.

And so things had transpired. They had found the harbor, and three of the rowers had carried the girls ashore. Diomedes had slogged through the gentle surf to say his farewells. Embracing each of the three in turn, he struggled valiantly to keep his voice steady as he rehearsed Lysander's directions with them and gave them the purse. He also warned them about getting off the road if they heard anyone approaching and made sure each girl showed him her dagger. It was at that point that Aglaophone said the first words she'd uttered since the sad voyage had begun.

"Say goodbye to Aganus for me."

"I will, Lady," said Diomedes—and that was all he could manage. Blinded by tears, he resolutely turned his back on the trio and waded back to the ship.

Finally, the vile wind started to die down, and the girls began to make better progress. Peisinoe and Thelxepeia walked side by side, trying to keep their spirits up, hoping with each twist and bend in the shore road that the villa they'd been told about would materialize. The real trouble was Aglaophone. After her brief remark to Diomedes, she'd lapsed back into the morbid, total silence that she'd maintained for eight days and nights. They were beginning to be afraid that she'd never snap out of it. Then what would they do?

Peisinoe turned and looked back to where her younger sister lagged a hundred feet behind, her head bent down, apparently taking no notice of anything.

"Come on, Phonny!" she called. "You've got the food! I'm hungry!"

The girl lifted her head and obligingly quickened her pace. When she reached the other two, she unslung the food pouch from her shoulder and handed it over without interest. The three sat down wearily under a bent old oak tree and dug out some stale bread and cheese. As they ate, they stared out across the sunny blue water toward Aetolia. Thinking of the parents they would never see again, Peisinoe and Thelxepeia began to cry. Then pulling themselves together, they passed around the wineskin and took carefully rationed sips of water.

"We'd better find that house soon," said Thelxepeia. "Or at least a spring."

With a sigh, Peisinoe got to her feet. The other two joined her. The girls took turns going behind the tree to relieve themselves then resumed their journey. An hour later, toward mid-afternoon, they crested a steep rise in the hilly road and saw it. Off to the left, at the foot of the hill behind a grove of fruit trees, stood a sprawling, flat-roofed, three-storied building of white dressed stones trimmed with red timbers.

Thelxepeia started to cry again. "It looks like Father's palace," she whispered.

A moment later they entered the unguarded grounds and approached the villa. As they walked along, they glanced with curiosity at the fruit-laden trees that lined both sides of the path. The boughs held hundreds of little round orange-colored spheres.

"I wonder what they are," said Peisinoe. "They look like the golden apples that Heracles went looking for in the story."

Silently, Aglaophone stepped to the side of the road, picked three of the mysterious apples from their boughs, and popped them into the pouch.

Now as they drew near the house, they saw that the big double doors were wide open. They began to feel apprehensive and wondered how they should proceed. The twins reviewed between them the laws of hospitality as they sized up their bedraggled appearance. This was going to require some finesse. It was decided that Thelxepeia with her honeyed tones would make the initial pitch to their hostess. If more persuasion were needed, Peisinoe, with her orderly mind and somber demeanor, would take over. Ordinarily, perky Aglaophone would have been a natural to close the sale, but in her current listless, uncommunicative state, she would be of little use.

They approached the doorway and heard the raucous laughter of men inside. They took a step back and shared a worried look. Then taking a deep breath, they entered the house, Aglaophone trailing behind. Peisinoe and Thelxepeia instantly spied what they were looking for and scurried, heads bowed, toward the huge circular hearth in the center of the large and colorful tiled hall. There they sat down in the ashes on the rim of the pit as befitted their status as suppliants—exiles or wanderers seeking a night's shelter. Aglaophone joined them.

A sudden silence had fallen over the room.

Then, "Well, what have we here?" purred a silky female voice. The girls looked up and saw a voluptuously beautiful woman with long, blazing red, circleted tresses and wearing a pale green gown. She was lying on a low-slung divan with a handsome, pouting young man. They were sharing a golden beaker of wine. In a distant corner of the room, several other men interrupted their dice rolling in response to this sudden diversion.

The three girls stood up but stayed where they were.

"Please, Lady, we are suppliants," said Thelxepeia. Her voice quavered and stopped.

"I'll say," drawled the woman. "But are you legitimate? Or just three little beggar girls from down Catania way. You're filthy, the lot of you!"

"Yes, Lady," Thelxepeia plunged on. "We were set ashore down the road yesterday. It's been a long walk, and there was a wind. We're exiles, my sisters and I."

"Shall I get rid of them, Circe?" asked the young man.

"Alexandros, be a dear and shut up. Approach, the three of you! Exiles? Where from? You're accent is Greek."

"Yes, Lady," said Peisinoe. "We're from Aetolia."

"Are you? But there are Greek colonists now all up and down this coast. As I said, you might just be three scurvy little runaways."

Peisinoe drew herself up to her full height. "That's a slander, Lady. We are princesses, higher born than you."

Circe shot off the couch, suddenly enraged. "Why you insolent little. . . !" Then she caught herself and smiled unpleasantly. "Princesses, huh? Does that include the little tongue-tied one? What is she—dimwitted?"

"Hardly that, Lady. She's devastated at being torn from her family and home—as we are," Peisinoe faltered and bowed her head.

"Now come the tears, I see! Well, I must admit you're clever little actresses—but no more. You may sleep outside on the porch tonight, if you wish. But by morning I want you gone."

Thelxepeia gasped. "You deny us the right of hospitality as decreed by the gods?"

Circe screamed, "You dare lecture me, girl? I am Circe, whom men fear and call an enchantress!"

"Then they are fools!" cried Aglaophone, pushing her way forward between her sisters. "It's easy to see that you are a fraud! An enchantress would have recognized US! For we are Aglaophone, Peisinoe, and Thelxepeia—royal daughters of King Achelous and Queen Terpsichore of Aetolia! And men call US the Seirazein!"

"The Siera . . ." Circe had turned pale and sat down. "But you're children!"

"Not for long, Lady, not after what we've been through this past week! Now, are you going to extend to us the rights of suppliants? Or do we leave you here to the judgment of the gods and the pleasure of your present company?"

Alexandros flushed bright red and bestirred himself. "Circe, shall I . . . ?"

"No," Circe said absently. "You and the boys run outside and find yourselves a javelin to heave."

Sulkily, Alexandros got up and motioned to his fellows to follow him out. Circe, meanwhile, had recovered somewhat and smiled pleasantly at her guests. She rose.

"Come, young ladies. Let's get you all a nice bath, some fine clothes, and a warm bed. And perhaps after supper," she said, putting a companionable arm around Aglaophone's shoulder and marching her upstairs, "you'll sing us a song or two."

Following behind them, Thelxepeia grinned at Peisinoe. Nodding in the direction of their sister, she said softly, "She's baaaaaccck!"

Eight

It had taken the better part of an hour, but finally Circe had stopped shaking and was beginning to calm down. She had had, she judged, a close call. Her secluded lifestyle and the arrogance it had bred in her had seduced her into a potentially very dangerous lapse in judgment. That afternoon she had flouted one of the most sacred laws that governed the relations between humans and their gods—the law of hospitality. This stricture stated that it was incumbent upon any homeowner to welcome at any time strangers of whatever rank, even the humblest, into one's dwelling—to provide them with a bath, a meal, and a bed (as well as gifts if the strangers proved to be of significant dignity and able to reciprocate in kind). Only after they had been made thoroughly at home was it permissible to ask them their story and their business with you.

This time-honored convention was not simply a matter of politeness, for history (or at least legend) had provided numerous instances of the gods disguising themselves as beggars or even lower life forms in order to test the kindness and humane instincts of mortals—with severe punishments, even eternal damnation, meted out to those who proved insolent and cruel. Now admittedly, the little princesses who this evening shared her dining table with her were not goddesses—but they were already celebrities throughout the far flung regions of the Great Sea, their fame exceeded only by their mystery: the Sirens, they were called, musical spellbinders whose singing and whose beauty moved audiences to tears of longing and unfulfilled desire. That they were little girls had never occurred to Circe.

But then little girls got bigger every day, and the transformation that a bath and brightly hued, Egyptian-cut gowns from the wardrobes of her handmaidens had wrought upon their appearance was stupefying. She could no longer doubt that the dirty ragamuffins who had appeared on her hearth earlier that day were indeed royalty. All three of the girls were stunners, whose poise and graceful mannerisms matched their outward beauty. The twins were of medium height and had ringleted auburn hair dressed in the Minoan manner that she herself had abandoned long ago upon her flight from Crete to escape the mighty purge there of the Great Mother's priestesses. Theirs was a sensual, earthy glamour that in many ways mirrored her own looks. The youngest sister had an entirely different appearance—she was blond, small, and sweet-faced, with enormous blue eyes that radiated blazing intelligence and, oddly, lurking danger.

Aglaophone bore watching.

Not at the moment, though. As they dined with her on roasted venison, Circe was struck by the sadness that inhabited every gesture and glance of her guests. They were unfailingly polite, which bespoke their good breeding—but except when expressing childish delight at the sweet taste of the orange slices that were a side dish ("The golden apples!" Peisinoe had exclaimed), they seemed distracted. More than once, she caught each of them turning her head away and wiping her eyes. And more than once, she felt at such a moment an uncharacteristic lump in her own throat.

Finally, Circe could contain herself no longer.

"Young mistresses," she began, "this afternoon when you first arrived here, I was extremely, unforgivably rude to you—in obvious defiance of sacred law. I repeat my apology to you now by way of excusing a second transgression of the same law I feel I must make. As you know, I'm supposed to wait until you've had your meal to ask your business here. But you poor children are so obviously distressed. Won't you tell me your story so that I may . . . ?"

That did it—she had opened the floodgates. Suddenly, all three girls burst into loud, uncontrollable weeping. Circe's half-dozen male companions, who on this occasion had been shuffled off to a servants' table in a distant corner of the hall, looked up from their meat and wine, startled and annoyed.

Over the next half-hour, between sobs, sniffles, snuffles, and ungainly hiccups, Circe was able to elicit some sort of co-herent narrative from her guests. When one girl was momen-tarily too overcome to continue, one of the others picked up the thread of the story. They told her of the raid on the Maiden Kore's shrine by King Odysseus of Ithaca, their failure to save the Goddess, the savage drought that the Mother Demeter had brought to Aetolia as a result, and their subsequent condemna-tion to death at their own father's hand—which everyone seemed to think would mollify the Mother and spare the land. As sacred king, it was their father's duty to protect his people, no matter the personal cost. In an attempt to convince Circe of her father's obligation, Aglaophone told her that there was a tradition among the Habiru people on the far eastern fringes of the Great Sea that told of an ancient king named Abraham who'd been commanded by their sky god Yahwah to sacrifice his own son Isaac.

Their story concluded, Circe stood up and the princesses followed her example, though none of them were quite con-scious of their movements. Then she hurried to embrace the girls and hold them to her.

"As it turns out, we are not so dissimilar, after all," said Circe, proceeding then to relate her own tale of exile and loss. As a girl, she, too, had been a priestess of the Mother, in service at the great palace of Knossos with the royal princess Phaedra, younger sister of Ariadne. After the Athenian prince Theseus had slain the Minotaur and made off with the older girl, something had gone terribly wrong. At first it was believed that Theseus was a cad, who'd used Ariadne, then unceremoniously deserted her at the first island stop heading back to Athens. Then dark rumors began to circulate about Ariadne, who'd always had a wild streak, falling in with the orgiastic Maenads, the drunken, promiscuous worshippers of Dionysus, and thus being deserving of her fate.

Be that as it may, in a few years, Theseus, now king in Athens, returned to Crete at the behest of the High King Atreus with express orders to conquer the island, assert mainland rule over it, and, most importantly, suppress the Great Mother and destroy her shrines. Only Circe's friendship with the Cretan princess, Phaedra, had saved her, as Theseus, now besotted with the younger daughter of Minos, married her and willingly spared the life of her best friend—as long as she quit Crete for good.

Not needing any further hints, Circe had booked passage for Sicily in the far west. Arriving at Catania on the southeast coast, she had used her beauty to ensnare a local merchant prince who had made her his bride and brought her home to his villa. He had died a few years later, and here she'd been ever since. The young men sharing her home, she concluded lamely and blushingly, were . . . just good friends.

At the mention of the men, who had finished their meal and were growing loud with wine, the princesses looked warily in their direction. Circe noted their concern and nervously tried to minimize it.

"Men!" she scoffed. "Feed them, give them a few drinks—they invariably make pigs of themselves!"

That hardly seemed to give the girls a sense of comfort. Then Circe had an idea—one that might allay the remaining shreds of doubt in her mind about the legitimacy of her youthful houseguests.

"Tell you what!" she said. "Why don't we conduct a little test? Your fame as musicians is widespread. Why don't you perform for us, and we'll see if it's true that music soothes the savage beast? We have a few prime examples right here, as you can see."

She was pleased to see the three youngsters grin mischievously at each other.

"Great!" said Peisinoe. "Wait right here while Thelxepeia and I get our instruments!" The two older girls ran, giggling, upstairs. A moment later they returned, Peisinoe carrying her flute, her sister armed with a small lyre that easily fit into a portable leather pouch.

Circe descended from the dais and arranged herself gracefully on the divan, beckoning the wine-sodden young men to gather around her at her feet. Meanwhile, Peisinoe and Thelxepeia sat on the dais step while Aglaophone stood between them.

What followed in the next few moments, to Circe's mind, defied credence—set the laws of nature at naught. The combination of the youngest girl's voice joined in concert with her sisters' or in counterpoint to their gifted playing staggered the aesthetic senses of their listeners. When the contemplation of their physical beauty was thrown into the mix, the overall impact was an ethereal giddiness wedded to an ache in the breast that was as delicious as it was excruciating. To hear these girls was to be simultaneously beatified with joy and damned with an unquenchable longing for something that could never in a thousand centuries be attained or even defined.

When they had finished their final song, the story of Demeter searching the wide world over for her lost daughter Persephone, there wasn't a dry eye, including their own, in the house. Timidly, Alexandros asked Circe if he might approach the princesses. Tears streaming down her face, not trusting herself to speak, she nodded yes. The young man got to his feet, went to each of the sisters in turn, and kissed their hands. In his wake, every one of his companions followed suit.

Afterward, there was nothing to be done but for everyone to go to bed. As the serving girls doused the torches, the young men prepared their pallets in the lower reaches of the hall. That one of them should share Circe's bed this night seemed somehow profane. The princesses, yawning mightily, made their way to the chamber that had been prepared for them, undressed, and climbed into their pallets. Circe, too, went to her room, where she sat for a long while and wept and wept.

Then when the entire house was sunk in peace and slumber, she arose and made her way in the dark to the guest chamber. By the flicker of a single lamp vessel that rested on the window ledge, she located the bed occupied by Aglaophone. She watched the sleeping girl for a moment then, furtively, as if ashamed to catch herself in the act, bent and kissed her forehead and drew the coverlet up further around her chin.

"Circe?" the child said sleepily, making her hostess jump back with a sharp intake of breath.

"Yes?" she answered, frightened and embarrassed

"Would it be all right if we stayed—just for a day or two?"

Circe thought she would die. "Oh, yes," she said. "I'd like that. That would be . . . wonderful!"

There was no response from Aglaophone, who had drifted off again. Circe returned to her own chamber and her own bed, where she spent the rest of the long night wailing bitterly.

Early the next morning, before the princesses were astir, she went downstairs and drove the young men forever from her home. Thereafter, she would remain celibate for many years—until the day when Odysseus would come, ransack her villa, rape her, and then drive his bronze sword into her soft belly.

Nine

As it turned out, much to the happiness of everyone, the princesses stayed with Circe for well over a year. Very quickly, in the first couple of weeks, a mother/daughter bond developed between her and all three girls—but even at that early stage, it became clear that Aglaophone and Circe were becoming particularly close. Quite often, after Peisinoe and Thelxepeia yawningly called it a night, the older woman and the youngest princess would sit talking over a cup of wine almost into the dawn.

One fascinating and crucial conversation took place only three nights after the girls' arrival. Circe and Aglaophone began to discuss their respective experiences as priestesses of the Mother. Circe made the point that she'd felt abandoned by the Mother when she'd been forced to flee Crete, her homeland, and as a consequence had never bothered to set up a shrine here in her home, even though worship of the Goddess was still prevalent in Sicily. The young princess shook her head.

"I don't feel that way."

"But, Phonny," protested Circe, "how can you not resent Her when She actively sought your destruction? You and your sisters have lost EVERYTHING because of Her."

"Not everything. We've found YOU."

Circe felt her eyes moisten.

"No, Circe," the girl resumed, "the Mother didn't destroy us. Men's irrational FEAR of her did that. Men in their superstitious insistence on assigning a god to everything we can see and feel made an illogical connection between the theft of Kore's image, us, and the drought that followed. I don't believe there was a connection. I think it was all coincidence."

Circe stared open-mouthed at her.

"How can one so young possibly know that?" she finally asked.

"I just sense it," the girl said quietly. "Circe, I think the Mother is INSIDE us—all of us—even men. I think we ARE Her—each of us is a part of Her. You don't need to build Her a shrine. You've already done that, inwardly. It's just a matter of opening your heart to Her again."

Circe could only wait for what would next pop out of this incredible child's mind. The wait wasn't a long one.

"When you were a priestess, did you ever sacrifice a dove to the Mother? Behead a dove with a tiny labrys?"

"Yes," said Circe, having no idea where the girl was headed now.

"So did I. It grossed me out, but I did it. Now, if it disgusted ME, why wouldn't it disgust the Mother? I mean, what woman would consider a headless bird a desirable gift?"

Circe suddenly began to scream with laughter—and then so did Aglaophone. When they stopped clutching their stomachs, they each took a sip of wine, only to spit it out as laughter engulfed them again. Finally, they both calmed down for good, and the girl went on with her ruminations.

"Sometimes," she said, "I get these very weird notions. I sense things that are true, but nobody knows about them yet—except me. Isn't that strange?"

"Like what?" asked the older woman.

"Well, for instance, if you were to walk out the back door of this house and walk westward all the way to the other side of Sicily, then sail further west THROUGH the Pillars of Heracles, then sail completely across the huge sea that's there, to a mighty land that no one knows about yet, and cross that till you get to another even BIGGER sea, and sail across that till you got to more land—and so on, do you know where you'd end up?"

Circe shook her head.

Aglaophone grinned. "Coming in your own FRONT door! Isn't that wild?"

"Phonny, that doesn't make any sense. Maybe you'd better not have any more wine right now. What do you mean?"

"I mean the world is ROUND, Circe—not flat."

Circe scoffed. "That's impossible! What's it resting on? Why aren't we all off balance and sliding and falling all over one another if it's round?"

The princess frowned. "Well, you've got me there. I don't know—yet. But I know I'm right. The Mother has told me."

She was quiet for a little while, then asked. "Circe, you said the other day that you were an enchantress. Are you? Has the Mother given you special powers?"

Circe frowned and didn't respond immediately. She stood up and walked over and refilled her cup from a clay ewer. When she sat down again, she appeared to be weighing whether or not to speak.

Finally, she said, "Well, I have encouraged that reputation—that my beauty was so extravagant that men became my . . . slaves. There's even a rumor about me that I can turn men into animals—swine, for instance. As if they needed any help doing that! It helped give me an edge, an advantage, when dealing with those . . . friends I've just sent away. It all seems silly and pointless now." Her voice drifted off.

Aglaophone knew enough to keep quiet.

"But, yes, I do have the ability—a very limited ability to SEE things—things that are happening elsewhere or WILL happen in the near future."

Her young companion was all ears now, sitting on the edge of her chair, her eyes sparkling. "Tell me!" she pleaded.

"Well, I know things about the big war that's going on back east—the one they're fighting over the Lacedaemon queen, Helen. I know, for instance, that the Greeks will win after a long, terrible struggle."

"At Troy, yes. King Odysseus was on his way to join up with the High King's army when he made a little stop off at our palace and casually destroyed the lives of my sisters and me," Aglaophone said.

"You must hate him for that," Circe observed.

"No, not really. That wasn't his purpose. We were just . . . - collateral damage."

Aglaophone looked confused and dazed for a moment, as if she might faint.

"Phonny, are you all right? What an odd phrase that was! Where did you get it?"

The princess blinked and shook her head. "I don't know. It just came to me from somewhere—out there. As if from another world, another time . . . I told you I sometimes get these ideas. . . ." The girl looked frightened.

"What is it?" asked Circe. She reached over and grasped her arm, steadying her.

"Circe," she whispered. "The voice that planted those words, 'collateral damage,' in my head just now. It was HIM! It was Odysseus!"

"Sweetheart, let's get you to bed right now!" said Circe. "You're just over-tired, still, from all you've been through."

"Yes, all right," said Aglaophone. Then she got up, set her wine cup down, and let Circe guide her upstairs to her room.

Five minutes later, Circe was back downstairs pouring herself another glass of wine. *That poor child and her sisters,* she thought. How could she tell them what else she knew about the end of the Trojan War? Of the terrible and conscienceless man that it would, through the remorseless twists and turns of

Fate, send their way, send to the very corner of the world they quietly inhabited, meaning no harm to anyone? How could she tell the little princesses about Odysseus of Ithaca—who was coming to Sicily one day to be the death of all of them?

With the amazing, eternal resilience of youth, Aglaophone put the distress of that late evening quickly behind her—and it wasn't mentioned again by either her or her hostess. One afternoon a week later, the princess was about to return to Circe's villa after a pleasant hour of picking oranges when she heard the low rumble of thunder far to the southeast. Storms had always fascinated her, and she turned around to wait for the inevitable lightning stroke. When it came, it triggered in her an interesting sequence of conjectures.

Men had for generations now insisted that their sky god Zeus was master of the lightning bolt—and could send it unerringly to destroy any mortal who had offended Him. But these same men also acknowledged that Zeus was the GRANDSON of the Mother. If so, didn't that logically entail that She was the ultimate source of lightning? And, to take things one enticing thought further, couldn't that mean that Aglaophone herself, whose being enclosed the Mother, had some say over the direction a particular lightning bolt might take?

Intrigued by the idea, the girl stood on the pathway to the front door and watched. When the next thud of thunder sounded, she deliberately waited for the subsequent flash of light—then she counted. She got all the way up to twenty-five before the next thunder rumble. She counted again. Twenty-one this time before the next concussion. Again. This time the interval between the flash of light and the sound was only nineteen. All the while, she noticed, the sky to the southeast had grown increasingly dark and ominous. The storm was getting closer, and the time intervals between the lightning and the thunder were growing shorter.

Aglaophone felt the tingle of a monumental discovery enveloping her now. The closer the storm came, the less time between lightning and thunder—or was it the other way around? Warily, she retreated to the doorway of Circe's villa. Within a few minutes, the atmospheric violence seemed immediately overhead—and just as she'd hoped, the time lapse between the frightening, lurid flash of jagged light and the crash of sound that accompanied it had virtually vanished. Lightning and thunder were apparently the very same event. Did that mean that the ear was slower than the eye? Was sound slower than light? Or the reverse?

Aglaophone felt herself shivering with excitement for the rest of the afternoon. That night at supper she mentioned to her sisters and Circe that she had a little . . . game or experiment in mind that she'd like them to take part in with her next time there was a thunderstorm. Circe blanched and tried to beg off, saying that she'd always been terrified of lightning. The princess assured her that she'd be perfectly safe—that she wouldn't, in fact, even have to set foot outside her door.

That night, Aglaophone didn't sleep a wink as she kept going over calculations and probabilities in her restless mind till dawn. She waited all the next day and was distressed nearly to the point of tears when no storm appeared. She nevertheless shored up her plan that evening by reminding the others of their arrangement.

Then, at mid-afternoon the following day, thunder sounded in the south. Ecstatically, Aglaophone rounded up Peisinoe and Thelxepeia and their hostess and hustled them all toward the double front door of the villa. She barely noticed the reluctance of her sisters or the downright panic of Circe. Standing in the open doorway as the glowering sky raced their way, she gave them their instructions.

"Now, listen. Let's all of us hold hands. . . . That's it. Now, the storm is getting closer and closer. I want you all to concentrate on that ash tree directly in front of us about a hundred feet out. You see it? Good. Let's give this a run-through. The next time you see the lightning—oops! There it is!—All right, the thunder—there! That was a count of six. When you see and hear the next sequence, I want you to THINK AND SAY to yourselves, 'Mother-lightning-tree!' Have you got that? And CONCENTRATE on each image separately as you think it! All right? When I say, 'Now!'"

Barely had she finished, when a ferocious jag of lightning forked down through the sky in front of them. Circe whimpered.

"All right! At the thunderclap! There it is!—aaannnd —Mother-lightning-tree! NOW!"

A livid, yellow-purple light and a deafening blast of sound swallowed their whole world as the trunk of the ash tree was vertically shattered in front of them, causing a third of it to crash to the ground.

"Yes! Oh, yes!" screamed Aglaophone, leaping free of the others out into the storm, clapping her hands, and laughing. "Now, THAT's going to come in handy! But maybe while I've got you all here, we'd better try it again. . . ."

She all at once became aware of the stillness behind her and turned around to see Peisinoe and Thelxepeia standing trembling and ashen-faced in the doorway, looking down at the crumpled, unconscious form of Circe. Aglaophone hurried and knelt down by the side of the stricken woman. Gently, she patted her face till Circe began to stir and revive.

"Probably she's just upset about her tree," the princess explained to her sisters.

But that turned out not to be it at all. After the girls had gotten Circe to her feet and helped her to the divan—and after they'd had one of the serving girls fetch a cup of water for her, she smiled sweetly and asked Peisinoe and Thelxepeia if they'd kindly excuse her and their sister. The twins somehow guessed that the request was in their best interest and quickly headed upstairs, though they stopped short of going to their room and hid just around the landing corner.

What they overheard Circe tell Aglaophone over the course of the next few minutes was absorbing and very intense, dwarfing in anger anything she'd said to them the day when they'd first entered her home.

"You little IDIOT!" she screamed. "What in Hades and Hecate did you think you were DOING out there? Were you deliberately trying to get us all KILLED?"

The girl, who sat meekly on the divan, cringed and kept her head down.

"ANSWER ME!"

"I was trying something out," Aglaophone said quietly.

"She was trying something out!" muttered Circe, raising her hands and looking at the ceiling. She said some Cretan words that neither the girl nor her eavesdropping sisters could make out—nor did they want to.

"And what would that be?" she went on with dangerous amiability.

The princess cleared her throat. "I wanted to see if I could control lightning."

"I see," said Circe after a moment. "And what would the purpose of THAT be? Do you figure Zeus is slacking off? That He's no longer up to the job?"

"I don't think He ever was," said the girl. "I think lightning is just part of nature, part of the Mother like everything else. I think someday people can learn to control it."

Circe found that her anger was subsiding and being replaced by active curiosity.

"Why would we want to do that?"

"Well, it would be a very effective weapon, for one thing."

"Oh, I see. You want to control lightning so you can kill people with it? Bronze swords don't do the trick?"

"Women don't use bronze swords," Aglaophone pointed out.

"Well, lightning's a little unwieldy and impractical, isn't it, Phonny? Rapists don't do their best work during thunderstorms."

"I was going to try that next," said the girl.

"What?"

"Creating a storm. Not necessarily to be destructive. Think of the possibilities of being able to control the weather. If there were the threat of a drought, you could simply summon the rain . . . instead of sacrificing a princess."

"Oh," said Circe, melting. She sat down beside Aglaophone then smiled and ruffled her hair. "What a wonder of a child you are! But, Phonny, I think you forget sometimes that you're only—what?—thirteen? You be careful with these experiments of yours. And, please! Leave me and my trees out of them!"

The princess smiled, relieved at being forgiven. "I promise," she said.

That night, when she fell asleep, Aglaophone had the strangest dream she'd ever had in her life—as exciting as it was puzzling and disturbing. In the dream, she was looking at a woman sitting with a man on a bench of some sort. They were near the water, and they were watching the sun come up. They wore strange-looking clothes, and behind them rose a tower far taller than any she'd ever seen before. The woman was small and pretty and had golden hair. She looked very familiar, somehow—and, for that matter, so did the man, who was quite handsome. And even though they spoke in a strange tongue she'd never heard, in the dream she could magically understand them.

They were talking about HER.

The woman's name was Daisy.

Abruptly, Daisy stopped talking and sat up straight.

Brian said, "What is it? Something wrong?"

Daisy looked distracted. "What? Oh, no. It's just that I had the oddest feeling a second ago." Then a dreamy smile settled across her face. "Oh, yes," she whispered. "Aglaophone!"

Brian said, puzzled, "Yes, you've been telling me all about her."

Daisy seized his arm and sighed happily. "Brian, I knew you'd be good for me! I just knew it! First, us last night. Then this beautiful bright new dawn we're looking at. Now the most wonderful thing of all!"

Brian smiled and shook his head. "I don't have a clue what you're talking about, Daisy," he said.

"Well, Brian, it seems this morning the Great Mother Herself is very much with us."

With that enigmatic offering, Daisy resumed her tale.

Ten

For the time being, Aglaophone decided to keep her bizarre dream to herself. She wanted time to try to puzzle it out, to try to unravel its meaning on her own. Maybe there'd be a recurrence the next night or the night after that, and she'd be given some further insight as to its possible significance.

In the meantime, she and her sisters settled into a comfortable, idyllic life as Circe's guests. Not wishing to impose, they offered their hostess the contents of the purse the generous stranger at the dock in Catania had given them, but Circe wouldn't hear of it, suggesting that they keep it for spending money. She had one or two shopping expeditions in mind in the near future that they might enjoy.

By and large, over that same time frame, Aglaophone kept her word about her meteorological experiments—technically. She never again involved Circe or her trees—or her own sisters—in any of her odd little projects. On the other hand, it was observed that she frequently went for long, solitary walks up and down the shore road. It was also noted that to an extraordinary degree during her absence fairly violent storms seemed to evolve very suddenly out of placid blue Mediterranean skies. Half an hour later, the princess would return to the villa, soaking wet and bedraggled but looking uncommonly pleased with herself. On these occasions, she would skirt quickly through the great entry hall and up the stairs to her room. She and everyone else in the household seemed to have arrived at some mutually agreed-upon arrangement.

Don't ask, don't tell.

*　　*　　*

One warm and balmy day, Peisinoe and Thelxepeia asked their sister if they might join her on one of her strolls. If she minded, she didn't give any indication and said instead that she welcomed their company. They decided to head north on the shore road. Once they had cleared the boundaries of Circe's estate with its orange, fig, and olive orchards, they could clearly see and admire the majestic mountain that loomed in the medium distance off to their left.

Their shock was considerable when, before any of them could comment on its beauty, the top of the peak erupted with a shattering roar. A gigantic plume of coal black smoke shot through with flame soared a mile or so into the azure sky before spreading out and blanketing it in darkness. The girls screamed and raced back the way they had come. Before they had quite reached the intersection with the path leading to the villa, the road beneath their pounding feet gave a shuddering lurch and they were tumbled to the ground. A couple of boulders twenty feet away sheered off and bounced down the cliff to the sea. Dazed and shaken but unhurt, the princesses picked themselves up. The twins stared wild-eyed at their sister.

"Well, don't look at me!" she cried. "I'm still practicing my thunder storms!"

A few moments later, when they burst through the front door of the villa, Circe comforted them and ushered them into the kitchen for a snack of barley cakes and sliced oranges. When they had grown calmer, she assured them that while the force of the mountain explosion had been impressive, it was not a significant event. The volcano, called Aetna, had a habit of erupting with a fair amount of frequency. This particular incident didn't appear to have done much damage, at least not locally.

Later in the day, the princesses ventured out again and this time successfully completed their walk.

On another occasion, Aglaophone had again been picking oranges. She returned to the house and made her way to the rear to enter through the kitchen. As she rounded the corner, she drew up short, noticing a big lout of a stable hand around her own age named Talos, pushing an eight-year-old named Epirus, the son of one of the cooks. It was obvious he was trying to goad the youngster into a disastrous mismatch of a fight. Stepping back out of sight, the princess ransacked her memory, thinking of all the times she had seen her father wrestle both in the amphitheater and in private practice matches. She had always watched him closely and avidly studied all his moves. She selected one now that she thought would do nicely.

Circling undetected around Talos, she came up behind him, raising her finger to her lips to insure that Epirus wouldn't give her away. When she was virtually parallel to the bully to his left, she suddenly sliced her right foot out, catching Talos just below his calf, simultaneously elbowing him in the side and upending him in the dust. As he yowled his pain and surprise, she bypassed him, barely looking down.

"If you're going to be a fighter, Talos, you're going to have to watch your back," she remarked. Putting her free arm around the little boy's shoulder, she said, "Want an orange, Epirus? Come with me to the kitchen."

Epirus, of course, would have accompanied her to the ends of the earth.

Then one day about two months into their stay with her, Circe piled the princesses and herself into her covered carriage. The sulky stable boy Talos had been assigned to steer the two horses. Circe announced that they were going on a visit to the village of the Cyclopes about eight miles to the north. The Cyclopes, she explained, were a group of extremely inventive and talented metalsmiths who, generations ago, had banded together into a tightly knit community at the foot of Mount Aetna with their families. She thought the girls might enjoy exploring their shops and perhaps find some attractive jewelry to purchase.

"'Cyclopes?" asked Peisinoe. "Doesn't that mean 'wheel-eyed'?"

Thelxepeia shuddered. "I think I've heard of them. Aren't they giants who just have one big eye right in the middle of their foreheads?"

Circe smiled. "And aren't the Sirens wickedly beautiful temptresses whose haunting music lays waste to a man's senses, drawing him inexorably to his doom?"

The girls giggled nervously. "Is that what they say about us?" asked Thelxepeia.

"At the very least, darling. You ladies are already the stuff of legend. So it is with the Cyclopes. The eye you've heard of is nothing more mysterious than a tattooed yellow disk centered above their noses. It's a sun disk in honor of Helios, the god who fuels their furnaces as well as the mouth of the great volcano which supplies their ore.

"On the other hand," she said a moment later, seeming to choose her words carefully, "I feel I have to warn you in advance about their . . . appearance. That third eye CAN be very disconcerting. Try not to look too startled—and try not to stare. The difficulty at first is that when you're conversing with one of them it's hard not to looking. . . ."

"Him right in the eye!" laughed Aglaophone.

Circe and her sisters groaned.

They were about halfway through their two-hour journey at this point. They all fell silent as they took in the wild beauty of the sun-drenched morning. Off to their left above a copse of poplars they could see the towering mountain. To their right was the sparkling blue of the Ionian Sea, the glare of sunlight winking off the waves making them squint and blink. Ahead of them were their driver Talos and the brown rumps of the cantering horses.

Eventually, the canter slowed to a trot and then a plodding walk, as the horses strained to tug the carriage up a steep rise. Then, as they crested the hill, the princesses caught their first glimpse of the Cyclopes' village, a hamlet a quarter mile away that sprawled on a plateau forty feet above the sea. Just at the approach to the settlement, a natural causeway fashioned ages ago by some ancient earthquake jutted at a right angle out into the sea for two hundred feet before terminating in a wide grassy hilltop. On this little plot stood a lone circular dwelling of huge unfinished stones with a roof of thatch. Next to the house stood a small outbuilding.

"What's that?" asked Aglaophone.

Circe grimaced. "Possibly trouble—at least at first. That house belongs to Ligeia, the village priestess. That's her shrine to the Goddess beside it. She has a touch of the Sight—not much, but enough so that she's undoubtedly aware of your current whereabouts."

Indeed, even as Circe spoke, a small dark form dislodged itself from the distant spur of land and began stalking determinedly toward them. Almost simultaneously, the great door of the palisaded settlement began to swing outward and people started to emerge.

At the head of the delegation was a man of tremendous height with, as Circe had promised, a sun disk tattooed in the middle of his forehead. Behind the giant, one individual or group after another filed from the settlement to make them welcome. Circe hadn't exaggerated. The sight of the delegation was hardly one for sore eyes. Or as Thelxepeia expressed it:

"Eeeeewwwhhh!"

She said it in a quiet voice, awed simultaneously, as her sisters were, by the majesty and the solemn mystery of the people who approached their conveyance and the grotesquely eerie vision they presented.

"Accursed!" screamed the creature rapidly closing the distance from the causeway to their right. Both this person and the people of the settlement were set to arrive in front of them at approximately the same time. The leader of the approaching party glanced nervously at the lone woman, apparently prepared to defer to her.

Still, ignoring her to the extent that that was possible, Circe spoke first to the gigantic chieftain.

"Greetings, Polyphemus!" she said.

"Accursed!" repeated the figure rapidly coming at them, who turned out to be an unkempt, wild-looking woman of indeterminate age.

"Does she speak for you?" Circe asked the leader with a hint of disdain in her tone.

"Let's hear what she has to say," said Polyphemus diplomatically.

Circe nodded with a solemn hint of irony. "Hello, Ligeia," she said.

"Accursed!" shrilled the woman for the third time. By now, she had approached them and was actively, if unintentionally, spooking the horses.

"We take your point, generally speaking. But could you get down to specifics?" said Circe.

"The Goddess has damned these young women!" shouted the woman excitedly. "They were turned away at Catania! They were denied sanctuary there! The Goddess has disavowed them! Do you deny it, Circe?"

"Now that you bring it up, not entirely. There were extenuating circumstances that the delegation at Catania were unaware of. Like you, they chose to condemn without understanding. Even so, the leader of the dockside contingent was moved to an act of charity and mercy. He saw to it that the young women were directed to me, and they have been my houseguests ever since—and most welcome ones, at that."

"They are the Sirens!" cried Ligeia, "Who damn all men's souls with their song!"

"Be sensible for a moment and look at them, Ligeia," said Circe calmly. "When all is said and done, they are little girls—unfairly victimized by a situation far beyond their control."

"It is common for monsters and enchantresses to be able to change shape at will," snapped the crone. "And in the case of the latter, to be able to shift the shape of others! You yourself have something of a reputation along those lines, Circe!"

"That's true," Circe said coolly, "and you'd do well to remember that. These are good girls, Ligeia—but they do possess certain impressive talents. Especially, the little one here," she remarked, jerking her thumb toward Aglaophone. "If I unleash HER on you, I can guarantee that you'll be house-hunting by lunchtime."

Ligeia's eyes widened and she took a hasty step back. This time she held her tongue.

"Ladies, enough!" said Polyphemus, raising his hands decisively. "Circe, do you vouch for the young women? Can you give assurances that the Mother won't take offense and harm my people if we admit you to the settlement?"

"Yes, Polyphemus, you have my word. You and your people have nothing to fear."

"Then that's good enough for me. You may enter," he said, nodding at Talos. "Ligeia, we thank you for your concern. But I feel that Circe speaks the truth and that everything will be all right."

Ligeia merely glared at him, turned on her heel, and stomped back across the causeway to her house.

Talos, meanwhile, shook the reins and steered the carriage toward the open gateway. As they made their entrance, the princesses were instantly agog at the unsuspected size and splendor of the vista displayed before them. Aglaophone noted that the huge, timbered palisade that surrounded the settlement was not rectangular, as one would expect, but rather oval in shape. Within its boundaries, which encompassed about a dozen acres, the town was arranged in three concentric rings. The outermost of these was comprised of forges, storage facilities, small barns, and open livestock pens, which housed sheep, goats, oxen, and hogs. Inside that was s second circle consisting of the community's shops and produce stalls. Finally in the center, arranged around a large, grassy common, were the dwellings, most of them circular stone huts with thatched roofs—like the one out on the promontory belonging to Legeia. It dawned on the princess that if she were standing part way up Mount Aetna, which towered above them only a mile or two to the west, the Cyclopes' village would look like a monumental eye staring up from the surrounding landscape.

Once Talos had brought the carriage to a halt, Polyphemus lifted each of the four women down. If the girls felt squeamish at his touch and the sight of the glaring yellow tattoo on his forehead, they managed to hide it. Taking a wide-eyed look around them, they found that they were now at the center of a genial maelstrom of noise and activity. Everywhere were the sights, sounds, and smells of a happy and prosperous community—cooking and furnace fires, the metallic bang of hammer and anvil, madly scampering, yelling, frolicking children, bellowing, baa-ing, barking animals, and delicious, aromatic food smells.

"Talos!" called Circe. "Come here, boy!"

As the stable hand made his shambling approach, his mistress opened her purse and shook a couple of coins into his hand. "There. Get yourself something to eat, and have a look around. We'll be wanting to leave by mid-afternoon."

The boy turned red with embarrassed pleasure. He bowed. "Thank you, Lady. I'll be waiting."

Polyphemus gave instructions for the care and feeding of Circe's horses then began to give his guests a guided tour of his settlement. Although the princesses at first continued to be a bit flustered at the sight of the bizarre tattoo that decorated the forehead of every male and female over the age of five, gradually their attention was siphoned away by other interests and concerns.

In the meantime, Circe chatted with their host. "How about that last eruption a month ago? Did it do much damage?"

"Not really," replied Polyphemus. "It panicked the children and the animals, of course, and there were some related aftershocks that did a little road damage outside. But there was no significant lava flow. Mainly, it was a matter of staying inside for a few hours till the ash cloud dissipated. A couple of people lost their roofs to the falling cinders, and we were raking up piles of the stuff for a week. It's good fertilizer, though, for our fields. Of course, we're lucky that we're virtually under the thing. If we were further away, anybody who got caught in the horizontal cinder flow would be turned into an ash statue."

Circe shook her head. "Sounds like you enjoy living dangerously."

The giant laughed. By this time, the party had reached the ring of stalls and shops. "I assume our young friends here would like to take a look at some of the jewelry we have on display."

"Indeed, they would," laughed Circe. "How well you understand the female heart."

Polyphemus stood aside at the door of a jewelry shop, ushering the princesses and Circe in ahead of him. Once inside, the girls were instantly mesmerized by the intricately worked bronze delights spread out on the shelves that lined the small store. After twenty minutes of agonized indecisiveness, Peisinoe chose a necklace with a lavishly scrolled circular pendant; Thelxepeia a star-shaped brooch; and Aglaophone a pair of wrist bracelets designed to replicate coiled snakes. The purchases half-depleted their coin supply, but they were ecstatic with their acquisitions.

After duly admiring them, Circe and Polyphemus began to head toward a sweet-smelling bakery a few doors down. Before they'd walked more than a dozen paces, though, Aglaophone eagerly asked if they could stop for a moment and take a peek inside the weaponry shop. Polyphemus shrugged with a perplexed smile and, while the other women waited outside, took her in. The girl spent a moment or two inspecting the bronze swords and daggers—and then her attention was caught by a sword unlike any other she'd ever seen. It was made of a heavy gray-black metal. She touched it gingerly, as if she expected it to bite her.

"What's this?" she asked softly.

"It's an experimental model," said her guide, "smelted from the iron ore we dig from the mountain."

"What would its advantage be, do you think? In battle, I mean."

"Well, simply put, an army furnished with these weapons would demolish an opposing force armed with conventional bronze swords."

Aglaophone gave that some thought. "How much?" she finally asked.

The giant burst out laughing. "It would take several more of that purse you and your sisters brought with you today!" He noticed the girl blush with embarrassment then said more gently, "Surely, Lady, you're not thinking of taking up soldiering."

"No," said Aglaophone quietly, "I just wanted to . . . study it."

"Oh," said Polyphemus, terminally puzzled.

Circe rescued him by sticking her head in the door. "All set?" she asked. When the party reconvened outside, it was decided that they'd split up for a short time—Polyphemus to tend to his civic duties, Circe to make some food and wine purchases, and the girls to explore. They agreed to meet for lunch in an hour outside a fruit stall where there was a picnic table. Polyphemus said he'd be happy to join them.

It was only when they met again at the appointed time that they realized that Aglaophone was missing. The twins said they hadn't noticed just when it was that she'd wandered off. After waiting a few minutes, they all went looking for her, her sisters going in one direction, Polyphemus and Circe heading back toward the main gate. As they approached it, Circe spotted Talos strolling around eating a handful of figs.

"Talos! Have you seen the Lady Aglaophone?"

"Uh, yes, Lady—about twenty minutes ago. I think she went outside."

"Oh, Hades and Hecate!" swore Circe. "NOW what's she getting into?"

She began to run toward the big settlement portal with Polyphemus tagging along behind. They burst through the gateway and hurriedly looked around. Then they saw a sight that truly shocked them. Coming back over the causeway that led to the priestess's little establishment was Aglaophone walking arm-in-arm with Ligeia. The two women were talking animatedly, as if they were mother and daughter.

Seeing Circe and Polyphemus, the princess grinned and waved. When she reached them with the skinny priestess in tow, she said, "I thought Ligeia might want to join us for lunch, so I went and got her!"

Overcoming her surprise as best she could manage, Circe smiled warmly. "Why that's wonderful! Come with us, Ligeia!"

Then Ligeia did something neither Circe nor Polyphemus had ever seen her do in all the years they'd known her. She smiled—shyly and, despite the absence of a couple of teeth, quite beautifully.

As they ate their snack of freshly baked bread, cheese, and figs, all washed down with cups of delicious dark wine from the Cyclopes' own vineyards on the lower slopes of Aetna, the chatter was lively and good-natured. The girls happily displayed their jewelry to Ligeia, who, to everyone's surprise, proved to be an interesting and vivacious conversationalist, once the wine had taken a bit of a hold. She also turned out to be, on second look, far younger—around thirty-five—and prettier than anyone had previously noticed.

When they were done, Circe exclaimed, "Now, Polyphemus, you must let us repay you for your kind hospitality! You must hear these girls sing!"

"Oh, no, Circe!" the girls chorused.

"We don't even have our instruments!" Thelxepeia pointed out.

"I'd love to hear you," said Ligeia.

"There! You're outvoted!" Circe laughed.

Groaning, the girls stood up and had a hasty conference to select their repertoire. They finally decided on two hymns. They began with a hymn to the Earth, which began

"The mother of us all
the oldest of all . . ."

Quickly, as their song progressed, a hushed crowd drew near to listen. As the ravishing voices lofted over the settlement, even shop owners were drawn out into the open, and tears spilled from every eye. In later years, legend would insist that even the tattooed third eyes wept.

For their second song, Aglaophone sang a hymn to Demeter, which ended with a plea to the Mother to "preserve this city." The audience response was similar, with Ligeia reduced to open sobbing. Without anyone noticing, Polyphemus momentarily disappeared. Then he emerged from the weapons shop carrying the iron sword. He came to where Aglaophone stood and mutely laid it in her arms.

"Oh, no!" she protested. "I couldn't!"

"Lady," said Polyphemus, his voice unsteady, "if I had ten of these, they would be insufficient payment for what you and your sisters have given all of us here today. Go with our blessing—and come again whenever you like. For, surely, no one cursed by a goddess could so look and sing like one."

      ✿   ✿   ✿

On the long drive home, Circe listened to the twins excitedly going on and on about the day's adventure. They kept admiring their new jewelry and chattering about the miraculous change the afternoon had wrought in the priestess, Ligeia.

"And, you know, those tattoo things weren't so bad, after you got used to them," Peisinoe said.

Thelxepeia wasn't so sure.

Circe, meanwhile, was watching Aglaophone with growing concern. The girl had barely said a word since leaving the settlement. Once they'd gotten underway, she'd untied the strange sword from the leather binding Polyphemus had wrapped it in. From then on, she'd just been staring down at it despondently.

"What's the matter, darling?" Circe asked quietly.

Barely audibly, Aglaophone said, "It's so sad. It's just so sad."

She hadn't had the dream again since the first time, but that night it returned with a vengeance. Dark swords smiting light ones. Fierce fires roaring over city walls. Dying groans. The shriek of women. Savage armies with angry, marching boots. A man in white hanging on a tree. Monster machines heaving boulders at walls. Iron tubes that roared and belched fire. Huge metal birds, dropping loud, orange death. And in the midst of all the carnage, the anguished face of the beautiful, golden-haired woman—which then disappeared in a frightening, blinding, mushrooming light like a thousand exploding Aetnas.

Aglaophone sat up in bed with a barely suppressed scream.

Now she knew EXACTLY who the woman named Daisy was.

Eleven

The next morning, Aglaophone arose feeling strangely disassociated from the world around her. Everything seemed out of kilter, as if she were a strange being from another place, someone neither her sisters nor Circe would any longer recognize. With a sense of leaden doom, she washed and dressed and, before any of the others were up and about, took the iron sword and wandered downstairs and out into the yard. She directed her steps toward the stable and sought out Talos. She found him brushing the mane of a horse.

"Talos," she called out.

Talos jumped, startled at her appearance, then hung his head, not meeting her eyes.

The girl, taking no apparent notice of his craven subservience, asked him if there were any old, discarded bronze swords on the premises, perhaps one belonging to some male servant now deceased. Talos mumbled that he'd go look and excused himself. Five minutes later he was back with the requested item. Aglaophone bade him follow her back out into the yard. There, after looking around, she noticed a tree stump used for mounting horses.

"Give me that, Talos, and you take this one."

"Yes, Lady."

They exchanged swords. The bronze weapon she'd been handed was scarred, bent, and rusted into a greenish tint. Aglaophone held it upright before her eyes for a moment; then laid the tip of it on the stump and, holding the hilt at arm's length, told Talos to strike down on the center of the old blade with all his strength. He hesitated.

"Do it, boy!" snapped the princess.

Finally, the youth's anger and resentment were ignited and, standing back, he raised the iron sword in a two-handed grip above his head and slashed brutally downward. The sword cleaved through the ancient weapon as if it were butter, and it shot with a clang from the girl's hand.

"EeeeeeeeeYOWWWWWW!!" she screamed and began hopping around in an erratic circle, clutching one hand with the other. Talos instantly dropped his weapon and fell abjectly to his knees as if he'd been pole-axed. Aglaophone moaned and whimpered then recollected her dignity, and, her eyes stinging with tears, picked up the ruined bronze sword. She examined it wordlessly for a short while and then nodded solemnly to herself. Tossing it aside, she picked up the iron weapon and headed for the back door to the villa.

As she reached it, she turned back and saw Talos still groveling in the dust, his head down, apparently waiting for some dreadful punishment to descend upon it. Laying down the sword, the princess retraced her steps.

When she stood over the youth, she said softly, "I called you a boy before. That was wrong of me."

Talos remained crestfallen and immobile.

"Talos, on his knees is not a good place for a man to be."

Having said that, she knelt before him and extended her still stinging hands to grasp his. Together, they rose to their feet.

She smiled, "Have you had breakfast yet?"

Mutely, Talos shook his head.

"Me, neither—and I'm famished! Come and join me! Do you like oranges?"

So saying, she led him toward the house.

By the time her sisters and Circe had arisen and were going about their daily business, the cloud of despair had again descended over Aglaophone. Not only did she not leave the house on one of her infamous walks, she spent the entire day in her room, emerging only at mealtimes. Then, instead of chirpily dominating the conversation, as was her habit, she replied to questions only in listless monosyllables. On a couple of occasions, Circe sent one or the other of the twins surreptitiously up the stairs to spy on her. They came back only to report with a shrug that the girl was sitting with the sword in her lap, downcast and brooding. Finally, it was agreed among them that Peisinoe and Thelxepeia would excuse themselves after the evening meal and leave Circe alone with her.

This was done. When the two of them were left to themselves, Circe asked, "What's wrong, Phonny?"

"Please, Circe, I'd rather not talk about it just now."

Still speaking gently, the older woman said, "Oh, but I insist. No moping in THIS house."

Aglaophone stared at her for a moment as if trying to bring her into focus, then said, "All right. Excuse me for a moment."

With that, she got up and went upstairs. While she was gone, Circe directed a servant to replenish the dying fire in the great central hearth. Then she drew two chairs over to it and poured two cups of the rich red wine she had purchased from the Cyclopes the previous day, liberally diluting the princess's drink, as always, with water. When the girl descended the stairs again, she was carrying, as Circe expected, the dark iron sword.

Approaching her hostess, she handed it to her and plopped down into one of the chairs.

"What do you see?" she asked dully.

Circe shrugged, perplexed. "An unusually heavy sword. What else?"

"DAMN IT CIRCE!" the princess shouted. "WHAT DO YOU SEE?"

Circe was stunned by the frantic savagery of the outburst. Then she recovered and fired back, "Don't you use that tone with ME, girl! Now stop this nonsense and explain yourself!"

Now it was Aglaophone's turn to look shocked. "I'm sorry. I'm sorry," she whimpered with her head down, close to tears. "But you said you had the Sight from the Mother. Circe? Can't you see?"

Circe relented and softened her tone. "My gift, Phonny, is a limited one. I don't so much 'see' the future as FEEL it, intuitively, I guess you'd say. I know there's a war, and I can sense who will be victorious and approximately when—and I'm pretty good at sizing up people, or at least I used to be. You and your sisters, obviously, threw me for a loop that first day." She handed the sword back. "Are you saying that YOU have the Sight? That you've just discovered it?"

"Oh, yes," breathed the girl sadly. She now raised the weapon upright before her eyes against the backdrop of the hearth flames. "It's all here, Circe. In this sword."

"What is?"

"The beginning of the end. The straight and narrow path to the destruction of everything on earth. Oh, I suppose you could make a claim that the first man who clubbed another with a tree branch, or the man who invented the bronze sword started the ruin—but now it will only accelerate."

"You see all this? In your head?"

"Like a flickering succession of images, yes. In the sword—and in dreams. Two of them—one the night I angered you with my lightning experiment, the other, much worse, last night. In a hundred years, Circe, swords like this will be in the hands of a race of savage soldiers who will descend upon all the lands of the Great Sea, slaughtering and destroying whomever and whatever they find. Then for several hundred years, there'll be . . . darkness. Nothing but fighting and surviving—or not surviving. Then humanity will slowly begin to pick itself up from the rubble again."

"What else?" asked Circe, barely able to breathe.

116

"Unfortunately, that will continue to be the pattern. Mighty new empires will rise only to fall when newer weapons are developed which are more and more deadly. Unimaginable weapons. Metal tube things, some hand-held, others bigger than a man, that send thunder and fire out of their spouts and knock down walls and buildings far away. Giant metal birds that drop explosions on people and towns. Huge, roaring arrows that fly over oceans. Then, finally, the worst of all—I think it must be the end of the world—a big, billowing cloud of blinding light that rumbles like a hundred earthquakes, as if the sun itself had burst upon the earth. Surely, nothing could survive such a thing."

Circe sat, shocked and silent. "Is there no hope?" she asked in a small voice.

"I'm not sure. I saw one man in last night's dream. I get the impression that he tried to save the world, but they nailed him to a tree and went on with all the killing. But then . . ."

Aglaophone stopped and sipped her wine then stood up, seemingly uncertain about going on.

"Yes?" Circe encouraged.

"Twice—once in both dreams—I saw . . . a woman. Last night I saw her just before the big fireball."

"What kind of woman?"

The princess was silent for a long time staring at the hearth flames. Then she turned to face Circe.

"Circe, like you I was brought up in luxury. I've had a mirror, as you do—and in its bronze surface, I've seen my face dimly reflected. I've gotten an even clearer look at myself in streams and pools—although the ripples cause some distortion."

"Why are you telling me this, Phonny?" Circe asked in an awe-struck whisper.

"Circe, the woman in the dream living in a strange land at the other end of time was about your age—but she wasn't you." Aglaophone audibly sighed. "She was me."

For a long while, the only sound in the big, shadowy hall was the pop and crackle of the fire.

Finally, Circe managed, "Are you sure?"

Aglaophone nodded.

"But didn't you just admit that our reflected images are indistinct—and that this woman was a lot older than you? Did she have your name?"

Aglaophone laughed mirthlessly. "No. She had a PRETTY name—though an odd one. Daisy."

"There. You see. She may not be. . ."

"Circe, in the first dream, she was with a man. He looked familiar, too, but I can't place him. Anyway, she was telling this man all about ME—as if, somehow, we were one and the same person, as if she were remembering her own childhood."

"What do you think it all means?" asked Circe, like a small child needing a sane and sure answer to a frightening mystery.

The princess took a deep breath. "I've been wondering the same thing—and I THINK I may have an idea, I think she's trying to keep the sun from exploding—and I think, through the Mother, she's trying . . . to get me to help her."

She took a step back toward her chair, when she suddenly gave a yelp, a happy sound, and dropped her cup to the tiles, where it clanged and rolled and spread its stain unheeded by either woman. With an ecstatic grin, she threw herself at Circe, hugged her, and nearly toppled her from her chair.

"Circe! Circe! She's FOUND him! She's WITH him! I'VE found him! The man she was with! It's Aganus! Oh, it's Aganus!" She began sobbing with joy.

"Who's Aganus?" asked Circe, patting the girl's back and finding her hysterical happiness flooding her own eyes.

"Aganus! The boy I loved back home! The boy I never thought I'd see again!"

Daisy abruptly stopped talking after telling Brian about the sword-testing incident with Aglaophone and Talos.

"Then what?" prompted Brian after a period of silence.

Daisy sighed and looked up at him. "Brian, do you mind if I save the rest for another time? The story gets awfully dark from here on in—and it's such a lovely morning. I'd like to hold onto it, if I can."

Brian gave her a hug. "Of course."

Daisy sighed again, happily this time, and snuggled against him on the bench.

"Say, Mister, you remember all that sex stuff you introduced me to last night?"

"Yeah?"

"Well, the way I figure it, I've got four hours and twenty minutes till check-out time—and I've got a few variations of my own I'd like to try. If you don't have anything better to do, of course."

How could he turn down the last of the red hot Sirens?

Laughing, they raced all the way back to the hotel.

Twelve

August, 2004

Arianna Dillon could not BELIEVE where she was! But it was undeniably true. She was in the middle of the third row of the Majestic Theater on West 44th Street in Manhattan watching THE SOUND OF GODDAMN MUSIC. And Jesus and Dionysus! There was no way to stop it—the star of the show, Daisy Crandall, and seven indescribably obnoxious children in dirndls and lederhosen were now going to start singing "Do-re-mi." How had it come to this?

She knew, of course. It came with the territory. She and her husband were now credibly positioned to become the new occupants of the White House, as of next January. That meant, among other things, they had to display some celebrity supporters. The Democrats had Streisand, Alec Baldwin, Cher, and Paul Newman. The Republicans could always trot out Bruce Willis, Tom Selleck, and Bo Derek. But so far, the only star of any wattage whatsoever to indicate sympathy toward Donald Dillon's Independent Party candidacy was the over-the-hill musical star, Daisy Crandall—Broadway's Sweetheart—adorable, still incredibly pretty in her mid-fifties, talented, but unfortunately, a total ditz.

Arianna reminded herself to strangle—no, dismember—her public relations director, Brendan Foley, for involving the Dillon campaign with such an obvious airhead as Daisy Crandall. Foley, a blond model Mel Gibson look-alike, had originally been assigned to profile the Dillons for *Trendsetter* magazine once Donald's inevitability as a national candidate had become evident. He had proven to be very suggestible and the piece that had been published had garnered Donald a lot of favorable publicity. Foley also demonstrated soon thereafter that he had a low integrity threshold, and Arianna'd been able to wean, if not seduce him, away from *Trendsetter* and onto her personal staff.

As it happened, the man had previously shared the same agent as Daisy Crandall, and he'd informed her that Crandall had unsuspected far-right tendencies and was still a big enough name to attract new adherents. Why not invite her to the next fundraiser at the Labyrinth on Long Island—and then attend the premiere of her six-week *Sound of Music* revival on Broadway? Arianna'd gone along with the suggestion. The raves, of course, and the upstairs sexual booby traps were long gone. The risk of exposure was now far too great. So any money-raising was now low-key and legitimate. If attendees and contributors were going to get high, it would have to be on booze alone.

That hadn't stopped Daisy Crandall, who'd managed extraordinarily well on several glasses of Spumanti. Inevitably, she and Donald had become exceptionally friendly—after all, being blond and petite, she was very much his type. By the end of the evening, they'd been calling to each other across a crowded room, as Rodgers and Hammerstein would say. They'd even coined nicknames for each other. She was Daisyducks and he was Donnydiddums. Fortunately, all the reporters and correspondents on hand were blackmailable, and none of this had ever made it into print.

So here she was, suffering through Little Debbie Cakes and a platoon of stunted Munchkins actually singing 'Do-re-mi.''

Calm down, she told herself. It could be worse. This was, after all, a fairly beneficial photo op. Admittedly, Daisy Crandall wasn't J.Lo or even Whitney Houston at her most wasted. But, like Lawrence Welk, in ages past, she had a direct pipeline to the sentimental hearts and votes of mid-America, who didn't give a rat's rear end WHO Liza was marrying this week or who Elton John's partner-du-jour was.

Arianna let her mind glaze over and start to consider the good things of life. First and foremost, of course, was the First Ladyship that was about to fall into her lap. Then there was the relief of having New Dawn fade, like a dimly remembered bad dream, into the irrelevant mist. It was almost as if the whole thing had been an Internet prank, a bad joke that had expired at its inception. Not since the day two years earlier when Rhonda, her assistant, had brought the list of frightening New Dawn names to her attention had there been even a single phone call referring to the Great Mother or any other unsettling message plainly targeting the Dillon presidential campaign.

Then, too, there was the matter of Kyle Webber, her chauffeur both in the limo and in bed, who was about to begin his third term as year-king. The man was incredible! She just couldn't bring herself to give him the ax. He was good for up to six orgasms a night. She had assumed that Brendan Foley would be his natural replacement—but he was proving difficult. Either Foley was gay, which didn't seem likely given her attraction to him, or he was incorruptible, which was patently absurd. Nobody since Adam and Eve or Epimetheus and Pandora had been.

In the midst of these musings, something clicked in Arianna's mind: Daisy Crandall, the woman onstage right now singing that abominable song. On the one hand, the evening she had recently spent in her company plainly indicated that the lady had the mental gravitas of a soufflé. On the other hand, something was definitely off-key here. The singer onstage was not only a total pro, but she was definitely in charge—scarily so. She effortlessly commanded the stage, the audience, and, most tellingly, her colleagues. You found yourself looking at no one but her. When she sang, part of you died because you knew she would stop, and you could never get back the moment of hearing her do THAT again. When she was offstage, nothing onstage mattered.

Arianna shook herself out of this poetic fancy. In another hour, she'd be thrown together with Crandall backstage and could easily satisfy herself again that the actress was nothing more than a brainless bimbo trying to hitch a ride on the Dillon Express.

And so it seemed. After the performance and Crandall's innumerable curtain calls, Arianna and Donald were whisked backstage for the kind of proleterian photo match-up that commandeered front-page headlines in *The New York Post* and *The National Enquirer*. As soon as they appeared in the doorway of the star's dressing room, it began.

"Donnydiddums!"

"Daisyducks!"

Jesus Christ! Where was Joan Rivers with her gag reflex when you needed her?

Donald and Daisy fervently embraced. Then Crandall acknowledged Arianna's presence.

"Adrianne! Good to see you again!"

"Arianna."

"Oh, sorry! Wasn't that silly of me? How'd you like the show, Donald?"

"It was wonderful," Dillon said dutifully.

Daisy swatted his wrist. "Donald! We have to train you better! When an actress asks how you liked her show, she's REALLY asking how you liked HER!"

Dillon grinned foolishly. "Oh, of course. You were magnificent. It goes without saying."

"Donald! No, no, no, no! It never goes without saying, you silly boy! Oh, look at him blush! Allison, this husband of yours is ADORABLE! I think I'm going to have to steal him from you!"

Arianna could only smile weakly.

"You know, it never really occurred to me before, but Don-nydiddums, here, looks a lot like Dennis Miller—you know, the TV comic? What do you think, uh, Arianna? Doesn't he look just like Dennis Miller? But Dennis Miller's a real potty-mouth—and I don't approve of that at ALL! Donald is a total gentleman, and that's what a lady likes, especially in a President!"

Arianna couldn't resist. "Are you a conservative then, Daisy?"

"Oh, I never trouble my head about politics. All I care is that the man I vote for thinks the way I do—and is good-looking, of course. I mean, who wants some fat little bald person representing us, you know, with overseas leaders and all? We want a man who LOOKS like a President!"

"Fascinating!" said Arianna. She definitely began to relax. Whatever doubts she'd entertained about Daisy Crandall earlier in the evening had been pleasantly resolved. The actress's IQ need no longer be a concern. Obviously, the refrigerator door was open and the light was out.

Meanwhile, back at the Labyrinth, the Dillon home on Long Island, two people were avidly searching for the key to the cellar, where they suspected the lady of the house had long been perpetrating high crimes and misdemeanors. One of them was Arianna's public relations director, Brendan Foley, previously known as the writer, Brian Ames. The other was Arianna's longtime assistant and confidante, the part-time TV actress, Rhonda Raveneaux—who, as the Dawn Timer Hippolyta, Queen of the Amazons, was a highly prized member of the New Dawn council.

"Where can the damn thing BE?" groaned Rhonda, busily rummaging through one of the twin nightstands in Arianna's bedroom while Brian ransacked the other. For all the time Rhonda'd spent in the house over the past three years, she'd never been left there alone before. But Arianna had needed her to mail out some last minute invitations to another at-home fundraiser coming up and so had directed her to stay till the job was done. Rhonda had alerted Brian earlier in the day, and he'd made the two-hour drive from Daisy's house near Darien, Connecticut, and arrived there after the Dillons had departed for the theater.

"Keep looking!" Brian urged.

Then a man behind them cleared his throat, and both the intruders gasped and spun around. There filling the bedroom doorway with his formidable six-four frame was Arianna's lover, Kyle Webber, the ex-weight trainer.

Aside from simultaneously and audibly gulping, Brian and Rhonda could only stand there petrified. Then Webber lazily extended his right hand from which a small object protruded.

"Looking for this?" he asked. He came forward and handed it to Rhonda.

The very thing.

"Christ, Daisy! I must have had about eighteen heart attacks in those first two seconds after he showed up! Then, fortunately, he turns out to be one of the good guys!"

'Yes, but who?" Daisy puzzled, with her chin propped on her fist. They were sitting in Brian's study in the guest cottage on the Beaumont family estate. Brian had gotten home first and called Daisy at the theater, just as she was saying goodbye to the Dillons. She decided to drive home right then, rather than spend the night at the midtown hotel she'd booked herself into for the six-week run of her show. Before proceeding up to the main house, she'd stopped for an urgent wee hours conference with Brian.

"Rhonda's got the key?"

"Yes. She's having a couple of duplicates made. Then she figures to slip the original back to Webber the first chance she

125

gets tomorrow. Let's hope Arianna doesn't head for the basement before then. By the way, isn't Webber himself due again to go to the way of all flesh? His second anniversary as Arianna's year-king is coming up."

"True, but Rhonda's not getting any bad vibes. As you know, there are no replacements living down at the compound, and Arianna's in an extraordinarily good mood every morning. He must be exceptional in bed. Either that, or she realizes the risk of discovery now is too great. Another possibility, of course, is the fact that 'Brendan Foley' isn't coming across as she'd expected. He isn't, is he?"

Daisy meant the question to be humorous but felt a stab of anxiety, even as she asked it. Brian reached over and pulled her onto his lap. He kissed her and said, "In a word, no. Say, you want . . . ?"

Daisy laughed with ill-disguised relief and pushed herself up and away from him. "Not right now, O Lusty One!" She picked up again the glossy eight-by-ten of Kyle Webber that they'd had on file since Rhonda had faxed it to them two years earlier. She studied it intently.

"Who? . . . WAIT a minute!" Daisy's voice was suddenly vibrant with excitement. "Oohhhh, Brian! This could be a major, MAJOR boost for New Dawn, if this is who I think it is!"

"Who?"

"Not right now! I've got to check something out before I can be sure! There's someone special I've got to try to contact!"

"Well, do it here! There's the phone."

Daisy laughed as she headed for the door. "AT&T doesn't have the set-up yet to handle THIS call. It would blow every transformer in the state!"

Back in her own room up in the mansion on a hill overlooking Long Island Sound, Daisy anxiously and excitedly closed all the shades, blocking every nighttime glimmer from outside.

Then she shut off the lights and in pitch darkness lay down on her still made bed. She'd been daring herself to try this for a long time now—ever since she'd sensed Aglaophone "eavesdropping" on her and Brian that early morning back in Evanston—but had never really gotten up the nerve. She'd always felt that the disappointment of failure would be too shattering to endure. But the girl's life was at stake, after all. Waiting any longer would be unconscionably cruel to her psychologically and would leave no time at all to effect a remedy, if one were indeed available. Added now to that concern, her sudden, inspired suspicions about Kyle Webber's true identity had sparked her conviction that the Mother had started to orchestrate New Dawn's endgame and that it was up to her to implement it.

Closing her eyes, she lay straight and absolutely still. She emptied her mind of everything extraneous and focused her thought with laser-like intensity on an exiled, now twenty-seven-year-old princess approaching the end of her life in the year 1236 B.C.

Inner Time

(Are you there?)

(. . . ?!? . . . Yes?)

(Do you know who I am?)

(Daisy.)

(That's right.)

(I dream of you a lot. How are we doing this?)

(I'm not sure. This is the first time I've tried it. It seems that The Mother has opened up the Way.)

(This is wonderful!)

(Where are you, Phonny? Right now?)

(I'm standing outside our house on the promontory. It's late morning on a warm day. I like to come out here and practice my singing.)

(I'm a singer, too. I sang earlier tonight in a big theater here.)

(Tonight? But it's morning, I told you.)

(Not where I am—on the other side of the world. You were right. The world is round. You're six hours ahead of us there in Sicily. I can explain all this another time.)

(But where ARE you? WHEN are you?)

(Phonny, I'm in a country called America, thousands of miles across the Atlantic Ocean beyond the pillars of Heracles. I am living—I know this may be hard to accept—three thousand, two hundred and forty years in what to you is the future.)

(Oh.)

(I'm fifty-four years old.)

(That can't be possible. You're so very pretty in my dreams.)

(Thank you. I come from good stock. Phonny, getting back to your situation for a moment. You said you were in the shrine. Ligeia's dead by now, right?)

(Yes, she taught me—taught US—much when we came to assist her at the shrine. Do you remember Polyphemus had his builders enlarge the house for us?)

(Yes. Where are your sisters today?)

(In town. It's my day to offer sacrifices and libations to the Mother.)

(Ugh! Do you still have to behead the birds?)

(Yes, people still insist on the ritual. I HATE it! It's so . . . primitive and useless.)

(You're right, it is—and yet people have remained the same in that respect, all these centuries later—still looking for answers from gods through rote prayer and sacrifice. Phonny, the world I'm living in has become extremely dangerous. An evil man is trying to gain control of it. If he does, the whole world could . . . blow up!)

(I know. I've seen the pillar of fire.)

(Yes, our wise men have unwisely opened Pandora's box and unlocked the secrets of the sun. Anyway, I'm trying desperately to prevent this man from taking over. There are others who are helping me. Peisinoe and Thelxepeia live with me. Their names are Pamela and Teresa now. And, Phonny, Aganus is with me, too. His name is Brian. We're going to be married soon, although being a man, he doesn't quite realize it yet.)

(That's wonderful. But it makes me sad that I can't be with him myself. I still miss him terribly. I've never even been tempted to take a lover to replace him.)

(I know, Phonny. Your life has been hard in many respects, but you have achieved great things in your few years. But getting back to what I was saying, I think someone else from your time may be trying to help, too. Someone very important. Do you remember when that big handsome wine merchant from Thrace stopped at . . . Father's court for a few days—how you—how WE—drooled over him? His name was Dionysus, and people believed him to be a god because of his looks and the wondrous drink he provided. In fact, in some places, he was already being worshipped.)

(I remember. He was as tall as Polyphemus and had dark hair and piercing eyes.)

(Yes! I can picture him perfectly now! That's definitely him! He's here with us, too, and I think he intends to be a help. . . . Phonny, there's something else I have to tell you now—something very frightening.)

(. . . What, Daisy?)

(. . . Your time is very limited. I'm sorry to have to tell you this, darling.)

(What happens to me? I mean how. . . ?)

(I . . . can't answer that, Phonny. If I do, you'll try to change it. And that's never allowed—even in my time. We still don't know how to alter our destiny. If you tried to change yours, based on what I tell you, it might affect the future in unimaginable ways—just by ONE person being where she wasn't supposed to be.)

(. . . I see. . . . Can you at least tell me when it will be? I'd like to be . . . ready.)

(. . . Not long. A couple of weeks. . . . I'm sorry, darling.)

(. . . Oh. . . . Daisy, I feel so cold now . . . so afraid.)

(Phonny, listen. I can't promise. But I think there's a way we might be able to . . . CHANGE your life when the time of your death comes. You will see it coming enough in advance to select the manner and exact moment of it.)

(You mean—commit suicide?)

(Believe me, suicide will seem the natural culmination of a devastating day of loss for you, Phonny. But as I say, I think we can work out a way to bring you to ME at the precise moment when your death is . . . in progress. Then we can BOTH live out MY life in this time—as one.)

(That would be wonderful! You can do this thing?)

(I think WE can do it together, darling. I really think so. I have to go now—but I'll be back soon, and we'll plan this thing out. I promise. Have faith in yourself and the Mother, Phonny. You and She and I are, after all, one and the same.)

(. . . Thank you, Daisy. . . . Good-bye.)

(Good-bye . . . and be brave.)

Thirteen

Daisy should have felt elated by the epochal breakthrough she'd just achieved in psychic communication, but instead she was overwhelmed by sadness. She now understood first hand the age-old curse of humanity's creative and inventive instincts, the Frankenstein conundrum: for every positive discovery there were dozens of unintended negative consequences. For example: invent the automobile and create forty thousand deaths a year. Develop television and raise generations of passive, non-reading ignoramuses. Split the atom and risk wiping out the species. Drop in unexpectedly on a child living at the dawn of history and casually deliver her a death sentence.

That poor girl. She had awakened to a beautiful morning as full of promise as her vital young life, only to be informed by a motherly, authoritative voice in her head that what was left of her existence could be measured out in a handful of days. Worse, she had been denied even the most rudimentary information abut the nature of her approaching death or from what direction to expect the blow. Instead, she'd been provided only with a vague hope of mysterious, last minute, other-worldly salvation.

Would there really be any harm in letting Aglaophone know what was headed her way—so that she would have some sort of fighting chance? Daisy knew that the classic theory bandied about for generations by scientists and fiction writers was that any change, however small, inflicted upon the past by the present would disrupt catastrophically the flow of history; might even destroy the present. What if a time traveler had contrived to prevent Lincoln's or Einstein's parents from meeting, for example?

Should she risk it? Could the current state of the world possibly be any worse if a young woman in the ancient past were allowed to live to see her twenty-eighth birthday? If she had been some dim-witted peasant girl? Probably not. The trouble was that Aglaophone was not only royalty living in a time when such personages were held in semi-religious awe, but also a forceful, brilliant, and daring woman of the type that would undoubtedly make a significant mark upon history's stage, for good or conceivably for ill. The things she did, the marriage she made, the children she bore—all of these might ultimately weigh heavily in the unfolding of the world's story.

Daisy sighed. Better leave it alone. One thing she would do, though. She would devote every ounce of mental and physical energy she could spare from her fight to deny Donald Dillon the White House to managing that unique deliverance from death she had promised her Dawn Time self.

In the meantime, she would have to bestir herself and find out just where Kyle Webber, once known as the demigod Dionysus, fit into the scheme of things.

Two nights later, Daisy was wiping off the last vestiges of her stage make-up after her third *Sound of Music* performance, when she saw in her mirror that Donald Dillon was leering at her from her dressing room doorway.

"Hiya, Daisyducks!" He proffered her a cellophane-wrapped bouquet of roses.

"Why, Donald! What a surprise!" *And a totally unpleasant one at that!* "Oh, these are lovely! Thank you!"

" 'Donald'! We can do better than that, can't we?"

"Sorry, Donnydiddums. So, uh, Donny—what's the occasion? Is Arianna with you?"

"No. She's back home attending to her needlepoint. I happen to be spending the night in town and thought you might join me for a bite to eat somewhere."

"Well, Donny, that's very sweet, but I'm not terribly hungry. Plus, I've got a long day tomorrow—a matinee and an evening performance."

"Oh, come on! Why don't we just grab a cab up to Rosie O'Grady's for half an hour?"

"It's Friday night! It's likely to be packed. And you're a married man running for President. We'll be all over the tabloids tomorrow."

"I'll risk it for Daisybucks! No—seriously, can't a politician have a little public conference with a key supporter?"

"Well—okay, Donny, since you put it that way. Just as long as Arianna doesn't come after me with an ax or something."

Dillon froze. "What made you say that?" he finally asked.

Daisy reached up and brushed some imaginary lint from his lapel. "Why, Donnydiddums! If you were MY husband, that's what I'D do if somebody were trying to get you away from me!"

"Is that what you're trying to do?"

"You have to ask, you presidential frontrunner, you? But you'll have to leave while I make a personal call—and I'll have to sign some autographs outside. Hey, Donny, maybe they'll want yours, too!"

"You think so?"

"Of course. You're a major celebrity now! Besides, they can always sell it on eBay for ten bucks. Now, run along. I'll see you outside in a few minutes."

When she was sure he was gone, Daisy placed a quick call to her hotel suite at the Times Square Marriott. Arianna Dillon's public relations man answered.

"Brian? The Man Who Would Be King just dropped by my dressing room and insisted on a late supper at Rosie O'Grady's. You know where that is? . . . Right, corner of 52nd. Wouldn't it be intriguing if photographers from *The Post* and

The Daily News popped in and caught Mr. Married Frontrunner hitting on a, you should pardon the expression, famous actress?"

"Daisy, you sure you want that? It can't do your image any good to get caught that way."

"Darling, I must make the sacrifice in order to alert poor Arianna. Besides, inquiring minds want to know. Make the calls, okay?"

Brian laughed. "You're a piece of work, Daisyducks!"

"Don't call me that!"

"You must be pleased with your reviews," said Dillon. "They were sensational."

"Thank you, Donny. Yes, it looks as if my career still has a little kick in it."

They were sitting at a corner table on the upper level of a popular saloon-style restaurant in midtown, just north of the theater district. Predictably, their entry had created a considerable stir among the crowd of patrons, but now they'd been left to themselves. They each ordered a chicken salad sandwich and a glass of Merlot.

"Why wouldn't it? You're a wonderful performer and an astonishingly lovely woman."

"Well, thank you . . . but should you be noticing other women? I mean, a married man and a minister, running for President?"

"These aren't the Middle Ages, Daisy. People aren't concerned any more about clergymen . . . enjoying themselves, as long as it's not with little boys. And Bill Clinton proved a President can get away with murder."

"Do you think that's right? A President getting away with . . . murder?"

Again, Dillon seemed startled and gave her a dark look.

"I mean," Daisy explained, "the main reason I'm attracted to you—besides your good looks, of course—is because you seem, well, so moral. Don't you believe in being faithful to Ariel?"

"Arianna. Yes, of course I'm faithful. She's a wonderful woman. . . ."

"Very strong. You're lucky to have her. She doesn't seem as if she'd let anything get in the way of you becoming President!"

Dillon sighed. "You got THAT right!"

Daisy took a large sip of her wine and giggled, "Wow! Imagine me sitting here with the next President of the United States!"

With what was intended as a playful leer, Dillon said, "You can do a lot MORE with him if you like!"

Daisy looked shocked. "Why, Mr. Dillon! That's *awful!* . . . Oh, you were joking, weren't you?"

Dillon sighed again. "Yes, I was only joking."

Daisy pouted. "I don't like people joking about, you know, dirty things."

"But you said yourself back in your dressing room that you were trying to get me away from Arianna—and you said the same thing to HER the other night."

"Oh, but I was only . . . "

"Joking?"

Daisy raised her hand to cover her mouth and laughed nervously. "You must think I'm SOOO dumb!"

Dillon let that one slide.

"Gosh, though! What a kick it would be to be First Lady!" Daisy said dreamily.

"You'd like that?"

"Of course! What woman wouldn't. Sleeping in the Lincoln Bedroom, hosting Easter egg hunts on the White House lawn, meeting the Queen of England. It would all be a dream come true!"

"So, if I divorced Arianna and married you instead, you would go for that?"

Dillon thought Daisy would get upset again at the semi-playful suggestion.

"Well," she said, "I know you're teasing again. But that would be the ONLY way we could ever . . . become involved."

Dillon looked at her hard for a moment, as if considering the possibilities of what she'd said. Then he ruefully shook his head. "It doesn't matter," he said. "This is my last fling, so to speak—the last time I'll ever get to be alone with a pretty lady other than my wife."

Daisy looked puzzled. "What do you mean?"

"Well, next week the Independent Party is officially nominating me in Chicago. From then on, I'll be under Secret Service protection night and day. No more sneaking off by myself."

"Where there's a will there's a way," Daisy pointed out reasonably.

Just then they sensed a commotion headed their way from the lower level of the restaurant.

Daisy said, "Oh, look! Photographers!"

Alarmed, Dillon whipped around and raised his arm to shield his face against the blinding flash.

"You don't want to do that, Donald!" Daisy said with concern. "It'll ruin the shot—and it makes you look guilty, like you're trying to hide something. Don't worry, though. I think they got you!"

Fourteen

DONALD AND DAISY! DUCK! screamed the front page of *The New York Post.*

ARRIVIDERCI, ARIANNA? questioned *The New York Daily News.*

Both daily tabloids ran the identical photo under Kennedy assassination-size headlines. It showed a radiantly beaming Daisy Crandall sitting opposite a desperate, deer-in-the-headlights Donald Dillon cringing from the camera's exposure.

"Nice going, Donnydiddums!" snarled Arianna. "I haven't seen that expression on a human face since Janet Leigh ran into Anthony Perkins in the shower. Just the man America wants diddling with its nuclear arsenal!" The Dillons were sitting across the breakfast table from each other, and Arianna made her husband sit still while she read him *The Post*'s article, word for humiliating word.

"Presidential frontrunner Donald Dillon, about to assume the mantle of Independent Party nominee next week, was discovered late Friday night enjoying an intimate late night supper in a Manhattan restaurant with Broadway diva Daisy Crandall, currently enjoying a hugely popular return to the New York stage in a new production of the Rodgers and Hammerstein evergreen, *The Sound of Music.* The tête-à-tête took place at Rosie O'Grady's, just north of Times Square.

"There is every reason to believe the pairing was innocent, as Ms. Crandall is known to support Mr. Dillon's candidacy, and is, in fact, the only celebrity so far to do so. Why then, one wonders, did Dillon, with only a terse 'no comment,' bolt so precipitously from the restaurant, leaving his charming companion to fend for herself?

"Fortunately, the lovely lady was more than equal to the task and readily submitted to the questions of reporters—although some of her replies seemed a bit disingenuous. Were she and the very married presidential candidate a romantic item? 'Of course not!' replied Crandall. 'We're just good friends!'

"To the question of why Arianna Dillon was not present, Crandall professed ignorance, saying only that the candidate had told her Mrs. Dillon was home for the evening, apparently doing some sewing. Asked why she and Dillon were sharing a late night supper, Crandall would only say that Dillon apparently valued her interest in his candidacy and 'was seeking some input,' a comment that drew laughter from bystanders.

"One scribe wondered at Crandall's support of a presidential candidate whom many regard as far to the right of center. Did she espouse such extreme positions herself? The star replied that she wasn't quite sure about what 'positions' the question referred to—but that she was by no means totally 'sold' on Dillon yet and had actually made no financial contribution thus far to his White House bid.

" 'I'm adopting a wait-and-see attitude,' she said.

" 'Could she ever envision herself as First Lady?' a female reporter inquired.

" 'Certainly!' grinned the delightful star, 'but only if I were the President's wife!' The conversation then turned to Crandall's current resurgence as a born-again Broadway superstar in the new *Sound of Music*.

" 'Well, it's certainly very touching to think that the public still remembers an older performer who's been out of the limelight for so long,' she said. Responding to the mischievous question of how old she might be, Crandall ended the impromptu interview with a wink and a smile, 'Believe me, THAT you don't want to know!' "

Arianna felt like screaming. Only five months shy of the White House, and Donald Dillon was splashed all over the nation's front pages and the morning news shows looking like the poster boy for Cheat-of-the-Month Club—while Crandall the Cretin came out of it smelling like Broadway Daisy Rose. The little idiot had actually GAINED stature, judging from the fawning tone of the *Post* article.

"Okay, Mr. Moral Voice of America, now what?"

"Oh, for God's sake, Arianna, stop having a cow! Relax! Blow off some steam! Why don't you go down in the cellar and turn Kyle Webber into chipped beef?"

"This is no time for flippancy! Bill Clinton could TAKE this kind of heat. He was built for it. Everybody knew he was a horny frat boy going in! You're supposed to be the Voice of Goddam God, for Christ sake!"

Dillon said calmly, "I'll handle it. I'm booked on Alan Pope's CNS interview show Monday night before I fly to Chicago to pick up the nomination. I'll explain all about my little outing with Daisy Crandall—which you seem to forget WAS totally innocent, in spite of appearances."

"In case you haven't noticed it, politics IS appearances and show biz, too. It's a good thing Miss Cotton Candy Head isn't running against you. She'd win in a landslide!"

"She doesn't want to be President. She wants to be First Lady—remember?"

Arianna groaned. Then she said, "Too bad you couldn't croak her and ship her down The Old Mill Stream the way you did all your blond TV co-hosts."

Dillon lifted his head. "You know about all that? Well, forget it! Crandall's an international celebrity. Somebody might miss her."

"No reason she can't pull a Jimmy Hoffa."

Dillon suddenly sat up straight and got a faraway, reflective look in his eye.

"You actually considering it?" Arianna asked.

"Huh? . . . No. Arianna read over some of those quotes of hers to yourself for a minute. See if they sound like the remarks of an airhead, as you've always considered her."

His wife for once did as she was told. "I see what you mean," she said quietly. "What are you getting at?"

"Well, for one thing, HAS she made a contribution yet?"

"I'll ask Rhonda when she gets in—but, no, I don't think so."

"So, in other words, we've entertained her HERE, and we've suffered through that insufferable musical—and we've got squat to show for it?"

Arianna nodded. "Looks that way."

"How'd we originally tie into her, anyway? It was through your publicity guy, What's his face—Foley, wasn't it? Something about them sharing the same agent?"

Arianna was starting to get a bad feeling about all this.

"Do you know who it is?"

She thought a minute. "Yeah. The Aurora Agency. That means 'dawn' in Latin, doesn't it? A woman named Teresa Beaumont. Gorgeous looking. In fact, she has an identical twin, who heads up a big law firm for entertainment figures. Pamela, I think."

Dillon turned pale. "Uh-oh!" he said, not certain why. He stood up and went to the sink, where he stood looking out the window.

"What is it?" Arianna asked nervously.

"During intermission the other night, I took a minute to glance through Daisy Crandall's cast biography in the theater program. It said her real name was Beaumont . . . Beatrice, I think. Beatrice Beaumont. It said she started out as part of a

140

singing act with her older twin sisters. And I think those were their names—Pamela and Teresa."

Arianna had always assumed the cliché about feeling the room spin around you was dime-store literary exaggeration, but now she guessed it wasn't.

From far away, she heard herself ask, "Do you still have your program? I tossed mine into the first trashcan I came to."

Dillon mumbled, "I think it's still in my jacket." He went upstairs to look. All the while he was gone, Arianna clutched both sides of the kitchen chair so she wouldn't topple off. Her husband came back and handed her a copy of *Playbill* opened to the Crandall biography. Arianna gazed, mesmerized now, at the innocuous face of the little blond actress. Then she let her eyes wander down the column of information. There it was, about a quarter of the way down. Back three decades ago, Daisy and her singing sisters had billed themselves as New Dawn.

The truth came crashing down on Arianna. Once upon a time, millennia ago, Daisy Crandall had been Aglaophone the Siren.

Now she was the Great Mother of the New Dawn council.

Having come to that inescapable conclusion, Arianna DID scream. She fainted, too.

Excerpt from the transcript of *The Alan Pope Show* on CNS, August 23, 2004:

Pope—Reverend Dillon, you created quite a stir last Friday evening in New York City when you suddenly showed up in a crowded midtown restaurant in the company of musical star Daisy Crandall instead of your wife. Care to comment?

Dillon—Much ado about nothing, Alan, much ado about nothing. Obviously, a left-wing attempt to embarrass a candidate whose views are dramatically opposed to theirs—and who is leading the field in the presidential race.

Pope—But nagging doubts persist, Reverend Dillon. If your little get-together with Ms. Crandall was entirely above board, why did you hastily leave the premises, stranding her there, so to speak, and, apparently sticking her with the bill?

Dillon—I was legitimately angered at the uncalled-for media intrusion. And as a matter of fact, I contacted the restaurant the next day and settled my bill with them. They assured me that Ms. Crandall had so thoroughly charmed the entire establishment that there was no charge for her.

Pope—And do YOU find her charming?

Dillon—Of course. I'm a man, after all, and she's a beautiful and talented woman—but I must say, as I've learned to my sorrow, something of a disappointment.

Pope—Oh? In what way?

Dillon—I had been counting on her support—incidently, the only reason I was meeting with her that night. Yet, I see by the comments attributed to her in *The New York Post* that she seems to be distancing herself from me—and is taking a wait-and-see attitude towards my candidacy. I can't help but wonder at her change of heart. I'd previously had the impression that she was solidly in my corner.

Pope—Any educated guesses as to her apparent . . . defection?

Dillon—You'd have to ask Ms. Crandall—but I think she may have been disappointed that I obviously wasn't taking a . . . personal interest in her.

Pope—Personal. You mean romantic? Are you suggesting that Daisy Crandall was, as they say, coming on to you?

Dillon—I'm sure I can't read the woman's mind. But I do know that she made at least two joking comments about getting me away from my wife—and was constantly talking about how wonderful it would be to be First Lady. She must have gotten the message that I wasn't interested in the least in pursuing an illicit romance with her and so grew lukewarm about lending me her support.

Pope—I see. Well, I have to say, Reverend Dillon, that your remarks about Daisy Crandall border on the ungallant, not to say slanderous. I will certainly extend to her an invitation to come on the show and present her side of the story, if she so wishes.

Dillon—You do as you feel you must, Alan, but I assure you that unless we turn immediately to more serious and substantive matters regarding my political views and plans for the presidency, you will find yourself talking to an empty chair when you return from the next commercial break.

Pope—Very well, then, let's address those issues. I'm sure you're aware, Reverend, that many in this country are expressing concern about those very views and policies. Some say that your foreign policy announcements are so aggressive that they virtually amount to a declaration of holy war against the entire Muslim world, making no distinction between friend and foe. They also point out that you seem deliberately to be blurring the Constitutionally mandated separation of Church and State with your persistent references to God and Christ. Thirdly, they suggest that there's a distinct whiff of racial, ethnic, and gender bias in your campaign. There are no African-Americans or Jews among your many advisors and operatives—and only one or two women in minor posts.

Dillon—Well, Alan, that's quite a mouthful and quite an indictment. Let me begin to respond by pointing out that those expressing the opinions you so righteously cite are the media flacks and hacks who think they control political discourse in this country—those who aren't content unless they are tearing down this great nation and all its values and God-given ideals. Let me also point out that 68% of the American PUBLIC actively share those ridiculed ideals and support my candidacy, according to all the latest polls, including CNS's.

143

Pope—Be that as it may, how do you respond to these expressed concerns?

Dillon—Very well, let's take them one at a time. First of all, apparently neither you nor those whose accusations you mouth bothered to notice that three years ago on 9/11 the Muslim world declared war on US. Now, I know that the politically correct view holds that only a small percentage of Middle-Easterners are terrorists—but how do we know exactly WHAT that percentage is? I say it's better to be safe than sorry—and so I put that whole part of the world on notice. Once I became President, any act of terrorism against those sovereign shores will be met by MASSIVE retaliation against the entire Middle East.

Pope—That's insane! Does that mean nuclear weapons?

Dillon—No, it's blunt and realistic—and yes, moderate, targeted use of our nuclear arsenal would certainly be an option I'd seriously consider.

Pope—In spite of the fact that Israel is surrounded by Arab states?

Dillon—That is indeed regrettable—and I certainly hope that the terrible day never arrives when our nuclear capability will have to be deployed. But should it happen on my watch, I must tell you that that I would not be deterred by Israel's unfortunate geography. Too many Presidents in recent decades, including the incumbent, have allowed a small but vocal ally to hold our foreign policy hostage—with the full connivance of the media elite, whose ranks are filled to overflowing with Jewish producers, commentators, and performers—all of whom seem to regard America as an annexed territory, whose main goal is and should be the survival of Israel at all costs.

Pope—I believe, Reverend Dillon, that you can safely kiss the Jewish vote goodbye.

Dillon—I'm sorry to hear it. But if that is the price of plain-speaking as opposed to politically correct kowtowing, so be it! And if my unswerving opposition to such abominations as affirmative action, reparations for slavery, and abortion costs me the vote of every black American and every female American, as well, I'm prepared to pay the price.

Pope—I take it then, that you're staking the election entirely upon the support of white Christian males of European descent.

Dillon—If you're referring to the descendants of the giants who founded the greatest nation on the face of the earth—I believe there are indeed enough of them to provide me with a comfortable and enthusiastic margin of victory in November.

Pope—That is surely the single-most arrogant and crude pronouncement made by a political figure in the history of the republic.

Dillon—I'm sorry you're so easily offended, Alan—but if it won't give you the vapors, I'm prepared to make a major campaign announcement right this moment on your show.

Pope—Well, Reverend, you've already managed to insult and terrify at least two-thirds of our viewing audience, so go for it! Let's have it!

Dillon—I am hereby announcing that I am naming as my vice-presidential running mate, retired Colonel Oliver Dedwell, formerly of the United States Army . . .

"What?" shouted Daisy, flying off the sofa she'd been sharing comfortably with Brian in his bungalow. Whatever Alan Pope's reaction was to Dillon's declaration was lost on Brian amidst his wonder at the outraged consternation of the woman he loved. "He can't DO that!" Daisy yelled, jabbing her finger at the TV.

"What's the matter?" he asked. "Who's Dedwell?"

"Oliver 'Take No Prisoners' Dedwell," moaned Daisy, burying her face in her hands. "He makes Donald Dillon look like Winnie the Pooh!"

Brian continued to look puzzled. "Name doesn't ring a bell."

Daisy gave him an exasperated look, then explained, "Dedwell was in combat in Desert Storm back in 1991. A few months later, he was court-martialed for allegedly slaughtering a group of Iraqi soldiers who had surrendered. Unfortunately, he was acquitted. There was a rumor circulating at the time that none of his men would testify against him. They apparently lived in abject terror of him."

"Hmmm. I don't remember ever hearing anything about him."

"It only lasted a day or two in the news at the time. I probably wouldn't remember him myself—except that the whole affair made him a mini-celebrity, and ever since, he periodically crops up as a talking head on discussion shows, particularly when the topic is wartime atrocities. That's when he really comes alive. His basic attitude is that the entire concept of war crimes is a ludicrous fiction—that the battlefield is a separate universe that is the antithesis of civilization. A soldier who doesn't understand that is a dead soldier."

"Obviously, he and Dillon, with his gung-ho nuclear war philosophy, will make a dream team. I guess it shows anyone really CAN grow up to be President," Brian observed.

"Except if your voice is too high, and you have the wrong genitalia," Daisy said crisply. "Sorry," she smiled, "I didn't mean to go into feminist mode. Actually, I enjoy being a girl."

Brian said, "I've long gotten that impression. And may I say the feeling's mutual?"

"Oh, yeah? Well, stay out of my dresses!"

"Does that go for your pants, too?"

They both laughed. Then Daisy sighed. "Just when we're ready to close the book on the Dillons, now we've got Dedwell to deal with! If Dillon drops out, the logical thing, this close to the election, is to move Dedwell up to the top spot."

"So, Arianna finally caught on."

"So Rhonda says. SHE can hang in there a day or two longer, but, obviously you can't. You're the one Arianna's blaming for 'setting her up' with me. Your not showing up for work today makes you prime basement fodder."

'So what happens now?"

"I expect Arianna to make her move against me very soon—most likely this week while Dillon's in Chicago. My guess is that HE still views me as nothing more than an annoyance, a potential little fling that was stillborn. Rhonda has always had the impression that Arianna's never really filled him in on New Dawn—that she tried to do that early on, but that he scoffed at the whole notion as mystical, New Age nonsense."

Daisy rejoined Brian on the sofa.

"Are you sure you can handle her?" asked Brian anxiously. "I'd like to stick close. We KNOW she's a maniac."

"Don't worry, darling. I fully expect both you and Rhonda to be there for the grand finale."

Brian put his arm around her. "I hope you know what you're doing," he said. He kissed the top of her head.

Suddenly, Daisy sat upright. "Brian, do me a favor! Get on the Internet!"

"Right now?".

"Yes! Right now!" Daisy was already out of her seat and heading for the bungalow study.

Brian followed her. "What are we looking for?" he asked, sitting down in front of the monitor. He turned on the computer.

"Let's see what they've got on Oliver Dedwell. I particularly want to get a look at him."

They got lucky quickly. Apparently, as soon as Donald Dillon had made his dramatic announcement on *The Alan Pope Show*, the news services had gone into overdrive. The AOL home page had a biography of Dedwell already posted—accompanied by a recent color photo. Staring back at Brian and Daisy was a harsh, chiseled face with a hawk nose and piercing gray-blue eyes. The colonel wore his blond hair in a no-nonsense brushcut.

"Oh, yes," breathed Daisy quietly. "Oh, yes, I always thought he looked familiar whenever I'd see him on TV. It's all coming together, Brian—all of it! The Mother is bringing everything full circle."

Brian felt the back of his neck prickle. "What do you mean? Another Dawn Timer?"

"The biggest, baddest Dawn Timer of them all, as far as my sisters and I were concerned."

"Odysseus?"

Daisy nodded. "Odysseus."

Fifteen

Inner Time

(Hello, Phonny.)

(Daisy! Oh, I'm so glad you came back! I've been waiting!)

(. . . I won't desert you, darling, believe me. In fact, I think I have some good news.)

(Tell me!)

(I feel very strongly now that the Mother is with us—that She is very definitely working to bring us together. Not only the Goddess but the Fates as well. It's as if some grand design in which you and I are to play a central role is coming to fruition. I am so confident, in fact, that I'm going to take a chance that I wasn't prepared to take the first time I . . . spoke with you. Still, I feel I have to be cautious, and so I'll remind you of the frightening story Father used to tell us of his friend, King Oedipus of Thebes. Do you remember it?)

(Yes. I couldn't sleep for nights afterwards. That poor boy was given a prophecy that he would kill his father and marry his mother. He was so horrified that he did the only thing any sane, decent person WOULD do. He banished himself from his home in Corinth immediately, thinking to escape his awful destiny. Unfortunately, he didn't realize that the king and queen of that city were only his foster parents. He decided to head for Thebes, where he accidentally killed the king and then laid claim to the dead man's queen—not realizing THEY were his real parents. What kept me awake all those nights was the question—*why?* Why doom a baby that way from the day of his birth? It made me wonder if the gods and the Fates were insane. It made me think that in all the world and the skies above I was alone—and I resolved to rely only on myself from then on.)

(What about the Mother, Phonny?)

(I AM the Mother, Daisy! You and I and She—all one together. You said so yourself before . . . You say nothing?)

(. . . I am struggling to, Phonny. You move me very much, child, with your sad wisdom. Now, isn't THAT foolish? I call you "child," and yet you are my mother thirty or forty times over!)

(It's all very complicated, I guess.)

(Yes, it is. But what I was trying to say a moment ago, Phonny, is that I THINK the Fates are suggesting that I may offer you at least minimal assistance. I don't dare give you any specific details of what you're up against—other than this—the name of your assailant.)

(Yes! Let me know it so that I can strike him first!)

(No, darling, that's not the way. That's the way Oedipus would have responded. You must simply wait . . . and react. You may defend yourself, but you must avoid instigating a confrontation.)

(. . . Very well. I won't pretend I understand, though. Who is my enemy?)

(The man who has ALWAYS been—and now he is mine again, too—for I have just discovered his awful presence in MY world.)

(Odysseus!)

(Yes, Phonny! It seems it is our ultimate destiny to join forces to put an end to his evil. I believe the Mother is ordering it so. I think that's why She has forged this mental link between us that in spite of immense time and language barriers allows us to inhabit each other's mind so comfortably.)

(It must be so, as you say. Daisy . . . have you thought any more about how we can be together the way you said?)

(Yes, I have—though I'm still working out the details.)

(Daisy, what about Peisinoe and Thelxepeia? Are they supposed to die? Or can they be saved, too?)

(Darling, they must die—as must Circe and Polyphemus—all on the same day at the hands of this one man.)

(But if you think I can be saved, why not them, too?)

(I think you know the answer to that, Phonny. Your sisters are as precious to you as mine are to me. But they lack what you and I possess—infinite curiosity as to the *why* of things. They accept, as most everyone else does, the world that is presented to their eyes and ears and touch. You and I wonder at what lies behind the sunlit surface of the everyday. Rightly or wrongly, we try to amend and improve humanity's condition. If what we're planning works, it will be because you and I have forcefully interlocked our wills to create a timeless single consciousness. Neither your sisters nor mine, beloved by us though they are, have the vision or the spirit to transcend their everyday world. So you and I must be alone in this.)

(Very well, Daisy. I trust what you are saying and will obey you.)

(No, you mustn't take THAT attitude! From here on in you need to question me, particularly if you think I'm striking a wrong note. Remember that I'm new to all this, too. I'm very much feeling my way, and I'm going to need your insights as we go along if this is to work.)

(All right. There's one thing I HAVE been thinking of—though I'm not sure if it's a help or not.)

(What's that?)

(The manner of my death.)

(. . . . Oh. Go ahead, Phonny.)

(Well, I think poison would be too slow and unreliable. The pain might also hamper my thinking when the moment of . . .

transition? . . . arrives. I need to be clear and resolute then. The same thing with a self-inflicted dagger thrust. I might just give

151

myself a non-fatal wound—beside the point, so to speak. Jumping from a great height seems to me the best bet—say, off the promontory right here, if I can manage it. That will give me a few brief seconds between the leap and the . . . landing. That would be the logical time for me to come to you, if it can be done. What do YOU think, Daisy?)

(That's my girl! Though it grieves me that you have to expend your mental gifts in such a grim manner. As a matter of fact, I KNOW you've made the right choice.)

(I see. Well, I'm content then. Now, can we change the subject to something more pleasant?)

(Gladly! What would you like to talk about?)

(Your world! Tell me about it! I know I've seen terrible things—inventions—in my dreams—but there must be many unimaginable marvels, as well.)

(Oh, yes, there are, Phonny! Why we have horseless carriages that could take you to Circe's villa in six or seven minutes! We have flying machines that carry several hundred people at a time across oceans in a few hours! There are towering buildings in our cities that look as tall as Aetna, small handheld instruments that allow us to talk to people on the other side of the world, pictures that move and talk. . . .)

(Pictures?)

(Well, uh, like the big bull-dancer murals in our palace that Father had copied from those of King Minos at Knossos. Then there are machines that cook our food and wash our clothes. We have not only learned to control lightning, as you envisioned, but to CAPTURE it to light our homes and power all the machines I've mentioned. We have an instrument that, in a way, THINKS many times faster than a person can and allows us to read. . . .)

(Read?)

(. . . . Phonny, I can see we're in for a very long night. . . .)

Sixteen

Arianna rarely indulged in childhood nostalgia, but as she plotted Daisy Crandall's demise, she was reminded of one of her all-time favorite movie scenes. This was the moment in Disney's animated classic *Snow White* when the lethally beautiful evil queen, the heroine's stepmother, summons her loyal huntsman into her presence and orders him to take Snow White into the deepest, darkest part of the forest, kill her, and cut her heart out. Arianna had been deeply disappointed when the tender-hearted oaf had chickend out and let the saccharine little urchin scamper off unharmed to sing songs with bunnies and birds and dwarves.

She trusted that she would have better luck with Lyle Webber and Daisy. An hour before Donald unveiled his multi-faceted psychopathology on national television, his wife called her lover down at the compound, where for many months now—ever since the sudden disappearance of Dillon's last TV co-host, a giggly blonde named Wanda Beth—he'd had the bunkhouse to himself. When he answered, she asked him to join her up at the main house.

As Webber arrived, she invited him into the oak-paneled front sitting room, told him to have a seat, and in a paroxysm of egalitarian *bonhomie* offered him a glass of wine. When he mentioned that he'd prefer a Coors Lite, she told him not to push his luck. Pouring herself a glass of Chardonnay from an ornate crystal decanter, she sat down opposite him.

"So, what do you have to report?" she asked.

Webber looked down at his size fourteens, cleared his throat, then said, "Nothing much so far. I watched her from across the street after both the Saturday evening and Sunday afternoon performances. She signed autographs, then walked up the block to Shubert Alley. I followed her as she cut through, crossed 45th Street, then entered the rear door of the Marriott. I have to tell you, Arianna, there isn't much of a chance of making a grab. It's only a two-minute walk, and it's very well lit. There are people all around and nowhere to park a car. What am I supposed to do?"

"How should I know, dammit? I'm a KILLER, not a kidnapper! Forget I said that, by the way. Look, Kyle, I don't care how you manage it, but you have her here in this house by midnight Wednesday. My husband will be back Thursday, and I want her disposed of by then. He warned me not to do anything rash about Crandall while he was gone—but he hasn't a clue about what a threat she really is."

"I don't understand, Arianna. How can Daisy Crandall possibly be a threat to you?"

"Et tu, you brute?" Arianna set down her wine, got up, and draped herself lasciviously over the arm of Webber's chair, wrapped her arms around his neck, and kissed him long and hard. "Don't think, Kyle. You'll rupture yourself!" She planted another lingering scorcher on his lips and murmured, "And that's MY job!"

She did very agreeable things to him for a few moments and when he proved responsive, she purred, "Wednesday night?"

"Wednesday night."

Actually, Kyle Webber had his own, fairly straightforward plan for fulfilling his promise to Arianna and getting Daisy Crandall out to the Labyrinth with a minimum of fuss. However, there was a preliminary arrangement that had to be attended to first. That Wednesday afternoon he surreptitiously took delivery of a large item he'd leased for twenty-four hours from a neighboring farmer. This he placed in one of the old cattle stalls in the converted barn where he lived.

After assuring himself that it admirably conformed to his specifications, he left for the Isle of Joy to collect Daisy Crandall. He waited until Daisy had returned from the theater after the evening performance, went to her hotel room, and knocked quietly on the door. Promptly, the actress opened it.

"All set, Miss Crandall?" he asked.

"All set, Mr. Webber. Rhonda and Brian, here, will follow in my car."

"That's fine."

With that, all four made their way to the hotel's parking garage and from there headed toward Long Island.

✿   ✿   ✿

Arianna was aquiver with excitement and impatience as she waited for Kyle Webber to return with the evening's entertainment, Daisy Crandall. She sat in the front room, elegantly gowned in red and sipping Chardonnay. She'd done a little Ecstasy earlier and between the two stimulants was aglow with euphoric anticipation. She had denied herself, she now realized, the pleasures of her basement for far too long. She had allowed Kyle to live till he was now approaching the beginning of his third term as year-king—but, darn it! the boy deserved it! He was a priapic wonder, the kind of stud who came around once in a lifetime, if a girl were truly lucky.

Still, she didn't doubt that Dionysus must be growing impatient for his next blood sacrifice—and might consider her derelict in denying him his due for so long. So this would be a two-birds-with-one-ax night. She could provide the demigod with a suitable sacrifice and simultaneously rid herself of a formidable enemy.

She pictured for the hundredth time the agony and the ecstasy to come, once Kyle delivered the goods. Not for Daisy

155

the relatively easy death accorded Arianna's year-kings—swift decapitation before dismemberment. No, Daisy would experience a night that would send her shrieking and gibbering into the void. In the words of Arianna's favorite Roman emperor, the demented Caligula, Daisy would *know* that she was dying. Arianna intended to start with her victim's tiny feet and work her way upward. True, Daisy might quickly expire or lapse into unconsciousness from shock and blood loss, but Arianna was prepared to live with that.

Now her heart leaped, as she heard the crunch of car tires on the gravel of the circular drive in front of the house. She'd left the porch lights on so that she might treasure the sight of her victim's arrival. She wanted to witness firsthand Kyle popping the latch of the trunk and lifting Daisy, trussed and gagged like a Christmas goose, from the interior. Arianna rushed to the front hall and eagerly gazed out of one of the windows flanking the main entrance.

Damn! What was going on here, anyway? As the car rolled to a halt, the front passenger door opened, and Daisy Crandall stepped out, perfectly coiffed and poised, a vision in a flowing, sea-green dress, as pretty as you please—even prettier. What the hell was that nitwit Kyle up to? Take it easy. Maybe he was cleverer than she gave him credit for and had given Crandall the impression that this was some late evening soiree she'd been invited to. Sure, that must be it! Look how stylishly she was dressed. Okay, Daisyducks! Party time!

Arianna watched as Webber got out, came around the front of the limo and, taking Daisy's elbow, guided her with gentlemanly élan up the portico steps. Not bad, Kyle! The guy had style after all! Unable to wait, Arianna anticipated the pair's entrance and swung the door open for them.

"How nice that you could join us, Dais . . . "

"Evening, Arianna," said Daisy placidly, breezing past her as if her hostess were the maid welcoming her mistress home.

She walked to the center of the foyer and glanced into the paneled sitting room to her right.

"Ah, lovely! This will be fine! Bring Mrs. Dillon in here, will you, Mr. Webber?" From Arianna's perspective, the evening had abruptly taken on a surreal tilt—and before she could react, Kyle had grasped her roughly by the upper arm and propelled her before him into the room. A second later, she had been shoved down harshly into a chair.

"What the hell do you think you're doing?" Arianna snarled, although fright was beginning to seep deep into her marrow.

Daisy stationed herself across the room, leaning against the back of a sofa, her arms holding a manila folder to her chest. Webber went over and stood beside her. They both stood in silence, regarding Arianna with chilling objectivity.

"Well?" the puzzled woman demanded, her voice edging upward toward hysteria.

"We're here to put an end to you, Ariadne," said Daisy quietly. "Did I get the name right that time?"

"What if you did? I know who you are, too! You're Aglaowhoosis, the Little Mermaid."

"Ouch," smiled Daisy thinly. "But apparently you haven't experienced any epiphanies yet about Mr. Webber."

"I just GOT one! He's my ex-chauffeur! Beat it, Kyle! Pack up your jockstrap and your barbells and clear out! You're history!"

"He is indeed," said Daisy. Webber remained silent—ominously so—and made no move to go.

"The trouble with YOU, Arianna," Daisy continued, "aside from your utterly vicious dementia, I mean, is the way in which over the course of your life, both here and in the Dawn Time, you became enslaved to your appetites. Drugs and drink have so ravaged your mind that the most obvious insights dissolve before they form—in a brain-dead haze."

Arianna shot back, "Are you here to sign me up for a Twelve-Step program? Get to the idiotic point, whatever the hell of it is!"

"LOOK at ME, you shameless, murdering whore!" roared Kyle Webber, his eyes blazing, his huge presence seeming suddenly to blot out everything else in the room. Both women jumped. "You dare to ignore ME! You presume to make ME your sex toy! I, who commanded armies of revelers rioting throughout the ancient world—I, who effortlessly stole you from Theseus, King of Athens—I, your lord and master?"

In shock, Arianna shrank like a terrified five-year-old into the depths of her chair, very close to wetting herself.

"Dionysus!" she whispered.

"Yes, Dionysus," intoned Webber, his eyes boring implacably into her. "Lord of the vine, eternal consort-son to the everlasting Mother, the god forever dying, forever reborn. Now, I see, you know me at last."

Arianna, in abject awe and misery, nodded.

Webber seemed to relax. Turning to Daisy, he gave her a small courtly bow. "Sorry, Princess. I didn't mean to interrupt. I apologize if I was overbearing."

Daisy smiled a little nervously "Not at all, Lord. I think you provided us all with a much-needed moment of clarity."

At that, Webber burst out laughing. It was a pleasant, agreeable sound. "I remember hearing you sing once when I was your father's guest. What a little spellbinder you were! Too bad you were much too young for me. Even so, you filled me with a spiritual longing that has haunted me through the countless ages since—much more than thousands of nights of physical excess with soulless, earthbound beauties like *this* creature."

He cupped Daisy's chin gently in his hand, and the two seemed lost in each other for a moment.

Finally, Daisy said, "Well, I must admit, I spent more than one sleepless night myself, weaving childish fantasies around my father's handsome guest. But perhaps we're boring Arianna."

With a blush, she turned her attention back to their dispirited hostess. "Let's get to the point, Arianna." Daisy opened the envelope she'd been holding and withdrew three eight-by-ten glossy photographs. Crossing the room, she bluntly thrust them toward the seated woman. "Do you recognize those three men?"

"You know I do," said Arianna, glancing at the photos. Her spirits were beginning to revive. "Why else would you be subjecting me to this abysmal charade?"

"Gerald Anson, Jeffrey Mallon, Derek Dunne. Three young men, all your lovers, one after the other, each for exactly one year. Then, poof! Each vanishes without a trace. You know what that suggests to me, Arianna?"

"Astound me, if you must. What does it suggest to you?"

"Well, what I think happened was that each of them was taken down to the basement of this house, chained to a sacrificial altar, treated by you to a few final moments of frenzied intimacy, brutally dispatched with a double-ax, then buried piecemeal somewhere down there. How'd I do?"

"Splendid! But where's your proof?"

"Down in the cellar, which I'd like to inspect. Will you lead the way?"

"Will you get stuffed? You have no legal standing even to be here, let alone search my house."

"In case you haven't noticed," said Daisy smoothly, "we're all far beyond and above the constraints of ordinary American jurisprudence, here. Especially you. And I have to tell you, Arianna, this is as close as you're ever going to come to giving a White House tour. So how about it?"

"Sorry. The cellar's locked—and I can't remember where I left the key."

Daisy retreated to the sofa and rummaged for a second through her handbag. She located what she was after. Holding it aloft for Arianna's inspection, she said, "Then we'll use mine." She handed the key to Kyle Webber.

Within moments, both women, for diametrically opposed reasons, came to regret the descent into the basement of the Labyrinth that Daisy had so blithely insisted upon. As soon as the trio had reached the bottom step, Arianna saw that the jig was definitively up—and Daisy felt her stomach begin to churn and rebel.

Their mutual shock was all courtesy of Kyle Webber, who had unearthed and ransacked the ad hoc graves dug a few years previously by Reverend Dillon with the intention of shielding the public from the evidence of his wife's severe mental imbalance. What Webber had arranged was a display to enrapture the hearts of Jeffrey Dahmer, John Wayne Gacy, and Madame Tussaud. There, arrayed neatly and symmetrically on Arianna's altar were three pyramidal mounds of bones and limbs, some still looped with desiccated flesh, with each deposit surmounted by a decomposing skull. Brooding over the primordial horror of the scene, glinting in the wavering torchlight from the bracketed sconces, was the deadly bronze of the labrys, the huge double ax fixed to the wall.

Daisy had her proof and felt the worse for it.

"Oh, no!" she murmured to herself.

"I'm sorry for the shock, Princess," said Webber, throwing a comforting arm around her, "but how better to forcefully demonstrate her evil?"

Daisy smiled wanly, "You definitely got my attention. Well, Arianna, is this your work—or are you going to bother to deny it?"

Arianna recovered quickly, knowing instinctively that the good life was over. "I've been framed," she said sardonically.

Without further ado, Webber grabbed her cruelly by the elbow and dragged her to the altar. Yanking her arms behind her, he chained her standing to one of its outer corners. Then he strode purposefully to the wide wooden doors opposite that fed into the connecting tunnel and unbarred it. When he opened it, Brian Ames and Rhonda Raveneaux were waiting on the other side. Webber then turned and beckoned to Daisy. The group backtracked into the tunnel, where they examined the recently excavated mini-graves. Daisy nodded at the dismal evidence, and the party re-entered Arianna's death chamber to render their collective judgment upon her.

Watching their approach, Arianna sneered, "Well, well, the gang's all here. What the heck do I care? What the heck do I care? What's the matter, Little Mermaid? You're looking a bit peaked. If you can't stand the heat, stay out of the cellar, I always say!"

At that point, Rhonda stepped abruptly forward and swinging her arm, smashed Arianna open-handed full in the face. The prisoner fell to her knees with a cry, as the iron chain yanked at her arms. Then she wobbled to her feet, a rivulet of blood beginning to snake down her chin. "I guess this means we're no longer friends," said Arianna. "So how'd little Daisy Doodle, here, get her hooks into you, Rhonda? I don't quite see her as a daughter of Lesbos."

"Listen, beast!" said Rhonda. "There isn't ONE of us on the New Dawn council who isn't utterly devoted to this woman! She is our guide, our mentor, our inspiration—her very existence a warranty that the concept of the Goddess incarnate is more than a primeval mental construct. As for your worthless opinion of my sexuality, it is what I intended it to be. Don't you think I knew your shallow, drug-addled self-absorption would write me off as a mannish puppet you could purchase with a few revolting kisses? Well, absorb *this,* Arianna! Theseus, the king who abandoned you for the hedonistic riffraff you were ages ago—and have remained—MARRIED me, when I was Hippolyta, Queen of the Amazons, and sired a son with me!"

161

Arianna seemed shocked into silence for a moment but recovered quickly. "Is that so?" she smirked. "And when you died soon after, you pathetic weakling, my baby sister Phaedra seduced your grief-stricken widower into a ludicrous May–September union and destroyed both him AND your effete wimp of a son!"

"True," said Rhonda, though she looked stricken. "Phaedra had the tell-tale moral rot that was your family's only gift. She tried to seduce her stepson, failed, and in a vicious, petulant rage, hanged herself. But not before she left a suicide note accusing my sweet, innocent boy of assaulting her, causing Theseus to destroy him."

Daisy put her hand out and clutched Rhonda's wrist. "Don't let her upset you, dear friend. Destruction and evil are her only talents."

"She's right, Rhonda," said Brian, laying a comforting hand on the woman's shoulder.

His entry into the confrontation caused Arianna to direct her next effrontery to him. "Don't tell me, Brendan!" she mocked. "You're Zeus, right?"

"No," said Brian, untouched by her sarcasm. "And, actually, it's Brian—Brian Ames. Just an old friend of Daisy's. I knew her way back when."

"We were childhood sweethearts back in the Dawn Time, Arianna," said Daisy, giving Brian an affectionate hug. "We were miraculously reunited only two years ago, when he agreed to join our effort to bring you down. I suppose I have you to thank for bringing us together—for being the cloud to our silver lining.

"But enough socializing," she continued. "The four of us have come here to confront you with our knowledge—our PROOF—of your murderous depravity, the sickening signs of which are plainly visible in this room. We've amassed an impressive volume of evidence, which is now being forwarded to the

FBI through back channels—evidence not only of murder but of the wanton destruction of people's lives through blackmail and of the rampant adulteries of both you and your husband. We are also well on our way toward making a case against Reverend Dillon as the serial murderer of more than a dozen homeless young women, all in one-time residence on this property, all last seen in his company."

"Do you intend to kill us both?" Arianna asked, with an attempt at nonchalance. "If you do, how are you any better than we are? Or have you high-mindedly deluded yourself into thinking that your blatant vigilantism is a superior kind of justice?"

"Actually, that's not an inappropriate question," responded Daisy. "Since your husband is a 'civilian' in our terms, we're content to let the courts deal with him. But because you are, sad to say, one of us—a Dawn Timer—we feel justified in arranging your extinction. By brutally and mindlessly applying to the present day the savage rituals of a superstitious, long dead age—and doing so merely for your sick amusement—you have forfeited all right to benefit from laws you've consistently mocked and ignored. YOU die here—tonight!"

Arianna turned pale and hung her head. She licked at her bloodied lips. "What will you do to me?" she asked.

Daisy paused and her expression softened. When she spoke, her voice was subdued. "New Dawn will not have a direct hand in your death. Lord Dionysus, who has long been building his own case against you, has graciously relieved us of that onerous task. Your execution will be at his hands."

She turned to look at Kyle Webber. "Will it be quick for her?"

"Yes, Princess. Which is more than can be said for the death she had planned for YOU."

Daisy nodded. "It's cowardly, I suppose, but I don't want to . . . know the details—at least not now. We'll leave you to it then."

163

She took a step toward the doomed woman. Arianna raised her head, and they stood facing each other. Daisy spoke. "You were my heroine once. At my father's court, I used to make people weep with my adoring songs of you. How could you ever have become what you are?"

"Murder is no big deal once you get started, Little Mermaid. Remember that the next time you look in the mirror. You might just find me looking back at you."

Daisy flinched back, her eyes widened in horror at the remark. Arianna laughed. "Sweet dreams, Aglaophone!"

Taking a deep breath, Daisy said, "Goodbye, Ariadne. You, too, Lord Dionysus. I don't envy you your night's work."

"Goodnight, Princess. But you still have work of your own to finish, I understand—now that Colonel Dedwell has become a factor."

"Yes, I know. I had hoped our eradication of the Dillons would end the immediate threat to the world's security. How naïve of me. There's always one more monster out there somewhere, like the multi-headed Hydra that kept giving Heracles fits. Cut one head off and two replace it."

"True," said Webber, nodding at their captive. "Even this one will return sometime down the line in a new incarnation to haunt some hapless generation."

"Depend on it," Arianna interjected.

Daisy gave a mirthless chuckle. "And the tragedy is she won't have learned a thing. Because she's one of us, she'll have the capacity to REMEMBER this night, but, chances are, she'll block it out and take her murderous pleasures all over again."

She turned to Brian. "We're through here, love. Let's leave this place. I need some fresh air. Rhonda, would you mind bringing my car around from wherever you left it?"

Rhonda nodded to everyone, gazed darkly for a beat at Arianna, then crossed the cellar and disappeared into the tunnel. Then Daisy and Brian also quietly took their leave and ascended the stone steps to the house above.

And Ariadne and Dionysus were left alone to deal with each other.

Arianna was the first to break the silence. She smiled weakly. "So, Big Guy! The joke's on me, huh? You really ARE the Big Guy!"

Webber said nothing, his expression placid and unreadable.

Arianna gave it another try. "I mean, some god of wine! You drink Coors Lite, for Hades' sake! What's THAT all about?"

Webber smiled. "As I get older, I find wine disagrees with me. Acid reflux, or something. But again, Arianna, your dim sense of history has let you down, or you might have remembered that I started out as the beer god, Sabazias. Then I grew out of the frat boy thing and morphed into more of a sophisticate."

Arianna changed her stance to try to relieve the chafing strain on her shackled wrists. It didn't help.

"But getting back to me—what's YOUR stake in my destruction? What's with the 'holier-than-thou' bit? Not that thou aren't, of course . . . I mean, even though I didn't recognize you in person, I've always honored you with appropriate sacrifices. Look!" she said, pointing with her chin toward the grotesque mounds piled on the altar.

Webber shook his head in wonder. "Talk about not getting it! Arianna, you are one of those monsters of self-delusion who goes through life totally oblivious to anything that doesn't gratify her advancement, her pleasure, and her libido. You're totally isolated from the norm of everyday existence. Why would you think that any sane being in THIS time would demand that you chop people into mincemeat for his pleasure? THAT kind of spectacular cruelty had a place in a long-ago, frightening world when mortals identified closely and mystically with forces they couldn't comprehend—droughts, earthquakes, pitiless diseases, and the ever-present carnage of warfare. People rich and poor, high and low, lived every day of their short, brutal lives looking blindly for salvation. What better way to secure an angry deity's favor than to sacrifice your handsome young king—or somebody's pretty little daughter? But today, with a package store or a bar on every other street corner in urban America, why would you think the god of wine was yearning either for attention or for human blood?"

He turned to survey the grisly refuse nearby. "No, Arianna, you did THAT because it was fun. And for that you die."

Arianna appeared to reflect on this for a bit, then she smiled slyly. "Kyle, come on. Give me a break here! Why don't you just sweep all of that rubbish onto the floor, unchain me, and we'll have a little roll on the old altar. What do you say? You don't want to lose what we've had. Think of how good we've been together!"

"No," contradicted Webber. "I was good. You were merely insatiable."

At that, Arianna looked truly stricken. She bent her head, and in a moment her shoulders began to shake, tears spilling down her face to mingle with the drying blood on her chin. Webber reached out and stroked her hair.

"That was cruel of me," he said. "No, Arianna, there was certainly nothing wrong with either your loins or your technique. It was your total absence of HEART that was disturbing."

She mistook his decency for mercy and looked up, a wild hope shining through the watery sheen of her eyes.

"Give me another chance, Kyle. Please! I'll do whatever it takes to make amends—I swear it! Don't kill me! Please don't kill me!"

A darkness settled over Webber's features. He walked behind Arianna and grasped her firmly by her upper arms. Leaning over, he forced her to look at the human carnage she had created, speaking harshly into her ear.

"Look at them, Arianna! All that's left of three boys whose only crime was to incite your lust. *Look at what you did to them!* You stripped them naked, you chained them up like meat on a chopping block, you gagged them so the only pleading they could do was scream for mercy with their terror-stricken eyes, you used them one last time for your swinish pleasure, then you smilingly—SMILINGLY!—slaughtered them! You planned to do the same to me, if I hadn't pleased you—and much worse to Daisy Crandall. So, no, Arianna, there will be no mercy for you from the god whose image you defiled with these abominations!"

He let her go, knowing by her slumped shoulders that she understood at last.

"How will you do it?" she asked in a soft, choked voice. "The double-ax?"

"Only in the post-mortem phase, as a convenient means of reducing you to a fourth mound of rubble. That's the way the police and the FBI will find you, Arianna. You'll be ready for your close-up then—as shot by some crime scene photographer, who'll retire on the millions *The National Star* will pay him for sneaking them a copy of the Unmaking of a First Lady."

Arianna's head shot up in alarm. "You're going to torture me first? But you told Daisy my death would be quick!"

"And so it should be, if the killer is as efficient as I believe him to be. I've farmed the job out, you see. I've taken great pains over you, Arianna. Your execution will be an ironic master-piece, neatly encapsulating over three thousand years of your personal history and bringing everything full-circle."

Webber's mockery stung Arianna back to her old reckless self. "Enough of your vicious riddles! Bring on your killer so I can spit in his eye! Who is he, anyway?"

Webber smiled with mysterious malice. "Why don't we call him . . . Asterius?"

Arianna's mouth opened in shock, a vague, icy fear clamping her innards.

"Who?" she whispered.

"Ah! So our long-term memory kicks in at last! Tell me about Asterius, Arianna. Let's reminisce about the sweet, not-so-dead past."

"He was a monster," Arianna said dully.

"He was more than that, Ariadne of Crete. *He was your brother.*"

The miserable woman began to babble and sob simultaneously. "He was a FREAK! He brought shame to our whole family. My father Minos was a bull-king, a priest of Poseidon who donned the ceremonial mask of a bull when sacrificing to the god—just as Daisy's original father, Achelous of Aetolia, did. Then when my mother Pasiphae gave birth to Asterius—this deformed THING!—the evil rumor quickly spread that she had mated with an actual bull to produce him. The poor woman hid away in the palace in abject shame for the rest of her life. My father was so humiliated that he had a special room designed in the bowels of the royal basement to hide the creature. The thing actually had the LOOK of a bull."

"The Minotaur," said Webber. "A more enlightened society would have recognized that his affliction was the Proteus Syndrome, the Elephant Man's Disease, which produces large, hideous tumors and tusk-like protuberances on the head and body.

"So your brother was locked away in a dark recess of the Labyrinth. Two slaves, maimed and crippled bull dancers, were forced to be his guardians, feeding him goat's milk, since no woman could be found to nurse him, and raising him thereafter on scraps from the palace kitchen. Eventually, those slaves died, to be replaced by others. And so the story grew that Asterius had *cannibalized* his original keepers and would do the same with their successors. His infamy began to spread far beyond

Crete till it came to the attention of Theseus, Prince of Athens. Take it from there, Arianna. What happened next?"

"You know the whole story! Why are you putting me through all this? Bring on your hit man—whoever the hell he is—and let's get it over with!"

"Don't anger me further, Arianna!" Webber warned. "Do as you're told. It will help you to understand your death, if not to appreciate it."

Arianna glared at him defiantly for a moment, then wearily resumed. "Theseus was out to make a name for himself as a worthy and heroic future King of Athens. So he sailed to Crete bent on ending his kingdom's subservience to Minos's naval power. My father offered him the required hospitality. Theseus was bold in his demands, but Minos was amused and not at all frightened by his adolescent bravado."

"But what was YOUR attitude toward the young man?"

"He was very handsome," Arianna said with an odd dreaminess, given her present situation. "I loved him at first sight."

"Actually, you got the extraordinary hots for him—but let that go. The net result was that the two of you were quickly exchanging vows and bodily fluids in no particular order."

"Yes, we were."

"And then what?"

"Theseus began to realize that my father was patronizing him—was playing him for a teenaged fool. He began to think he would have to return, after all his boasting, without a deal, empty-handed to his father, King Aegeus of Athens, and I could see that he was beginning to panic."

"So you did what?" prodded Webber who had been in possession of the answer since the beginning of time.

Arianna fell into the hypnotized rhythm of the moment.

"I reminded him of my brother, the Arch-fiend, the Minotaur. I persuaded him that he could destroy the monster and win himself eternal fame as a hero."

"And your price for helping him win mythic glory?"

"Elope with me. Take me away from the abysmal shame of my family ties back to his homeland."

"Go on. Finish the story. I won't interrupt again."

Arianna sized up her interviewer, saw no sympathy there, and plunged on. "So I pumped him up. I told him how he might achieve historic immortality—how he could destroy the Minotaur, how I would lead him to fame everlasting."

"And he bought it."

"Of course—but you weren't going to interrupt."

"Sorry. Go on."

"I laid it all out for him—I chose a time in the wee hours of the morning when the Minotaur's guards would most likely be sleeping, showed him the secret passage to the thing's basement apartment—and waited. Armed with a candle and his sword, Theseus threaded his way down through the winding passageways of storerooms and wine racks till he reached Asterius's room. His adolescent adrenalin rush and natural fear of a fabled monster he'd heard about all his life must have been extreme. He killed the two sleeping slaves out of hand, then burst through the door of the creature's cramped room, slashing with his sword, sight unseen, in the flickering light of his candle. As he dismally told me afterward, he felt his sword bite into soft flesh and heard a single gurgling yelp of terror and pain as my brother expired."

"What did Theseus discover he had killed?" Webber quietly asked his captive.

"The Minotaur!—my freak brother, Asterius," Arianna said, feeling the full weight of the horror of self-discovery for the first and only time in thirty-three hundred years. "A defenseless, disease-ravaged, ninety-pound creature who had never known a moment of hope or comfort or love in his terrible, solitary life."

"So, by orchestrating your brother's death, you caused a young hero to cover himself in shame and self-loathing. Do you wonder that he abandoned you at the first opportunity on the way home—not just at your drunken licentiousness as one of MY creatures, but because you had made him, in his own eyes, a craven killer?"

Arianna lifted her head defiantly. "That's not the way history and legend record it!" she snapped. "Theseus is a towering mythic figure, and I am forever the beautiful princess he loved!"

"A fairy tale based on a foul and hateful lie. It is for THAT as much as anything you've done in your latest ignoble incarnation that you die tonight, Arianna."

"I see," said Arianna, "so my ugly, deformed brother, like a 1930s movie monster, has been dredged up from history's dungheap and recruited to kill me. Is that how we're playing it?"

"Only metaphorically, Arianna. Your gentleman caller is actually just a stand-in for Asterius—a pinch hitter."

"Well, I hope he's better-looking, at any rate."

"Oh, yes, he's a prime specimen, as a matter of fact—though, looking at your dress, I have to be honest with you—red is not his favorite color. I wouldn't plan on trying to save your life by seducing him."

Arianna smirked. "Is that so? Bring him on! If he's even half a man I'll be out of here in no time!"

Kyle Webber threw back his head and roared with laughter. "But what if he ISN'T?" Stepping forward suddenly, he grasped Arianna by the head and kissed her deeply and passionately.

"Time's up, Princess! Perhaps we'll meet again in the sweet by-and-by."

With that, he turned on his heel and strode across the room and into the open tunnel, leaving Arianna truly alone to contemplate her unknown but certain fate.

Seventeen

For the longest time, Arianna couldn't stop trembling. Even though Kyle had promised he wouldn't torture her physically, nothing had been said about mental anguish. And being chained in place waiting for an unknown killer to put a sudden end to her certainly qualified as a torment of a particularly awful intensity. For an hour or more, she remained rigidly fixated on the dark entryway to the tunnel leading to the barn/dormitory, watching and listening intently for the approach of her assassin.

Then as the second hour drew on—it must have been three-thirty A.M. by now—she began to feel a slight surge of hope. Perhaps, Webber and Crandall had joined forces merely to play some cruel, elaborate prank on her—designed to break her spirit and Donald's, so that they would withdraw from the presidential race for fear of criminal exposure. Or maybe she was simply meant to starve to death abandoned down here in the basement, the way her parents had been slowly starving Asterius through malnutrition in the cellarage of the ORIGI-NAL labyrinth. *That's it!* Kyle Webber was using "Asterius" as an ironic code word, a metaphor to indicate she'd be sharing the Minotaur's intended fate.

Suddenly, Arianna began to feel downright exhilarated. The fools! They hadn't bothered to check Donald's campaign itinerary and didn't realize he'd be returning home from Chicago on a mid-morning flight and would be here by noontime. All she had to do was hold out till then. When she heard him moving around upstairs, she'd start screaming her bloody head off!

But wait a minute. When all was said and done, the Minotaur HADN'T starved to death, had he? He'd been suddenly pounced upon out of the dark and . . .

What was THAT? That noise she'd just heard in the blackness of the tunnel entrance across the way? Her heart began to jump spasmodically in her chest.

There it was, again. A deep snuffling, snorting sound—the sound of a large—a *very* large—beast. Oh, Hades and Hecate! Idiotically, a child's nonsense jingle from *The Wizard of Oz* simpered through her consciousness—"Lions and tigers and bears, oh, my!"

But in the last moment of Arianna's life, it proved to be none of those but instead a huge, black, red-eyed, spike-horned Brahman bull that stepped, confused and uncertain, into the smoky, torchlit cellar. Aimlessly and stupidly it looked around, pawed at the earthen floor, snorting again then bellowing suddenly with dim and unfocused ill-will. Arianna felt her bladder let go as she saw the beast now become aware of her—not so much her as her fiery red gown. Now, she realized, its sense of purpose had been ignited.

Only fifty feet or so separated the tunnel entrance from Arianna's station at the far end of the altar at the opposite end of the cellar—certainly not nearly enough space for the bull to launch into a full gallop. But it made the most of the limitations imposed upon it and had speeded up to a ten-mile-an-hour lope by the time its 1,700-pound frame collided with the 120-pound woman, its curved and lethal left horn scything wickedly through her right rib cage as, with a half-realized shriek, she tried vainly to twist her body aside. Such was the force of impact that Arianna was ripped free of the altar shackle and, with the chain dangling from her wrists, borne aloft spitted on the bull's horn for a distance of ten feet before being smashed instantly—lifeless—into the unforgiving stone wall behind her.

But the bull Dionysus had named Asterius was not quite through with the red bundle of rags still affixed to its head. In its enraged efforts to free its horn, the beast smashed its burden to the ground, pawing at the limp carcass with its right fore hoof, and finally prising itself free with a violent upward wrench of its head. A residue geyser of blood erupted from the gaping hole in the newly dead woman's side.

Having solved its problem, the bull pawed and snuffled at the corpse for a little while, then lost interest. After that, it took to wandering around the cellar aimlessly until Kyle Webber came in, threw a rope over the creature's mammoth neck, and led it back to its stall, where its owner was due to collect it before sun-up. To ensure that the farmer would not commune with the tabloid press or come forward as a material witness in the days of excitement to come, Webber intended to slip him an extra few hundred dollars and break one of his hands.

Next he returned to Arianna, having donned a pair of rubber gloves that extended well up his forearms. He maneuvered her into an upright position and worked her stiffening body out of the doubly crimsoned silken gown. Since Arianna's craving for instant gratification had never brooked any needless impediments, there was no underwear to be removed. Setting the now naked carcass prone on the altar behind the remains of her former lovers, Webber removed the imposing labrys from its wall fastenings and began to deconstruct his late mistress. It took him no time at all.

Former Colonel Oliver B. Dedwell, acquitted in 1992 of slaughtering twenty-seven Iraqi soldiers as they attempted to capitulate to U.S. Army troops under his command at the tail end of Desert Storm, was having trouble getting to sleep—or rather he was experiencing a fear he'd suffered ever since late childhood of *going* to sleep. Tonight, his inability to drift off would be understandable, inasmuch as he'd just become the

Independent Party's nominee for Vice-President of the United States as the lower half of the ticket that featured the Reverend Donald Dillon—Jerk Extraordinaire in Oliver's humble opinion—as the Presidential candidate. But the excitement that would naturally attend such an honor wasn't the problem.

No. Not even the luxury bedding afforded by the Park Hyatt Chicago Hotel could assuage Dedwell's chronic late night affliction—because he KNEW that the moment he went to sleep he would be in HER realm—the kingdom of the lovely, haunting female creature who had filled his dreams with unbearable longing and desire (and ultimately hatred) for her for over forty years.

That was the problem, really. That an imaginary WOMAN—that most second-rate of beings as decreed by Holy Scripture, born as she was from Adam's rib—should have such ruthless and absolute command of his subconsciousness. Yet in the bleakness and desolation of the lonely night, there she was—always. Lovely yet eternally beyond his reach, singing her rapturous song while denying him her touch, her body, her love—weakening his resolve, his sense of purpose, all the while extending to him the vision of Paradise simultaneously attainable and forever beyond his reach.

What was most disturbing (yet in some fearful sense enticing) about the nightly assault on his male supremacy was its TIMELESSNESS—the thought that he and this woman-thing had been bound together for untold ages. In the dreams, she was forever dressed in some flowing gown, her blond hair arranged in triads of ringleted tresses down each side of her head. She was small—tiny, really—not at all in the tradition of lethal seductresses. Yet he felt she was capable of breaking him—that it was her purpose, immutable since Creation's inception, to *destroy* him.

Curiously, in the past week, the trauma had increased exponentially. In fact, he was sure that he could pinpoint the

175

moment when what had over many years devolved into a back burner concern, like a physical ailment one has learned to live with, had surged again to the forefront of his thought process. It had started four days ago on Saturday with the breaking of a slighty scandalous news story about his running mate, but had become overwhelming in the forty-eight hours since Donald Dillon had named him as his vice-presidential choice on Alan Pope's interview show.

Angry with himself for his sleepless restlessness, Dedwell kicked off the covers and turned on the bedside lamp. He seized his wallet and pulled from the back of it a folded-up newspaper clipping that he'd spent an unreasonable amount of time gazing at in stupefaction over the last several days. The article was highlighted by a candid shot showing Donald Dillon warding off the camera's gaze as if he were Dracula evading a raised cross. Opposite the wayward-seeming cleric was a radiant looking woman who was obviously basking in the attention—in fact, seemed malevolently to be enjoying Dillon's discomfort.

The woman was the stage and screen musical star, Daisy Crandall. And Oliver Dedwell all at once infallibly recognized her as the immortal girl of his dreams. How could that be? Was it just a matter of an uncanny physical resemblance? Or was she the actual incarnation of a lifelong figment of his subconscious? And what was she DOING in his subconscious, anyway—as if in some long lost age she had been a physical presence sharing space and time with him in another life?

Wearily, Dedwell shook his head and thought of tonight's earlier conversation with his running mate, The Jerk. After accepting their nominations at Chicago's convention center, they had had a mutually congratulatory late night supper and drinks in Dillon's suite two floors above him while their contingent of newly assigned Secret Service agents patrolled the hallways outside their respective rooms. They had discussed such routine matters as their separate traveling and speaking itineraries in the upcoming weeks, touched on the talking points they wanted to make to their audiences and the idiot media, and, most importantly, talked over their clandestine, backdoor ties to America's hate groups and paranoid militia organizations—the secret wellsprings of their political support, which must be kept beneath the radar of the effete, ever-suspicious news organizations—at least till after the election.

The serious concerns were finally set aside and after waiting for Dillon to drain off his third Grand Marnier straight up, Dedwell, still afraid of sounding foolish, nervously brought up the subject that was secretly causing him such inexplicable dread.

"Say, Don," he said, with an attempt at a chuckle, "tell me about this hotsy little chorus girl you got caught with last week? What's the deal, anyway? Did you nail her?"

He could tell from the feral look that suddenly gleamed in The Jerk's eyes that the man was about to lie. Then, oddly, Dillon seemed to grow despondent. He threw back a last, draining gulp of his drink and got up to prepare Grand Marnier number four. As he wobbled toward the suite's mini-bar, he shook his head.

"No," he said back over his shoulder.

When he returned, drink in hand, he sank back in his chair and closed his eyes as if that ended the matter.

"Why the hell not?" asked Dedwell, not about to let the matter drop. "I mean, what are women for other than to service our lust and to shoot out babies? You certainly aren't going to claim that you were after the droppings of her dim, insipid little mind, are you?"

Dillon looked at him sharply and spoke with some asperity. "Are you really such a consummate ass as to write off so disparagingly more than half the human race? They DO vote, you know. How have you arrived at the conclusion that all women are sight unseen so inferior?"

"Why, Reverend," said Dedwell mockingly. "How do I know? The Bible tells me so. Have you forgotten Adam's rib, Eve's brainless curiosity, Delilah's evil body heat?"

"All mythological rubbish, Colonel—which curiously enough brings us right back to Daisy Crandall. Tell me, what do you think of my wife? A brainless idiot?"

As a matter of fact, Dedwell thought quite a lot about the beautiful and rapacious Arianna Dillon, reputedly a thoroughly promiscuous bitch and, quite possibly, insane. However, he had to admit he owed his current rise in stature to her. It had been Dillon's wife who had seen him several times on the discussion show *Crosstalk*—so called because the panel usually shouted angrily at each other, as if decibel level equated with political truth. She had liked his views, she said, and had invited him to her Long Island home for a get-acquainted chat one weekend when he was in New York and Dillon was off somewhere. She had sent her chauffeur, a huge, muscular Schwarzenegger wannabe by the look of him, to drive him out there. He had happily contemplated putting the spurs to his hostess throughout the ride but was deterred the moment he got out of the car. As he emerged from the back seat of the limo, the driver politely held the door for him. Then while Mrs. Dillon, lounging like some sleek panther against her front door frame, smiled a raunchy welcome to him, he felt an iron hand drop to his shoulder and squeeze it mercilessly and painfully. "Listen, you evil bastard," murmured the chauffeur, "she's mine! Lay a hand or anything else on her, and I'll tear you limb from limb!"

As this had been the identical intimidation tactic he himself had used on countless men throughout his life, Dedwell appreciated the high seriousness of the warning and kept Arianna at several arms' length throughout his visit. Even though he could sense that she was baffled by his standoffishness, she must have held out high hopes for some future erotic tussle, for the visit went well—and in the end she had persuaded Dillon to invite him on the ticket.

"Colonel?" said Dillon snapping him back to the here and now.

"Your wife? An exceptionally good looking woman, obviously. And I'm certainly grateful for her active support of me. But does that mean we have to take her seriously in a political context? I can't buy that."

"Are you suggesting that in convincing me to pick you for my running mate she was not astute?"

Dedwell grinned and threw out his hands in mock helplessness. "Touche!" he said. "But what has she do to with this Crandall woman?"

"Colonel, my wife is not only brilliant but exceptionally dangerous, a fact you'd do well to keep in mind. Up until a few days ago, in fact, I would have stated unequivocally that she was the most dangerous woman alive. Now I'm considering demoting her to second place."

"Oh? Why's that?" Dedwell felt his scalp tingling with nameless dread.

"Because SHE'S convinced that Daisy Crandall is!"

"Why?" Dedwell asked, hating the weak, hollow sound of his own voice.

"Colonel, my wife is, as I said, brilliant and lethal. She also has several hundred major screws loose. She is oddly convinced that she is the reincarnation of a mythical Cretan princess named Ariadne, who millennia ago helped the Greek hero Theseus slay this half-bull, half-man creature."

"The Minotaur," said Dedwell quietly, as if to himself.

Dillon raised his eyebrows. "Colonel, you surprise me. Yes, the Minotaur. But that's not all. Ever since I've been running for President, Arianna's been trying to convince me that she's not alone, that there are other 'Dawn Timers,' as she calls them, living among us—that there is, in fact, a secret society of mythological women who have banded together to deny me the White House. The group call themselves New Dawn—and according to Arianna, their ringleader is Daisy Crandall. Until last weekend I had always dismissed her fears as mystical, heathen garbage."

"Something changed your mind?" asked Dedwell, his mouth dry, his throat hoarse.

"You could say that. In retrospect, I've come to the conclusion that Crandall set me up for that unfortunate photo in the restaurant last week. Plus, I checked out her biography in a theater program I have. She and her two twin sisters used to be a singing group calling themselves New Dawn."

Dedwell felt unwell. "Getting back to your wife's . . . delusion that she was this princess—what was the name?"

"Ariadne."

"Right. So does she have a theory as to who Crandall was back then?"

"She does indeed. She says Daisy and her sisters were in fact the Sirens—you know, the beautiful mermaid-like creatures, who according to the myth, sat on a rock near the sea and lured sailors to their deaths with their haunting voices. The hero Odysseus used trickery to escape them. I can't remember Daisy's name—it was some ungodly long thing . . . "

"Aglaophone," said Oliver Dedwell, as he sat now, suddenly drenched in sweat on the edge of the hotel bed. The doom-laden name had erupted without warning from the darkest, deepest caverns of his psyche—and he knew with certainty that he had correctly identified the dream creature who had haunted his sleep since childhood and now was threatening to overwhelm his every waking moment as well.

But he suddenly knew something else for a certainty, too. He would NOT be beaten or driven down by a mere woman. He would do unto Daisy Crandall before she did unto him.

He would kill her, if he had to.

His plane was rapidly approaching JFK. This should have been—so far, anyway—the supreme moment of his life. He was now the official nominee of the Independent Party for President of the United States. The poll numbers of the current President and his Democratic rival were in the sub-basement at this point, and so he had every reason to believe that he was a virtual shoo-in as the next occupant of the White House. *So why,* Donald Dillon wondered, *didn't he feel better?*

As he lay, head back, in his reclined first class seat on the U.S. Air morning flight taking him back to New York from Chicago, he thought to himself, *let me count the whys.* First, he was hung over like a bastard from the innumerable heavy duty Grand Marniers he had tossed down the night before. Secondly, he was now joined at the political hip to a militaristic troglodyte in the person of Vice-Presidential candidate, Oliver B. Dedwell—a man who actually BELIEVED in the Holy Scriptures that Dillon himself peddled without credence or conscience to the hinterland masses. Thirdly, he was headed home to contend, as always, with his wife Arianna (the Wicked Witch of the West, East, North, And South And All Broomstick Flight Paths In Between).

Oh, well. The plane was beginning to head into its descent pattern, so he'd better put on his game face. There was bound to be a significant cadre of reporters, officials, and supporters on hand to greet him as he strode into the terminal. Yes; in fact, as the plane angled down, he could see already the flashing roof lights of official cruisers and a small army of uniformed officers—an honor guard of some sort, no doubt.

Close, but no cigar. When the plane landed, it taxied to an atypical stop far short of the terminal-connecting ramp. The Reverend Dillon was then approached by a pretty but seemingly tense flight attendant who smiled nervously and asked him to follow her to the exit door. More impressed with himself than he'd ever been in his life, Dillon graciously acceded to her request, retrieved his carry-on bag, and magisterially walked down the length of the cabin, failing to notice that his Secret Service detail had remained seated. At the door, as the attendant stood aside, he discovered that a staircase apparently intended for his use alone had been rolled into place.

Then the oddest thing happened. As he descended the steps to the tarmac, a pair of uniformed United States marshals grimly and unsmilingly approached him, seized him roughly by the arms, and brusquely placed steel restraints upon his wrists. He was under arrest, he was informed, as the chief suspect in the axe murder of his wife, Arianna Dillon. He was pushed into the back seat of one of the cruisers and, flanked by the two officials, was whisked away, with sirens wailing, towards his Long Island home.

There, he found the approach to the Labyrinth cordoned off with yellow crime-scene tape, behind which concerned men and women in various law enforcement uniforms moved purposefully back and forth on the lawn and in and out of the house. An ambulance and a couple of vehicles belonging to the nearest medical examiner's office were pulled up in the circular drive before the front door. It goes without saying that the road fronting the Dillon property was snarled and clogged with local and national news media figures, their microphone-and-camera-wielding minions, and a fleet of mobile television vans sporting a wide range of network and affiliate logos. Things were really popping.

Dillon was hustled from the car to the front door to the accompaniment of shouted questions from the distant perimeter of the scene. Inside, he was escorted directly and firmly to the cellar door and down the stairs. At the bottom, a half-dozen or so people were busily collecting evidence, shooting crime scene photos and video, and conferring in quiet, sepulchral tones.

Without delay, the presidential hopeful was led to the raised stone slab at the far side of the room. Displayed on its surface were four neatly arranged mounds of human bones and skulls. Three of the piles were bleached with age and had evidently been there for some time. The fourth, surmounted by the recently beautiful head of Arianna Dillon, was, comparatively speaking, in mint condition.

"Is that your wife?" asked the FBI Special Agent in Charge.

Agog with wonder, Dillon said yes, it was.

"How about these others?" asked the SAC.

"Huh?" asked Dillon, apparently suddenly suffering from Attention Deficit Syndrome.

"The M.E. says these other . . . remains . . . all belong to young males in their twenties."

Dillon looked as if he understood and said, by way of explanation, "Oh, those are Arianna's year-kings."

A bright young woman from the medical examiner's office gave a low whistle, and someone else muttered, "Hoo-boy!"

"Ok, buddy, let's go!" said the FBI man, turning him around by the arm and nodding to the marshals to remove the prisoner from the premises.

And so the presidential candidacy of Donald Dillon summarily came to an end; and that of Colonel Oliver B. Dedwell just as precipitously came into being.

In the next hours, the media conflagration that attended the sensational murder of Arianna Dillon and the arrest of her husband as the evident perpetrator dwarfed anything previously seen in the realm of celebrity scandal, including the Manson murders and the O.J. Simpson trial. Facts and speculation were rapidly and hysterically brewed into a heady mix of journalistic overkill. Then while the maelstrom of coverage was still swirling madly throughout the public's circulatory system, Fox News turned the screws an insane notch or two tighter by broadcasting a contraband crime scene close-up of Arianna's fragmented remains—a quantum leap in bad taste that had thousands of people all over the country, including Daisy Crandall, locking themselves in their bathrooms for half-hours at a stretch and kneeling in heartfelt communion with their commodes.

Through all the madness, the outline of the crime and its discovery began to take some sort of shape. In the early morning of Thursday, August 26, 2004, the fax machines at the FBI headquarters in Washington, D.C. began to be flooded with documentary and pictorial information from anonymous sources purporting to show that presidential contender Donald Dillon and his wife Arianna had for many years been engaged in staggeringly criminal behavior ranging from drug trafficking and blackmail to serial murder. As a gesture of good faith verification of these charges, the tipsters—a trio self-designated only as R, B, and K, who presented themselves as having been close personal assistants to the Dillons—informed the Bureau that if it inspected the Long Island estate of their employers forthwith, evidence of some of the charges would be uncovered in the basement of the main house. While reluctant to act on information furnished by shadowy sources of unknown reliability, the material provided was so thoroughly and starkly compelling in its presentation that the Bureau felt justified in obtaining the necessary search warrants and going ahead with a daybreak raid on the Labyrinth.

The break-in itself had been staged by the FBI's Long Island Field Office located in Melville and led by Special Agent in Charge Delbert Grimm. Grimm and his team had found the house locked and, upon forcing an entry, unoccupied. Following the suggestion of the anonymous informants, they'd located the cellar stairway and a moment later discovered the charnel house below. After Agent Grimm, no longer feeling so Special or particularly In Charge, had queasily cell-phoned Washington, the FBI Director himself ordered the Reverend Dillon intercepted at Kennedy the moment his plane landed.

Initial findings by both the entry team and the medical examiner's people were discouraging in their amorphous complexity. There could be little doubt that Arianna Dillon and most likely the three other victims on display had all been forcefully vivisected by the awesome looking double-ax hanging on the wall behind what appeared to be a makeshift sacrificial altar. However, at least in Mrs. Dillon's case, the application of the weapon was judged to be subsequent to her actual death of causes thus far unknown. While there were evident substantial blood stains splashed on the stone slab and spilling in wide streaks down its front, the most recent of these rust-colored rivulets were found to be at least a couple of years old.

However, there was a massive, much more recent stain on the rough stone wall ten feet beyond the northern edge of the altar. Curiously, the top of this discoloration was nearly seven feet ABOVE floor level, whereas the victim was known to have been a woman of no more than five-and-a-half feet in height. Yet the large patch of blood that had seeped into the dirt floor at the base of the wall at that point could leave no doubt that Mrs. Dillon had been killed by a brutal collision with its stony surface while not in contact with the ground.

Then there was the curious matter of the many scuffed imprints still vaguely discernible on the basement's earthen floor. The crime scene technicians determined that there were SEVERAL pair of both male and female shoe prints still embedded faintly in the ground. However, even more mystifying was the fact that superimposed over THESE and smudging and partially obliterating them were the hoof prints of a large mammal—possibly a cow or a bull.

Finally, given the fact that Arianna herself was in such total disarray, there was no reliable way to pinpoint the time of her death beyond the logical supposition that it had occurred within the past twelve hours—a fact that favored Donald Dillon, in that everyone knew that he'd been in Chicago until that morning. Still, his physical absence from the crime scene didn't preclude him from having pre-arranged his wife's murder.

Because of the horrific severity of the crime and because of Dillon's national importance, he was transferred, much to Delbert Grimm's relief, from the jurisdiction of the FBI's Long Island office to the New York City headquarters in lower Manhattan, where Assistant Director In Charge Orville Durvish took over the investigation. It was Durvish's first procedural duty to oversee his illustrious suspect's initial interrogation.

At first, two male agents took turns questioning Dillon while Durvish watched the proceedings from behind a two-way mirror. For a long time, the suspect seemed soporific, as if in a daze at the dispiriting turn both the day and his fortunes had taken. After accepting a second cup of coffee, though, he began to focus and seemed willing to cooperate—in fact, waiving his right to an attorney, claiming the Good Lord would testify in his defense. The agents smiled. It was shaping up to be a wonderful day.

"So, Reverend," asked Agent One, "can you walk us through that business in your basement a little bit? You told Special Agent Grimm out on Long Island that the male victims—who had apparently been buried for some time in a tunnel adjacent to the cellar—were your wife's"—here the agent referred to his notes—"'year-kings.' Care to enlighten us about that? What's a year-king? And if they were buried, who dug them up and arranged them, so to speak, alongside the remains of your wife?"

"Well, to address the second matter first, I have no idea who disinterred them. I buried them myself after she killed them."

That seemed to give the detectives food for thought. Agent Two eventually cleared his throat. "So you knew about that? You were her accomplice?"

"Of course not!" snapped Dillon. "That was HER pet project! I just cleaned up after her, that's all."

"But why would you do that instead of calling the police? Wasn't it obvious that your wife was a psychopathic killer and needed to be stopped?"

"I was already contemplating running for President, for Christ sake! You think I wanted the public to find out my wife was a total looney-toon? No political party's going to consider a candidate with a wacko spouse!"

Agent One and Agent Two exchanged glances. "I see your point," said Agent One diplomatically. "But let's get back to my original question. Explain the year-king business, if you will."

At this moment, a petite, very pretty blonde in her mid-twenties joined Assistant Director Durvish at his observation post behind the window.

"Mind if I watch, sir? It's my lunch break, and I thought I might pick up some pointers on interrogation technique."

Durvish, a big, homely man with a puffy face, owlish glasses, no social skills, and a terror of attractive women, felt himself flushing and wondered if his armpits smelled.

"Of course, Agent Abbott," he said, hoping his breath was okay. Dulcie Abbott was a very promising interning agent that the training academy at Quantico was fast-tracking and had assigned to New York for the summer. She was a bright and smiling ray of sunshine, who worked in a small cubicle outside his office and was onboard mainly to observe and act as an intra-office gofer. And since she'd arrived, Durvish couldn't wait to get to work in the morning.

Now as he and Agent Abbott re-directed their attention to the little interrogation room, it became apparent that Agents One and Two were losing it. Dillon was giving them a crash

187

course in what appeared to be Greek mythology, claiming that his wife had insisted she was the Cretan princess Ariadne and that it was her duty to sacrifice young male consorts to the wine god Dionysus.

"Golly!" said Dulcie Abbott.

Suddenly, the interrogating agents turned panicky faces toward the window. They wanted out—now!

"Damn!" swore Durvish. "NOW what do we do?"

"Sir," said Dulcie, "I was a Classics major at Yale before switching to Law Enforcement. I don't want to be pushy or anything, but why not let me take a crack at him? I understand the mythological references he's making. Maybe I can get something useful out of him."

Durvish looked at her in wonder. "Sure!" he said. "Why not? Can't hurt."

Meanwhile, Agents One and Two made a dash for the exit, crowding each other in the doorframe like a pair of silent movie comedians. Once they'd squeezed through, Dulcie moved past them into the room with Dillon. Then, as the three detectives looked on, they saw a strange transformation come over the suspect. His mouth fell open, and he stared, bug-eyed, at the young intern.

Dulcie approached the small, gun-metal gray table and took the seat opposite Dillon, extending her hand as she did so. "Good afternoon, Reverend Dillon. I'm Agent Abbott . . . "

"You!" said Dillon in a shocked, hushed voice. "You look just like her! Are you her daughter, or something?"

"Sir?" said Dulcie, puzzled. "I'm afraid I don't . . . "

"Now I get it!" shouted Dillon. "Arianna was right! She's behind it all! She sent you here to kill me, didn't she?" His voice cracked, and he seemed on the verge of hysteria.

Dulcie shot a quick glance at Durvish behind the one-way window. "Who, sir? Who are you talking about?"

"Daisy Crandall!"

"Daisy Crandall? The musical star? What does SHE have to do with any of this?"

"She's behind it all! Arianna was right! She's always been out to destroy us! She and her secret organization!"

"Secret organization?"

"Don't play innocent! You're in on it with her! New Dawn! THAT'S what you call yourselves! It's all a vast Dawn Time conspiracy!"

Dulcie shrugged her shoulders at the window and came out into the corridor to join the others. Obviously, everybody was now in a brand new ball game. Then, while the three men conferred in a muddle of supposition and confusion, ignoring her, Dulcie stole back to her work cubicle. There, checking over her shoulder several times to make sure she wasn't being observed, she placed a hasty phone call to a midtown hotel suite.

Eighteen

Orville Durvish was more frightened than he could ever remember having been in his life. At the age of forty-two, he was
well-positioned to become the next Director of the FBI once
the aging incumbent retired—an event thought to be only a
matter of a year or two away. In over twenty years of service,
he'd won a solid reputation for leading investigations that had
netted some of the worst killers and bank robbers in the nation's
recent history. Then five years ago, he'd been given the New
York City field office, a sure sign that he'd been earmarked for
the ultimate professional assignment in the Bureau.

But none of that seemed to matter at the moment. Midway
through a day when he'd been handed the most explosive, reputation making-or-breaking case of his career—possibly of *anyone's* career since Pontius Pilate's—Durvish found himself
walking down an ornate, plushly carpeted corridor on the
twenty-first floor of midtown Manhattan's Marriott Hotel. He
felt just now like two hundred and ten pounds of ambulatory
Jello. Previously, he'd faced down serial killers, rapists, drug
smugglers, and international terrorists. But never—
NEVER—till this exact moment had he been called upon to
confront Daisy Crandall, the ninety-five-pound musical theater
actress he'd had a soul-rupturing crush on since the onset of
puberty. But an evident madman named Donald Dillon had
now made this encounter a necessity—for Dillon had just accused Broadway's Sweetheart (and Durvish's own secret inna-
morata) of having engineered his wife's grotesque murder. Dear
God! *Could it possibly be true?*

But there were even more traumatic concerns than Daisy's guilt or innocence to be addressed in these final seconds before knocking on the door. Accordingly, in the blessedly vacant elevator that had carried him up from the lobby, he had downed fully a third of the miniature Scope bottle that he always toted in his jacket pocket. Now, looking left and right and seeing no one approaching from either direction, he gave each of his armpits a desperate final sniff. The results were inconclusive but would have to do.

Showtime.

Durvish rapped on the door to room 2110 and stood back as if expecting it to explode. Instead it was opened by . . . his little intern, Dulcie Abbott. What the hell was SHE doing here? Then he realized he was mistaken—this woman was far older and far more beautiful than the undeniably pretty Agent Abbott. This woman was obviously an immortal of some kind. Durvish felt his pulse sink. Who was he to cause stress to, and possibly enormous legal difficulties for, such a creature? Yet if she were indeed implicated in the bizarre and grisly saga of Donald and Arianna Dillon, he had no choice but to follow through with the full weight of his professional authority.

"Mr. Durvish?" said the woman, flashing an uncertain smile that nevertheless undid him with its vulnerable beauty. Maybe he wasn't cut out for this hardnosed FBI stuff, after all. Maybe he and Daisy Crandall could run off to Vegas or some such place together, round up a Justice of the Peace, and . . .

"Yes, Ma'am. I called earlier." *His words,* he thought, *had emerged with remarkable fluidity.*

"I feel a little silly asking this—but could I see some ID? A woman can't be too careful these days, you know. At least that's the way you always see it on television, so I guess I really should ask."

"Oh, sure! No problem!" the FBI man said, reaching suavely into the wrong jacket pocket first and producing his

Scope bottle before successfully locating his credentials and presenting them for her inspection.

She smiled, "That's fine," and opening the door wider, stepped aside to admit him. Then she led him into the spacious living room area of the lavish suite overlooking the mad, lively swirl of Times Squares many stories below. Over her shoulder, she asked him if she could offer him something from the bar.

"Oh, no, Ma'am. I'm on duty, you know."

"Of course. I should have known better. I guess I'm just a little nervous, to tell you the truth—about your visit, I mean. Have a seat, uh—I'm not quite sure how to address you. Inspector? Detective?"

"Orville will be just fine, Ma'am." He'd always hated his nerdy name, never more so than at this extraordinary point in time. At least with her sitting now on the sofa a good ten feet away, he could relax a bit about his breath.

"Oh, thank you," the goddess said, spreading her hand above her bosom in a feminine gesture of relief. "That sounds so friendly. I feel more relaxed now. Oh, I'm Daisy, of course."

Durvish nodded in complete agreement.

"This Dillon business is so upsetting to me! I've been glued to the TV—at least, till they showed that awful, awful picture of . . . I'm afraid I was sick. I mean, I suppose you could say I KNEW them . . . " Daisy stalled in mid-sentence.

Durvish picked up the dropped ball. "Yes, Ma'am . . . Miss Crandall . . . I mean, Daisy. That's why I'm here, actually. As I explained on the phone, Reverend Dillon sort of freaked out, I guess you could say, at one point and began . . . well, babbling about you in a very specific way, seeming to implicate you in this whole sorry business . . . Ordinarily, we wouldn't take him seriously—but then there WAS that little flap in the papers last week about you and him . . . you know, being caught . . . I mean *seen*—SEEN together, that's all . . . so I thought I'd better just check everything out with you personally . . . "

By now, Daisy had the situation pretty much in hand. Actually, she found herself liking Orville Durvish.

"Orville," she asked softly, "should I call my lawyer, maybe?"

"Oh, no! no! Nothing like that!" Durvish protested. "I'm sure you and I can just have a little chat and clear everything up."

"Very well. I trust you, Orville."

"Well, . . . Daisy, how well did you know the Dillons? Why don't we start there?"

"Not well at all, really. I attended a single fundraiser at their Long Island home where Mrs. Dillon was . . . you know. Then they were kind enough to come to my show, and I saw them backstage—and that was it."

Durvish cleared his throat. "But what about your appearance at the restaurant alone with Reverend Dillon?"

"That was entirely HIS idea!" Daisy said somewhat flintily. "He simply showed up unexpectedly in my dressing room that night and was very insistent that I have supper with him. In retrospect, obviously, I should have refused. The papers, by the way, were quite accurate afterwards in reporting my remarks."

"I'm sure they were. Did you ever see MRS. Dillon again, on any other occasion?"

"I can't say that I did."

(She had, of course, but obviously she couldn't SAY that—so, technically, not a lie.)

Daisy crossed her legs, allowing her pale blue skirt to ride up an inch or so above her knee. She trusted that would deflect Orville's attention from her face, in case her expression fleetingly betrayed her. She figured she had several more upward inches in reserve—but that was a finite strategy at best. She wasn't Sharon Stone, after all.

Durvish pulled uncomfortably at his collar. "Does the name Dulcie Abbott mean anything to you?"

Daisy shook her head after a show of reflection. "The name doesn't ring a bell."

(Liar! Liar! Pants on fire! . . . No, actually no! She was being strictly honest. Names, after all, didn't go around literally ringing bells, did they?)

"Why do you ask?"

"Well, we have a young intern—an agent by that name—working for the summer out of our New York office. Her resemblance to you—except for her age, of course . . . I mean, she's not as beautiful as you, Miss . . . Daisy, not at all! But the resemblance is, well, quite striking, now that I see you in person."

"I see. And is this relevant in some way, Orville? To the case, I mean?"

"Actually, Daisy, yes it is," said Durvish, leaning forward intently with his arms on his knees. "You see, at one point in his interrogation, Reverend Dillon began to speak very oddly about a delusion of his dead wife's—that she thought she was a princess out of Greek mythology, and that she was routinely sacrificing young men who worked for her and her husband to one of the gods—Dionysus, I think he said!"

"How bizarre!" Daisy observed.

"True. But here's the thing. My two agents handling his questioning were obviously getting way out of their depth when Miss Abbott, who was watching through a one-way mirror with me, volunteered to take over. It seems she has some background in that area. But the minute she entered the room and approached him, Dillon started shouting and comparing her to YOU, claiming that she must be your daughter whom you'd sent there to kill him—that you were the head of some secret organization bent on destroying him and his wife—and particularly his presidential candidacy."

194

Daisy's skirt rose through inches three and four. "I see," she said. "And what was this group called? Did he say?"

"Actually, he did. He referred to it as New Dawn!"

Daisy suddenly laughed with relief. "Oh, THAT explains it!!" she said. "Well, I mean it doesn't explain this wild delusion both these poor people seem to have been suffering regarding me—but I can account for the name New Dawn . . . "

"Wait a minute!" Durvish interrupted with a big grin, like an excited schoolboy who'd just dredged up a correct answer out of nowhere. "That was the name of your singing group, wasn't it? When you started out in show business with your sisters back in 1971!"

"Why, yes, Orville! How flattering! Are you a fan of mine?"

"Like you wouldn't believe! Daisy, that must be IT! Dillon must have read about you somewhere and incorporated New Dawn into his sick fantasies!"

"You think so? Why that's brilliant detective work, Orville!"

Durvish rose from his chair in triumph. "Thank you! I KNEW there had to be some reasonable explanation for Dillon's bizarre behavior! Well, I see no reason why we have to prolong this interview, . . . Daisy! I believe we've both stumbled onto the source of Dillon's fixation with you!"

"Well, that's very comforting, Orville—and I'm glad you're satisfied about my . . . non-involvement in this awful mess. But I hate to see you go! I always get such a kick from talking to my fans!" By this time, she had risen, too, and seizing his arm, had him halfway to the door. "We actresses are very vain, you know! Say, how would you like a couple of front row tickets to *The Sound of Music?*"

"Oh, I couldn't, Ma'am! Daisy! That would be unethical!"

"Of course! How silly of me!"

"Besides, I've already seen you in it three times!"

"In one week? Isn't that sweet! Tell me, are you too ethical to accept an autographed photo?"

Durvish beamed. "No. My ethics have their limits."

"Fine! You wait right there!" Daisy disappeared into another room for a minute then returned with a glorious eight-by-ten glossy of herself in costume as Maria von Trapp. As she bent over a table and wrote, he looked at the soft, swanlike grace of her neck, smelled the delicate scent of her perfume, heard the haunting, unnamable tune she hummed, and felt that he might pass out in a delirious fit. Then she straightened up and offered him the picture on which she'd inscribed:

To Orville—a future FBI Director?
Fondly, Daisy Crandall

Then they said a cordial good-bye, and while Durvish floated toward the elevator, Daisy closed the door behind him. Contented that everything had gone as well as could be expected, she went into the suite's bedroom and immediately placed a phone call.

"Hello!"

"Hi, Daisy! How'd it go?"

" . . . Er, is this a—what do you call it—a safe wire?"

"Huh? Oh, a secure line. Yes, it is. Don't worry—I'm trained to tell if a phone line is bugged. So what do you think of Orville the dweeb?"

"Dulcie, that's not nice! Actually, I thought he was very sweet. And I wouldn't underestimate him if I were you. He didn't get where he is by being a fool. If he didn't have a crush on me, I'd probably be downtown being fingerprinted by now."

"So, bottom line, you think it went all right?"

"Yes, I do! Thanks for calling me before he did. It gave me an edge with him. And, Dulcie, I can't tell you how much we appreciate your expertise, everything you've done for us seeing that all our . . . material got into the right hands and wasn't traceable to our three friends or to the rest of us."

"Glad to do it, Daisy! That's why I infiltrated the Bureau, after all."

"Well, keep up the great work. How's the O.D. project going? We're going to have to deal with HIM very quickly. We don't have much time."

"I'm on it. I've got him on my monitor right now, as a matter of fact."

"Good. I won't keep you then. Thanks again for everything."

"You're very welcome, Daisy. Goodbye."

Clever girl, thought Daisy. Assuming New Dawn hung together beyond the current situation and became a permanent organization, she was seriously thinking of grooming that young woman as her successor. Dulcie'd certainly proven to be a pleasant surprise with her initiative and hard work. Back in the Dawn Time, she'd been Euphrosyne, one of the pretty little princesses, along with her sisters Aghaia and Thalia, known as the Three Graces—representing all the sweet, benign aspects of femininity. Dulcie had been the Grace of Happiness—and earlier Daisy had written her off as a decorative lightweight on the council. It just went to show how wrong it was to judge people based on first impressions.

Actually, as Daisy would soon learn to her sorrow, she still didn't have the correct read on the girl. For Dulcie Abbott was as black of heart as she was fair of face.

Choices! Choices!

After concluding her phone conversation with Daisy, Dulcie Abbott swung her computer chair around and, immensely pleased with herself, grinned, leaned back, and clasped her hands behind her head. She thought back to a favorite child-hood memory. Her mother had taken her, when she was eight or nine, to see her first Broadway show, a Wednesday matinee performance of the musical *Peter Pan,* starring Daisy Crandall as the irrepressible airborne youth from Never-Never Land. Daisy had launched into her first big number "I Gotta Crow!" with the boastful self-appraisal, "Oh, I'm clever! Oh, the clever-ness of me!"

Exactimento! thought Dulcie, applying the sentiment to herself.

Her future suddenly was spread out dizzyingly before her, limitless and exciting, in three divergent but equally enthralling scenarios. First, she could easily picture herself succeeding Daisy as the Great Mother of New Dawn, should the group evolve into a permanent organization. Daisy was a wonder in her way, of course, but the poor old dear was a dinosaur not really equipped for the twenty-first century, hung up as she was on saving the world from itself rather than developing the techno savvy that Dulcie herself possessed. These were the skills that could convert New Dawn into a force to be reckoned with and feared—a ruthless female Mafia composed of the world's most powerful women, controlling men, money, and govern-ments in a way the strident feminists of the previous half-cen-tury with their endless whining about equal pay and glass ceilings had never dared envision.

Still, it would be a mistake to underestimate either Daisy's brilliance or her tenacity. She could easily hang in there for another ten or fifteen years. The council revered her, so a palace coup designed to overthrow her was, for the foreseeable future, out of the question. There was always murder, of course—but Dulcie felt she wasn't quite there yet in terms of confidence or will. Daisy had been very sweet to her, after all. Moreover, there were awed whispers among the council members about the old woman having dark powers beyond the ordinary that would make her a fearsome enemy—though specifics were hard to come by.

Of course, given the knowledge Daisy had entrusted her with, she could easily encompass her mentor's disgrace—but that would bring New Dawn itself into disrepute, so what would be the point? Well, there WAS one, actually, feeding directly into enticing Option Number Two. What if she were able to contrive an end run around awful Orville? Sneak back to Washington with the packet of illicitly obtained Dillon evidence, reveal to the Director himself the identities of anonymous sources R(honda), B(rian) and K(yle), and as a consequence, implicate Daisy and her group in the Dillon debacle? Orville Durvish would be shown up as the clueless oaf she felt him to be (in spite of Daisy's warning) and suffer the FBI chief's disfavor. And might the Director not then turn for his successor to the masterful young woman who'd infiltrated a highly suspect, possibly criminal cabal on her own initiative and brought it to his attention?

Jesus, Dulcie! *Get real!* Clarice Starling was a fiction. No one was going to make a young female intern head of the FBI, an organization infamous for its zealous devotion to in-house loyalty, its covering up of operational incompetence, and—in spite of J. Edgar Hoover's reputed fondness for satin, furs, and heels—its macho posturing. When all was said and done the quickest, surest way for her to advance in the Bureau would be to hit the old sackerino with Orville Durvish. And that desperate she wasn't—yet.

But then, Possibility Number Three bloomed forth in her inner vision. She certainly wouldn't mind mussing the sheets of the man whose chiseled features stared hypnotically back at her from her computer screen. Oliver Dedwell, by all likely odds the next President of the United States. While the Constitution stated emphatically that the President must be at least thirty-five, there was nothing in the law of the land that insisted that his wife couldn't be a comely twenty-seven. And she was, after all, a bone fide member of the "I Want Everything And I Want It NOW!" Generation. Why wait for Daisy Crandall to shuffle off to the Old Sirens' home, or for Snoreville Orville to collect his retirement Timex? If she impressed O.D. sufficiently by providing him with inside information critical to his political survival—convinced him that there was a concerted effort to bring him down on the part of one small, insidious group that had already destroyed the Dillon campaign, wouldn't the colonel be grateful? How could he not, then, take her to his heart, to his bed, and to his next residence?

Dulcie Abbott Dedwell, First Lady of the United States From Sea To Shining Sea . . .

How awesomely, totally cool!

Dulcie had the good sense to tremble for a moment at the scope of her hubris. Then she slid out the tray of her computer desk and needlessly re-read Oliver Dedwell's home number, which she had pasted there several days ago. Next, with a shivering prayer to the dark god of boundless ambition, she reached for the phone.

Nineteen

Oliver Dedwell was so happy, so elated, so full of the awesome destiny that now seemed to be his for the taking that he almost smiled. In a little more than two months, he was going to be elected President of the United States. Everything had fallen dramatically into place with a swiftness that was dizzying—and he hadn't yet lifted a finger on his own behalf. Having flunked the FBI interrogation yesterday with extremely high-flying colors, Donald Dillon had been arraigned on a charge of multiple homicide and remanded for the foreseeable future to the psychiatric ward of Manhattan's famed Bellevue Hospital for extensive testing to see if he were competent to stand trial. One staff psychiatrist, speaking strictly off the record (as he believed), said that it was his professional opinion that the reverend would never see the inside of a courtroom since he was "obviously crazier than an outhouse rat."

It was a good thing, of course, reflected Dedwell, that Dillon's candidacy had disintegrated before it had begun. That meant that he wouldn't have to be exploiting his Al Qaeda contacts to organize the picture-perfect double assassination he'd conceived to eliminate both Dillon and his wife just before the reverend took the Oath of Office. That event would also entail hiring a couple of hate group snipers to take out the two nutso towel heads before they decided to make it a trifecta by adding Dedwell himself to their hit list. Then, of course, the hate group guys would have to be waxed—so the whole thing would have ended up draining an unacceptable amount of his presidential energy—energy that could much better be deployed in directing a military assault against the Middle East that would reduce that misbegotten section of the world to the irradiated, rubble-strewn desert the Old Testament God had always intended it to be ever since His fiery onslaught against Sodom and Gomorrah.

That still left him with one problem, though, that he hoped he was on his way to solving this very night. Daisy Crandall. The woman insistently continued to inhabit his dreams and gnaw at his emotional vitals. It was intolerable! That's one thing he had to give the camel jockeys—they knew how to mishandle the opposite sex. The Bible, as he read it, from Genesis to St. Paul vehemently asserted the superiority of Man over Woman. Why should he—destined now to become the most feared leader in the world—find his psyche permanently enslaved to a female, and one he'd never met, at that?

Of course, it was another woman who had suddenly come forward to offer him a chance to rid himself of Crandall. Some little tramp of a would-be Delilah had called him at his rural home in upstate New York the previous night. In a simpering little girl voice she had explained that she was a government employee in a confidential position with access to sensitive in-formation on the Dillon murder case—information that not only showed Daisy Crandall to have been complicit in the nominee's downfall but that she was even now re-setting her sights on Dedwell's own destruction. Would he be interested in getting together and seeing what she had? This last comment was punc-tuated with a pathetic, risqué giggle meant to be alluring.

"What's your name?" Dedwell had snarled. He could hear the girl flinch over the phone. It was very gratifying.

" . . . Let's just call me D, as in Daisy!" Still being cute!

"WHAT'S YOUR NAME, DAMMIT?!"

"Dulcie. Dulcie Abbott!" said the girl, her voice quivering, all the snotty assertiveness gone now.

"Dulcie? What kind of stupid name is THAT? What do you have in mind, Dulcie?"

"Well, I thought if I could just come up there, you know . . . to see you, I could show . . . "

"No way! I'll come to YOU tomorrow night. Where are you, anyway?"

"Well, I live in Darien, Connecticut."

"That's an hour-and-a-half drive for me, Dulcie! What you're selling better be damned good! Any quiet, out-of-the-way motels down there?"

"Well, uh, yes. There's the Cozy Spot. It's pretty dead, even in summer," the girl said, glad to be of help. "As a matter of fact, it's only half a mile from Daisy Crandall's estate."

THAT certainly got Dedwell's attention. "Are you serious?" he asked, his voice heavy with menace. Then after a moment, "Is there a back way onto the property? Unguarded?"

"Well—yes. There are woods all around and no walls. Hey, wait a minute!"

He could hear the girl swallowing nervously.

"You're not thinking of DOING anything, are you? . . . I mean, to hurt Daisy?"

"Isn't that the general idea, here? You called ME, remember?"

"But my intention," the girl protested, "was mainly to help you avoid any damaging . . . revelations coming out, you know? I admire you very much—and I'm anxious to see you become President. But I don't want to get involved if there's going to be violence."

As much as he'd hated to moderate his tone, Dedwell hadn't wanted to frighten the little bitch off—not if she were truly in possession of some documentary dynamite Crandall had on him; and not if he could terminate Crandall herself with REALLY extreme prejudice and exorcise the woman-thing once and for all from his head, from his dreams. If Dulcie hung up on him, he'd have a rough time tracking her down. She might have been clever enough to give him a phony name.

203

"Look, Dulcie, is it?" he asked reasonably. "Sorry if I came on a bit strong there. Truth is, the events of the last couple of days have got me kind of pumped up and on edge. I promise. No one's going to get hurt."

It was an outright lie, of course. So what?

There was a pause. "Well, all right then." The little fool was hooked. He smoothly reeled her in.

"Good. So why don't you tell me where this motel is and get us a room? For, say, ten o'clock tomorrow night? Be sure the room's isolated. I can't afford to be spotted in a compromising situation with an attractive woman, you know."

Mollified by the abrupt change in his manner, the girl had eagerly agreed to make the arrangements and hung up. Earlier tonight, his new security detail had naturally protested that he couldn't go anywhere without them, so he'd had to convince them that the thing was do-able by first beating them up and then duct-taping them to two of his kitchen chairs.

Now he saw the flickering blue neon light of the C-zy -pot Motel up the road to his right. *How symbolic,* he thought with satisfaction. Soon, the lights of Dulcie Abbott's insipid little life would be flickering out, as well. That would be after her rape, of course—assuming she wasn't a total cow.

Then it would be on to more of the same with Daisy Crandall.

He pulled into the motel lot and drove down the length of it to the only lighted room in the row and parked next to Dulcie's red Subaru wagon.

Dulcie had never been so nervous in her life. Ever since her phone conversation with Oliver Dedwell the previous evening, she'd alternated scenarios of seduction and romance with schemes of utter flight to some far distant pinprick on the globe where neither Oliver Dedwell nor Daisy Crandall could ever track her down. She'd had a couple of stiff scotches at home half an hour ago, but they hadn't helped.

She was sitting rigidly on one of the motel room's thread-bare twin beds. *What a dump,* she thought, echoing an old movie line that had lodged in her subconscious. The room's depressing anonymity emphasized how over-dressed she felt in her sexy, low-cut, black cocktail dress with heels to match. It gave her some comfort to realize that whatever else Dedwell would think of her, he certainly couldn't help but be impressed by her looks.

Unless he were gay, of course. And that wasn't totally un-likely. It was rare, after all, for a major presidential candidate to be unmarried, if only for photographic purposes. Moreover, none of the vast amount of material on the colonel that had been pumped out by the media in the past week—nor anything that New Dawn or the Bureau had come up with—had made mention of any women friends, past or present. If speculation about Dedwell's sexual orientation had not yet surfaced, it couldn't be more than one Drudge Report away.

Her heart suddenly leaped in her chest. A car had just pulled in next to hers. A second later its engines and its lights were killed. Dulcie stood up, tottering unsteadily on her heels, and gave herself one last nervous appraisal in the mirror. She couldn't know it, of course, because the subject had never come up on the phone, but the fact that the colonel had no idea what she looked like was about to become a definite minus.

Dulcie closed her eyes in prayer as she heard the firm, no-nonsense rap on the door. She counted to three then moved forward to answer it. Swinging the door open, she found herself facing the colonel for the first time. She barely had time to take in his blue polo shirt, his light tan slacks, and his massive, sculpted biceps before she saw a look of rage sweep across his features.

Storming across the threshold and abruptly slamming the door behind him, he snarled, "What the hell IS this?"

Dulcie shrank back, alarmed. "What are you talk . . . ?"

"You're HER, aren't you?"

He grabbed her roughly by the upper arm, causing her to wince and cry out in pain.

"WHO?" she shouted.

"Daisy Crandall!"

Dulcie felt relief surge through her. "Oh, I know what you mean! Everyone tells me I look like her."

Dedwell wasn't convinced or placated, but he let go of her. "It's more than that—though now that I look at you, you're younger. Are you her daughter?"

"No, honest!" Dulcie said, rubbing her arm. "Daisy doesn't have any children. She's never married."

"You seem to know a lot about her. And how is it, you just happen to live in the same town?"

"Well, we do know each other."

"I think you'd better tell me everything, Dulcie. Starting with you. What's your job that you mentioned, and what's your connection to Crandall?"

Dedwell took the room's only seat, while Dulcie perched tentatively on the nearer bed. She took a deep breath, licked at her lips, and began.

"I'm with the FBI," she said. "I'm a trainee. This summer I'm working out of the New York office in Manhattan, and I was there yesterday when they brought Dillon in. I watched him being interrogated. In fact, I took a hand at questioning him myself—or started to. But he did the same thing YOU just did. He went berserk when he saw me—accused me of being Daisy's daughter."

Dedwell said nothing but Dulcie could tell by his look that she'd moved up a notch or two in his estimation. She pressed on.

"That fact is I'm a plant. Oh, I went through the full training course at Quantico—did very well, too. But I'm not for real."

"Who planted you?" Dedwell asked, sitting forward in his chair.

"Daisy did."

Dedwell pursed his lips and made a blowing sound.

"So it exists. And you're part of it."

"What?" Dulcie asked.

"New Dawn."

Now it was Dulcie's turn to look startled and impressed. "How did you know . . . ?"

The colonel forestalled her with a raised hand. "Dillon started babbling about it the night we were nominated. Said Crandall was out to destroy him. Looks like she did."

Dulcie could feel renewed confidence seeping back into her blood stream.

"It gets better than that," she said.

"How so?"

"She killed Arianna Dillon."

Dedwell sat with his mouth open.

"Oh, I doubt if she literally did the killing. That's not her style. But I know she was there in that basement the night Arianna died. She presided over her execution, let's say. She knew Arianna was pure evil and felt justified in judging and condemning her to death."

"Where does Crandall get off being so high and mighty? She sounds as nutty as Dillon and his wife."

Dulcie bristled. "Daisy's a great woman! She's a Dawn Timer. We all are!"

Dedwell sneered. "I guess that means you all think you're retreads of ancient mythological characters? That's what Dillon said."

"Mythological characters were actually nothing more than ancient royalty transformed by their deeds, their awed subjects, and the old poets into larger-than-life figures. And we've all led past lives, Colonel. It's just that we women of New Dawn are more introspective, more in touch with our psychic roots. We acknowledge the Mother, and through her we remember the Dawn Time."

"The Mother?" Dedwell smiled condescendingly.

"The Great Goddess, who created all things—including the Judeo-Christian God," Dulcie said with quiet satisfaction.

Instantly, Dedwell was on his feet, his face a bright scarlet. "That's a blasphemous, heathen lie!" he roared.

Now it was Dulcie who had the upper hand. She remained calmly seated and stared at him as if he were a tantrum-throwing child.

"Are we here to discuss theology, Colonel? Or do you want to see what I've brought you?" She indicated a manila packet on a nearby side table. Dedwell calmed himself with a visible effort then walked over and snatched up the material. Ripping it open, he pulled out the contents. These, he saw, included the transcript of his court-martial, detailed speculation as to his suspected intimidation of witnesses against him, and, more recently, the names of key leaders of America's dark army of hate groups and the times and dates of his meetings with them.

No doubt about it. Daisy Crandall was good. *She'd have to go.*

"How do YOU happen to have this stuff—personally, I mean?" he asked Dulcie, straining to be civil for just a few minutes more.

"I'm the one who channels it to the authorities. That's how they got all the evidence on the Dillons."

"And you're offering this to me first? Everything you've got?"

"Except for my own copies, naturally."

Dedwell grew very still. "What's your price, little girl? What are you after?"

Confident now, Dulcie rose to her feet. "I want in on the presidential action, Colonel. I want to be a major player in your campaign." She moved closer. "Ultimately, of course, I want YOU."

Dedwell just stared at her for a moment. Then he asked, "Is Crandall home tonight?"

Dulcie was puzzled. "Why do you ask?"

Dedwell punched her hard in the face.

"ANSWER ME!"

Dulcie screamed with shock and pain and fell to her knees on the carpet. Something had broken in her cheek. She knew it.

"What are you doing?" she blubbered.

"Let's call it foreplay. Where's Daisy Crandall—AT THIS MOMENT?!"

"She's got a performance tonight!" Dulcie said, trying not to cry.

Dedwell smacked her backhanded in the mouth. "You got me all the way out to this godforsaken place for NOTHING?" he screamed.

"NO! NO! Tonight she's coming back here!"

"What do you mean? EXPLAIN, you little tart!"

"She took a hotel room in the city for the run of her play. But she's coming back tonight. She's called a meeting of her council for ten tomorrow morning. It's about you. She's obsessed about you—ever since Dillon announced you for his running mate."

"So later tonight she'll be back here?"

"Yes."

"Tell me about her routine when she's home. Give me the location of her room!"

Dulcie intuitively knew she was done for. She had betrayed Daisy, the Mother, and herself. She had forsaken her kind and chosen to engage men on the aggressive political field of play that THEY had dominated for nearly four thousand years—instead of exploiting the gifts particular to her own sex. She had gambled foolishly, recklessly, and lost. Under ordinary circumstances, she could have physically annihilated Dedwell, who had no clue about his own majestic Dawn Time pedigree. That was the key—KNOWING you were of the same stuff as the gods. But Dedwell made up for his ignorance by being a violent, self-absorbed maniac with a mission, and the Mother she'd denied would not help her withstand him now.

So, craftily, she told the truth, knowing that against Daisy Crandall Colonel Oliver Dedwell didn't have a prayer.

"Your best chance is tomorrow morning. When she's back here she likes to walk her private beach alone as the sun comes up. She's very corny. She says seeing a real new dawn energizes her—keeps her in touch with the Goddess."

Out in the open, she knew, Daisy would see him coming and be ready for him. Dulcie realized the finality of her situation now and prepared to take her punishment. And now that Dedwell had all from her that he had needed, he was only too happy to oblige.

"You said a moment ago that you wanted me," he crooned insanely in her ear. "Well, get ready, little girl, for more foreplay."

With that, he went to work. For fully three minutes, he punched and kicked Dulcie Abbott in the face, in the breasts, in the stomach, in the ribs, in the groin. When he had done, he threw her on the bed like a broken doll. Dulcie's last, hazy, remotely conscious thought was of the woman she had betrayed.

"I'm sorry, Daisy," she whispered brokenly through puffed and bloodied lips.

Dedwell stopped and checked the little woman's pulse and saw that her eyelids still fluttered. Good! He wasn't a pervert, after all. He wanted her alive for at least another three minutes or so. Savagely, he yanked her dress up and ripped off her underpants. Next, he unbuckled and unzipped himself. Then he fell on what was left of Dulcie and exuberantly perpetrated the primal outrage of Man against Woman.

Hey, he reasoned, *no one could say she hadn't asked for it.*

Twenty

Lying in bed beside the sleeping Brian, Daisy gazed sightlessly into the darkness of the bungalow bedroom, trying to hang on. She was, to put it succinctly, in a close to total dither, her mind awash in unsettling, discomforting images. She needed to be calm now, she chided herself. It was essential that she establish contact with Aglaophone tonight and make final arrangements for her alter ego's . . . well, final arrangements. If the unprecedented transmigration of being the two women were anticipating were to have a chance of becoming reality, it had to be effected roughly five hours from then—when Aglaophone's death was, according to Daisy's calculations, scheduled to occur.

Brian snorted, and Daisy wrinkled her nose in distaste both at the crude sound and at the sour, acrid smell of scotch on his breath. In the two years they'd been together, she'd flattered herself that she'd inspired him to bring what had been a serious drinking problem under control out of love for her. He rarely drank now except in moderation on social occasions—but he'd certainly made an exception tonight by going on a world-class bender here in the bungalow. When she'd returned from the theater an hour earlier, she'd found him lurching around the mini-bar unsteadily aiming the neck of a bottle at the rim of his glass.

"Oh, Brian!" she'd remonstrated softly, setting her hand-bag down on a chair.

Brian gave her an unaccountably hostile look, then raising the bottle and glass he held in his hands, he glanced from one to the other, "Well, boys! I guess it's last call! Her nibs, the

Great Mother, has returned! And she doesn't want I should drink any more."

Daisy stared at him, hurt. In all their time together, he had never before mocked her. Incredibly, they had rarely ever exchanged more than a few cross words born, now and then, of some fleeting irritation.

"Why are you doing this?" she finally asked.

"What? Drinking? Well, let's see. First off, I AM a bona fide alcoholic recovering from a long hiatus from the sauce—a recovering alcoholic, if you will, trying to get his game back. Secondly, I'm attempting, I guess you could say, to console myself for the loss of my manhood—for the fact that I've been a perpetual flunky to a goddess from whom there is no escape, as she very early pointed out to me. Oh, and one final tidbit. In this lady's service, I have now become an accomplice to murder."

"What did you say?"

"Murder. That's what they call it when you take someone down into a cellar, chain her up, and arrange her utter destruction. Don Corleone couldn't have managed it better."

"That's unfair!" Daisy cried. "You know what an unmitigated monster Arianna was! She DESERVED to die!"

"That's why they have judges and juries, Daisy!" Brian shot back. "And electric chairs and gurneys and needles!"

"Oh, right! We're not in Texas, Brian! Arianna committed her crimes in New York—liberal la-la land! Assuming you could find a jury with the guts and the intelligence to see through the legalistic obfuscation of some smarmy, high-profile defense attorney and actually convict her, the only way she'd die in prison is if she choked on a plate of tofu!"

"Then so be it! That's the luck of the draw, the way the civilized cookie crumbles. Christ! We can't even claim self-defense! Arianna never directly harmed either of us."

"She certainly meant to after she discovered who we were and what we were up to!"

"So that's your defense?"

"Look, Brian. I'm not proud of what happened, and I had no intention originally of doing anything more than we did with Dillon—gather the evidence against her and have Dulcie take it from there with the FBI. But then when Kyle Webber interjected himself into the whole business, he convinced me of the rightness of executing her out of hand. That it was . . . "

Daisy stopped and felt herself blushing. She turned her back to Brian.

"Divine retribution?" he finished for her.

She faced him again defiantly and tried to make a little joke. "Well, semi-divine, anyway. Dionysus is a demigod, after all."

Brian wasn't smiling. "And what about YOU, Daisy? Are we having a little identity crisis these days? Am I actually talking to the Great Mother Herself?"

"In the abstract, yes!" Daisy snapped. "All women have the right to identify with Her! It's just that they haven't yet reached that level of self-realization."

"Nobody but you in the entire world? You have the audacity to make that claim?"

"There's nothing audacious about the truth, Brian. All my instincts tell me that in this regard I stand alone among women currently alive. And tomorrow my situation may be even more unique."

At that pronouncement, Brian set his glass down. *Well, at least I've accomplished THAT much,* Daisy thought.

He sank into a nearby chair. "What happens tomorrow, may I ask?"

"You'll find out then, if I'm successful. You'll be the very first to know, in fact." She smiled in an attempt to lighten the moment. "Let's just say I'll be a new woman."

Brian was unamused. "So I'm not worthy of sharing this knowledge? You're into some new 'Great Goddess' enterprise, and you're shutting me out."

"No, Brian," Daisy sighed. "I promise that whether I succeed or not I'll tell you all about it tomorrow. But for the next few hours I really need to be alone and concentrate. Why not go to bed now? I'll be in in a bit."

Brian shot to his feet. "Fine! I'll go to bed! Mother knows best!"

"Perhaps I'd better sleep up at the house tonight," Daisy said quietly.

Brian headed for the bedroom studiously trying not to stagger. The effort wasn't successful. He waved her off. "Do as you please, Daisy. You always do."

"I love you, Brian," she called after him He didn't appear to have heard.

She'd stayed.

Now, as she continued to stare blankly into the darkness above, she could empathize with Brian's feelings of discontent. She knew that increasingly he had come to feel that he had ceded his masculinity to her. She had, after all, loftily proclaimed at the outset of their partnership that he was in essence hers to control. She didn't suppose that even her later confession that she was just as besotted with him had really restored his pride. Then there was also the fact that the danger supposedly inherent in the Dillon project hadn't panned out. She hadn't meant to recruit him to her cause by hyping the perils involved, but she had vastly over-estimated Arianna's level of general awareness, thanks to the woman's remarkable self-absorption and drug-induced lack of focus. In the end, Rhonda and Brian had penetrated the Dillon campaign with little effort, and once Kyle Webber had weighed in, the entire enterprise had become a total piece of cake. Brian had been left feeling like a lightweight appendage rather than a vitally needed cohort.

On the other hand, she now consciously acknowledged for the first time that she had originally deluded herself, as well—out of her lifelong yearning for him. She had fraudulently convinced not only herself but her entire council that Brian was an essential cog in their plans to undo the Dillons—when that hadn't really been the case at all. She had simply wanted him on board out of her desire for him.

She felt herself smile. So TELL him that, you little idiot! That should go a long way towards smoothing over this little rough patch between them.

Satisfied that she'd solved one problem, Daisy flipped over on her other side in the bed and made a renewed effort to focus on Aglaophone—to reach that level of intense self-awareness and mental isolation that allowed the psychic connection to be established. But again, distractions intruded.

First Brian snored.

Then the stomach-turning image of Arianna's dismembered remains popped unbidden into her head.

How could Kyle Webber have done such a thing? She hadn't bargained on anything like THAT degree of brutality.

Well, why not? He was Dionysus, after all, the ancient Lord of Misrule.

Kyle Webber.

She remembered the molten exchange of glances they had shared in Arianna's sitting room that had left her blushing and weak-kneed—followed, moments later, by the electric tingle of his comforting arm briefly around her in the basement. He could protect her, shield her from Arianna's inhumanity, the gesture had said.

Could Brian have?

Unlikely. She'd have had to do the protecting.

With an inner snarl of desperation, Daisy leaped from the bed, not caring if she awakened Brian or not. She didn't. Grabbing her pillow, she stalked with the aid of a baseboard nightlight into the living room and arranged herself on the sofa. There, finally, after a few moments of superhuman mental focus, she brought herself to where she had to be . . .

Inner Time

(Aglaophone? I'm sorry, darling. It's time.)

(I've been expecting it, Daisy. I'm ready, I guess. I'm heading for Circe's villa right now. Something you said earlier when we communicated—that she would die, too—led me to think Odysseus would strike from the south, from down Catania way. There's nothing much to our north—and there he and his ship would have to contend with the treacherous strait separating Sicily from the land to our east.)

(That sounds logical.)

(Daisy—I want you to know that if what we've planned doesn't work, you're not to blame yourself. I'll die knowing you've done your very best for me.)

(Don't think that way, Phonny! Be positive! The Mother won't fail us. She's creating a great work on the world's stage, and we are Her instruments. I FEEL it! I KNOW it!)

(Then I know it, too, Daisy.)

(Fine. Now let's review the basics. You know your enemy, and you know he's arriving soon. Fight him with all your great daring and brilliance! Improvise! You will inflict great pain and humiliation on him, I promise you that. Then when you've exhausted all your options, make your jump. As you leap, use the same principle that we used in our first lightning strike. At Circe's villa. Remember?)

(Yes! Do you remember the scolding we got?)

(Do I! Anyway, as you jump, link together TWO triple images of the Goddess in your mind—one ideal, the other real. The ideal, of course, is Kore, the Maiden; Demeter, the Mother,

217

and Hecate, the Wise Elder. For the real, combine yourself mentally with me and with Ligeia, our mentor. The psychic energy you release that way should do the trick—briefly freezing time and fusing our identities. In the meantime, I will be in an isolated place—my very favorite spot where I feel most in tune with Her and with the world She created untold eons ago—and I will open my mind to receive you. Together we can do it, Phonny!)

(Daisy, I just got the worst feeling that I've made the wrong choice in heading for Circe's. What should I do now? Keep going or turn back?)

(————————————)

(Daisy?)

(. . . It doesn't matter, darling. Your enemy is the cleverest of monsters. He has attacked both places simultaneously. Everyone you love is already gone. Go where your heart and the Mother take you—and in the end, I'll be waiting for you.)

Daisy arose just before dawn and, careful not to wake up Brian, returned to the bedroom. There, she slipped into a bikini and a turquoise beach dress. She grabbed a towel as well, although she doubted she'd be doing any swimming that morning. Then she left the bungalow and hit the beach. As she descended the attractively fashioned stone stairway to the sand, her entire being vibrated with anticipation and dread.

What if it didn't work? What if all her assurances to Aglaophone were empty lies, all her mathematical computations silly, ill-founded guesswork? Long before she had ever successfully contacted her Dawn Time alter ego, she had been hard at work on the chronology. She had consulted with calendar experts to determine as exactly as humanly possible the year, the day, the very hour of Aglaophone's death. She had accounted (she hoped) for the differences in the Julian and Gregorian calendars and considered the arbitrary eleven-day subtraction effected in

Europe in 1752 to reconcile the two. Based on all her efforts, she had concluded that the girl had perished on the equivalent of August 28 in the year 1236 B.C. If Daisy were correct, Aglaophone was now entering the final half-hour of her life.

But what if her plan miraculously DID work? How could she possibly calculate how her own life would change should she suddenly find herself sharing the same body with a primitive, raw, untutored young woman from a far distant time and culture—a girl whose energy and metabolism were far more hectic than her own? Wouldn't she, like Dr. Jekyll, eventually find herself being displaced to the point of annihilation by a dark, unruly inner twin?

What if the moment of psychic transfer—or whatever you'd call it—killed her? Well, she thought wryly, at least she'd made arrangements with her sister Pamela to run the ten o'clock council meeting she'd called if she were unavoidably "detained."

Oh, stop it! Everything was going to be fine.

Uh-oh!

Maybe not. Suddenly, just as the sun began peeking over the Long Island Sound horizon, Daisy noticed a dark form crumpled on the sand about a hundred feet in front of her. She stopped dead, irrelevantly aware of the cool morning sand oozing between her toes. When her heart started up again, she drew nearer and saw with dread the body of a young woman, lying twisted and still. Approaching nearer still, she gave a soft cry. The girl was battered and bruised almost beyond recognition.

Almost.

But through the still dim light and all the distortion caused by ugly, purplish bruises and puffed eyes and lips, Daisy discerned a younger version of herself. It was Aglaophone. Something had gone horribly amiss. The girl must have jumped to her death as planned and somehow succeeded in projecting

219

her PHYSICAL being forward in time—but not before she'd smashed onto the rocks below her Sicilian promontory. Daisy'd been off in her calculations by at least half an hour.

She sank now to her knees in utter desolation. Only then, through the glimmer of her tears, did she notice something way off base—two things, actually. The dead girl was wearing a black, low-cut cocktail dress that was certainly not the rage in the thirteenth century B.C.—and stuffed into her cleavage was a thick, folded manila envelope. Now Daisy peered more closely at the ruined face.

Dulcie Abbott.

With trembling fingers, Daisy extracted the packet from the top of the dress. As it unfolded in her hands, she saw scrawled on it—*in blood? no, lipstick*—three words:

"She betrayed you."

Oh, Dulcie.

Unsteadily, she unclasped the envelope and half withdrew its contents. She saw that it was the material New Dawn had been collecting on Oliver Dedwell. With ice sluicing through her veins, she dropped the papers back inside the packet.

He was here. Behind the line of scrub pine trees bordering the upper reaches of the sand. Very well, let him see what he was dealing with.

Slowly, Daisy rose to her feet and held the packet, which had the thickness of a good-sized magazine, aloft. Facing the trees sixty feet away, she calmly and effortlessly ripped the envelope and its contents in half and then in quarters before dropping each piece, one by one, to the sand.

"Time to pick on someone your own size, Colonel!" she called.

Nothing. Dead silence, except for an errant morning breeze riffling the trees and stirring the sand. What to do? She could smoke him out, of course, with a couple of bolts out of the blue, but that would wake up Brian. He'd wonder why she was up to her old tricks and come running to investigate. Damn! She needed to be alone right now more than at any other time in her life, and here all hell was breaking loose! A dead body on her hands and a stone killer lurking in the nearby brush She had twenty minutes at the outside before Aglaophone's ETA.

Then suddenly one problem was solved. Oliver Dedwell stepped out from his hiding place. In spite of the semi-darkness, Daisy could discern his cruel smile.

"She betrayed you," he said.

"I can read, Colonel." She sighed. "The girl let her ambition overpower her, obviously. But I can understand ambition and even treachery. At least they're HUMAN defects. There's nothing human about what you did to this child."

"She's just collateral damage in the everlasting war we righteous must wage against the heathen forces of darkness. Of which I understand you're exhibit A, Ms. Crandall—or should I say, Aglaophone the Siren."

Daisy started. How had he identified her? Had she accidentally let the name drop in one of the dreams she'd been hounding him with lately? This was bad! If Dedwell knew who HE was, and had learned how to tap into the power of Zeus or the Christian God the way that she could access the Mother, she was in for a very rough morning.

She strove for calm. "Did SHE tell you that?" she asked, indicating Dulcie. She hoped it was as simple as that.

"No," Dedwell said, apparently surprised into honest wonder. "The name just came to me the other night out of nowhere. I'd been talking to Dillon. He got that Siren stuff from his fruitcake wife. But apparently she was onto something. Your girl there corroborated Dillon's comments about New Dawn, your little ladies' club."

"And you believe it?"

"I don't know. Something's sure going on. I've been dreaming of you just about every night of my life—or someone who looks just like you. It's as if we were together in an earlier life."

Daisy breathed easier. Dedwell was clueless. No harm in giving him a little history lesson. He wouldn't be leaving the beach alive.

"We DID run into each other a couple of times," she said. "You'll be pleased to know that you were essentially the same psychopathic thug you are today. You managed to ruin my childhood, rape and kill my sisters, and destroy my two dearest friends."

Dedwell grinned. "And just for that you're out to destroy my candidacy?"

Daisy nodded. "The Independent Party seems to have a thing for homicidal maniacs this year. I figure the American people can do better."

Dedwell held his smile. "You've got spunk, little lady. And that stunt you just pulled with the envelope was impressive. Unfortunately, it won't stop you from ending up like your silly little one-time friend. But before I rape and kill you, how about telling me who I was way back whenever?"

"Actually," Daisy said, "you were a very impressive figure—with excellent public relations skills to camouflage your villainy. You were Odysseus, King of Ithaca."

Dedwell's eyes widened in awed surprise. "The *Odyssey* guy?"

Daisy barely suppressed a grin. She nodded. "The *Odyssey* guy. But what makes you think I would have spent these last few nights invading and orchestrating your dreams, drawing you inexorably to this time and place just to have you kill me? Don't you think it might be YOUR life that's hanging in the balance? And by the way, Colonel, haven't I in fact been an inescapable part of your nights from your earliest, bed-wetting days on?"

She exaggerated, of course. She certainly hadn't envisioned nor wanted him anywhere near her at this particular moment.

The bed-wetting shot had been a guess, a casual, morale-breaking cruelty, but she could tell from Dedwell's expression of mixed fear and embarrassment that she'd nailed him hard.

Just then, they were both startled to hear a barely audible whimper from Dulcie Abbott.

"She's alive!" Daisy breathed, falling to her knees beside the moribund young woman.

"Damn!" said Dedwell. Then while Daisy was distracted, he launched himself across the intervening distance, bowling into her and sprawling with her in the sand. Daisy was momentarily stunned, as her breath *whooshed* out of her. Groggily, she rolled clear of her assailant and began to wobble to her feet, struggling for balance in the uneven, yielding sand.

Now she was mad.

Dedwell, too, was pushing himself to his feet only to find that now HE was the one under attack, as the little actress hurled herself toward him before he'd regained his equilibrium. As he put up his hands to ward her off, she clasped them in her own. Three thousand, two hundred years of cumulative female synergy ignited in Daisy's brain and coursed through its synapses on its way to the nerves and arteries and muscles of her arms. Dedwell shrieked as the knuckles, fingers and veins in both his hands cracked and imploded under an iron, implacable pressure. Relentlessly, Daisy squeezed as the colonel's eyes bulged from his scarlet face, and white froth bubbled from his slack lips. His scream had now subsided to a high-pitched wheeze as his fingers fused amorphously, and his hands attained the doughy consistency of suet.

Then sensing Dedwell was about to lose consciousness, Daisy relinquished her grip in order to seize his right wrist. Lifting it and waving the pudding-like appendage attached to it in his face, she grinned savagely.

"Look at that, Colonel! Imagine raising THAT to take the

oath of office next January! I don't think your fellow Americans are going to be overly impressed, do you?"

Flinging both his arms and the colonel away from her, Daisy then made her way back to attend to Dulcie Abbott.

Twenty-One

1236 B.C.

Aglaophone found herself beginning to climb the steep rise that led to the home she shared with her sisters just outside the village of the Cyclopes—and realized she had no idea how she'd gotten there. She was dazed with shock. She had just walked for two hours returning from Circe's villa eight miles to the south but couldn't recall taking a single step along the way. Now that she took stock of herself and her situation, though, she'd obviously made the trip. Her feet were swollen and blistered; every one of her bones ached; and her mind screamed for mercy from a world from which that quality seemed permanently to have disappeared.

Circe was dead.

Just as Daisy had said—only three hours ago—she would be.

Which meant that over the next hill she would discover that Peisinoe and Thelxepeia were dead, too.

And the gentle giant, Polyphemus, the chieftain of the Cyclopes, who for the past dozen years had been like a father to her.

"Everyone you love is already gone," the sweet, all-seeing goddess within had told her. Shortly after her last communication with the mysterious woman from the far future, the truth of her dismal tidings had become evident. As Aglaophone had continued with a leaden heart toward Circe's, she'd suddenly become aware of the clattering drum of hoofbeats approaching from the south, indicating a substantial party of horsemen moving rapidly in her direction. She'd leaped quickly into the brush along the roadside to avoid discovery. A moment later, twenty or so armed men had charged by on their mounts. Many wore their war helmets, but their grim-faced leader rode bareheaded. The girl recognized a handsome, bearded, nightmare face from her lost childhood.

Odysseus—the savage suppressor of the Goddess's worship, whose long ago actions had sent three young princesses into permanent exile. Since the war against Troy had been successfully concluded with a famous Greek victory a couple of years earlier, rumors had reached far off Sicily that the High King Agamemmon had gotten a nasty surprise on his return home to Mycenae, the chief kingdom of the Greek confederation. In his absence, his queen, a former priestess of the Mother, had re-instituted the Old Religion and replaced him with a younger consort/lover, his own nephew. Together, they had ambushed Agamemmon at his homecoming and ritually slain him with a double-ax. Enraged at his brother's fate, the new High King, Menelaos of Lacedaemon—who had just recovered his own errant wife Helen from her Trojan captors—had reassigned Odysseus to the task of rooting out the Mother's worship throughout the lands of the Great Sea. The brutal warrior had finally brought his campaign to the far west. Presumably, after destroying the shrines presided over by the enchantress Circe and the fabled Sirens on the eastern coast of Sicily, Odysseus would be free to return to his own kingdom and queen, having made the world safe for Zeus and the other male gods—and the kings they protected.

When the men had disappeared in a dust cloud, Aglaophone had stepped back onto the road and, sick to the depths of her soul, walked her final mile to the old villa. Long before she reached it, she saw the plume of dark smoke wafting lazily up into the azure of the late morning sky, and the smell of burning wood assaulted her nostrils.

Within moments, she'd reached the house. The fire, having fed on the timbered framework of the stone and tile dwelling, was already guttering out, and Aglaophone entered the smoke-shrouded interior. Immediately inside, she nearly stumbled over the corpses of Talos, the stablehand, and Epirus, the young cook. Both had evidently died attempting to defend their mistress and the rest of the largely female household. Both had been run through with swords, their own bronze weapons lying nearby.

As she'd penetrated further into the villa's large entry hall, the horrors of sight and odor increased exponentially. Dimly, through the eye-smarting haze, she saw the naked, gutted bodies of dead and violated serving women from adolescent kitchen girls to elderly attendants. She'd been friendly with them all. Now the smell of their spilled entrails made her gag, but still she pressed on, looking for Circe. She believed she knew where she'd find her, just as Odysseus had.

Although Circe had originally been a priestess of the Goddess herself during her youth on the island of Crete, she had been forced to flee from religious persecution there. When she'd come to Sicily for asylum, she had given up on the Mother she felt had abandoned her and had then given herself over to a life of luxury and promiscuity. That lifetstyle had ended abruptly the day Aglaophone and her sisters had first entered her home. Since then, she had built a small shrine to the Great Goddess at the rear of the villa and re-instituted Her worship, serving as priestess and submitting offerings and petitions to Her on behalf of her servants and her occasional visitors. It was toward this shrine that Aglaophone made her way through smoke, fallen timbers, and debris.

And so she'd found her old friend—dead, naked, violated, and disemboweled, the small, shattered clay image of the Goddess spilled next to her on the tiles. Eyes stinging with more than smoke now, the girl knelt and brushed her lips to Circe's forehead. Then quickly she rose and rushed from the room and from the house. For an indeterminate amount of time, she simply stumbled in aimless circles in the yard, her mind wandering and incoherent. She knew she should return home now, but why, exactly, eluded her. Should she see if she could find a horse in the stable? But she'd never learned to ride, had she? So she might as well start walking . . .

And now here she was climbing the hill at the summit of which she would be able to observe the rest of the wreckage of her life. Again, first there was the smoke that heralded the sights and smells of carnage and mass death. Only here, as she neared the top, there were sounds, too—the screams of the dying and the savage braying of jubilant male conquest.

Aglaophone stood on the crest of the road that dipped down to the concentric, palisaded settlement of the Cyclopes below. Several smoke streams spilled into the sky from the large enclosure—with one forlorn little cloud hovering over the singed ruins of the little home on the promontory she'd shared with her sisters till that morning. They'd be dead now, of course.

The girl stood for awhile on the hilltop till the numbness faded and an engulfing anger began to sweep through her. Then raising the iron sword Polyphemus had given her the day they'd first met, and which she always took with her for protection when she walked the shore road, she resolutely descended toward the village below. As she went, she noticed with no great surprise that a large ship that could accommodate at least sixty rowers lay anchored in the harbor on the far side of the promontory. From its masthead depended a lowered, furled rectangular sail emblazoned with the figure of a brown boar that identified its captain as Odysseus, King of Ithaca. The wily pirate had sent his main force here by sea, while he'd marauded up the shore road with a smaller detachment.

"He has attacked both places simultaneously," Daisy had said.

When she reached the bottom of the incline, Aglaophone made directly for the main gate of the settlement. She noticed that there were half a dozen inattentive men detailed to the palisade rampart, their backs turned to watch the ongoing pillaging and revelry within. No one noticed her approach. She was about to make her presence known, when she was abruptly halted by a visual horror that dwarfed anything she'd seen earlier that day at Circe's villa. Her hand flew to her mouth in revulsion, and her knees nearly buckled.

There, nailed spread-eagle to the left hand panel of the huge open gate was Polyphemus. His hands and feet had been pierced by large iron spikes, undoubtedly seized from one of his own forges. A fifth spike had been driven through the tattooed eye on his forehead, transfixing his skull to the wood behind it.

Aglaophone took several deep breaths to steady herself. Moving forward, she stooped and picked up a rock the size of her palm. Taking aim, she heaved it upward and grimaced with satisfaction when it clipped one of the men above in the shoulder. He yowled and spun around, as did his fellow guards.

"Pig!" shouted Aglaophone. "Tell your swineherd he has a visitor!"

At first, the men were stunned—then they broke into raucous laughter. Finally, the man she had hit, who seemed to be their leader, turned his back on her, and she heard him call, "Lord, you've got to see this! I think we've found her—or she's found us!"

A moment later, Odysseus himself appeared above the gateway. He smiled unpleasantly. "Who are you?" he asked lazily.

"Aglaophone is my name," she responded.

"Ah, the missing Siren. We had great sport with your sisters a little earlier. They put up quite a struggle before we raped them and tossed them off the cliff over there. I'm glad to see you recognize the futility of resisting and have made yourself available to us."

The girl gave herself a little time to absorb the body blow of her sisters' fate, then said, "You mistake my purpose. I've come here to offer you battle, not submission. Will you come down?"

More laughter from above, as a dozen more men joined the fun. Odysseus kept his bleak smile. "You're very pretty—and I believe I had the pleasure of hearing you sing once when you were a child. You were very good—extraordinary, in fact. But I don't quite see you as a warrior. Under whose banner do you fight?"

"The Mother's. But don't worry, jackal. I'm not authorized to kill you—only to 'inflict great pain and humiliation' on you. That's a direct quote, by the way."

There were a few more guffaws that dwindled into silly giggles. A growing sense of unease occasioned by the small woman's casual bravado began to take hold among her observers.

Odysseus, though, seemed unimpressed. "The Mother, huh? She's certainly enjoyed tremendous success against me so far, hasn't she? You'd better find yourself a more capable general, little girl."

"Nobody's impervious to sneak attacks, which are your specialty, coward. But since you doubt Her abilities, I'll provide a little demonstration of them. Do you see your ship behind me?"

"Yes, I do."

Aglaophone flipped her right arm up and back. From the clear blue sky shot a lurid, purple-white flash and a staggering bang of thunder. The thunderbolt scored a direct hit on the mast and the furled sail of the ship. The huge sail burst into flame and crumbled in blazing shreds to the deck. The mast itself split in two with the top half crashing down to crush three of the six sailors who'd been left on board. The other three were now on fire to varying degrees and rushed, shrieking, for the ship's sides and cast themselves overboard. The boat itself began to founder and take on water.

"How about now?" asked Aglaophone.

A stunned silence emanated from the cluster of men on the ramparts followed by cries of protest and fear. Odysseus had turned very pale. Finally, he turned to his lieutenant, the man Aglaophone had hit with the rock.

"Eurylochos, go fetch the witch, and bring her inside. She will die howling!"

"Odysseus," called Aglaophone, "unless you consider this lackey utterly dispensable, don't send him down. I'm under no orders to spare HIM. The Mother has seen how you have dealt with Her servants today and in the past and demands a heavy blood price."

"You are over-playing your paltry little hand, witch," replied the warlord. "Everyone knows that the male god Zeus controls the thunderbolt. You were just lucky in your timing. But evidently I've displeased Him in some way, and I'll have to consult His priests in order to make a proper restitution. It's a small matter."

"Placating a god a small matter? One wonders where you got your vaunted reputation for wisdom. Actually, wolf, what everyone KNOWS is that Zeus is only the Goddess's grandson. She gives Him an occasional toy to play with when He behaves. Otherwise, the earth, the sky, and all their elements are HERS!"

Odysseus turned to his ashen-faced second-in-command. "Are you defying my orders? I said to get her!"

Aglaophone called mockingly, "Yes, Eurylochos, come down and be sacrificed to the Mother. Your master obviously has no use for you, and you and he have made Her very thirsty today!"

Having said that, Aglaophone contemptuously turned her back on the men assembled on the palisade walkway and made a show of throwing away her sword. She knew that the hapless man being sent down to arrest her would by now be terrified. Figuring that her observers would be distracted by the motion of her throw, she quickly reached down into the neckline of her tunic and retrieved, unseen, the dagger that Diomedes, father of her long lost, beloved Aganus, had given her the day years earlier when he had deposited her and her sisters on the shore road leading to Circe's.

Aware of how frightened Eurylochos would be, her ostentatious disposing of her sword had been calculated to recall him to some display of manly courage. How could he draw a sword on a small, unarmed woman and not become a target of derision from his fellow warriors? At the very least, she needed him to keep the weapon sheathed until it was too late for it to imperil her.

Aglaophone, clutching the dagger low in front of her, walked away from the gate, a distance of some sixty feet. As she did so, she petitioned the Goddess to see to it that the skill and speed of her youth hadn't fully deserted her. Then she turned around.

Eurylochos, she saw, had disappeared from the rampart and would be emerging from the gate any second now. Ah! There he was! And the Mother so far was with her! His sword remained sheathed. She waited for him to clear the gateway which bore the grotesque form of poor Polyphemus—then she sprinted straight at him. She saw the rounded horror of his eyes and his sudden fumbling for his sword. Too late! Twelve feet in front of him, she bounced on her toes once and launched herself upward into a forward flip. As she began her descent, she straightened her body with her right hand extended upward. Then as she landed on the recoiling Eurylochos, she gripped his right shoulder with her left hand and plunged the dagger into his neck at the point where it met his shoulder. A geyser of blood spurted upward, and the dead man slumped precipitously to the ground. Springing back quickly, she pulled the dagger free and negligently tossed it aside. A few seconds later, and she had retrieved her sword.

Not giving her audience any time to recover, Aglaophone spoke loudly into the shocked silence from the ramparts.

"Well, that was quick! Now, which of you sheep will be the next victim selected by your craven cur of a leader to slake the Mother's thirst?"

Odysseus gazed down at her with a look of withering, undiluted hate. She smiled jauntily back.

"Come out and play, Odysseus!"

With an incoherent snarl, the King of Ithaca flung himself away from his men and made for the stairs that would bring him to the gate. While awaiting him, Aglaophone hastily reviewed her entire stock of knowledge about swords and sword fighting, which amounted to virtually nothing. For all her athletic grace and her forceful personality, she had always been a quintessentially feminine creature, soft-natured and compassionate, drawn to beauty. She had never felt any inclination to compete with boys or men in areas in which the male sex naturally predominated.

Even her initial fascination with the iron sword she held had been founded only on its mystical suggestiveness about the future course of the world's development. After she and her sisters had come from Circe's villa to serve the Mother with the priestess Ligeia in the Cyclopes' village, Polyphemus had offered to have her trained with the sword. She had thanked him but declined. Now, she realized ruefully that even her informal test of the superiority of the weapon with Talos in Circe's backyard had led her to a faulty conclusion—the advantage of the iron weapon over its bronze counterpart lay not in the metal's strength but in its cheapness. The ratio of iron to bronze swords that could eventually be produced would be on the order of ten to one. Whole armies of peasants equipped with iron would then be unleashed on relatively small numbers of elite, bronze-wielding warriors.

She had, however, sat politely through a couple of lectures from Polyphemus and recalled now the one fact about bronze swords that she was relying on to save her life—for another half hour or so, anyway. Most bronze swords were riveted at the hilt, and this made them brittle and restricted their blade lengths to no more than two feet. Greek warriors were still equipped with this type of weapon, and she trusted that Odysseus would be no exception. If so, her fighting strategy would consist entirely of holding onto her own weapon with two hands and seeing to it that her opponent broke his against it.

Here he came now. Yes, he was carrying a short-bladed bronze sword! Hastily, Aglaophone seized the hilt of her own sword with both hands. As she did so, she heard sneering laughter at her incompetent technique from the men watching from above.

Odysseus wasted no time but rushed straight at her, slashing viciously downward with his sword. The girl held her weapon sideways to meet it. So brutal was the stroke that her sword was slammed to the ground and she was driven to her knees. Through the stinging in her hands and in her eyes, though, she hung on to it. As she scampered to her feet, she heard bolder, hooting laughter now, as her opponent's followers anticipated a quick, bloody victory.

I can't take more than one more of those, Aglaophone thought grimly. She might be joining Daisy more quickly and under different circumstances than they had planned. Here he came again, chopping downward ferociously. This time the girl lithely sprang aside then saw with excitement that the force of Odysseus' swing had lodged the point of his sword in the ground. Quickly raising her own sword with both hands, she smashed it down on the bronze weapon just below the rivets that joined it to the hilt. Odysseus's blade snapped in two, leaving him holding a jagged, toy-like metal stump.

Instinctively, Aglaophone took advantage of the warrior's surprise. Quickly ducking low, she swung her sword horizontally like a scythe, slicing deeply into the back of Odysseus's left calf. The hero of Troy screamed like an adolescent girl and crumpled to the ground, where he rolled around clutching his leg in agony. Aglaophone sprang upright. With her foot, she shoved the fallen man's shoulder and rolled him onto his back. Then she nestled the point of her sword into the base of his throat. The only sound now was the guttural whimpering of her victim. His companions had once again subsided into awed and terrified silence.

"Hear me, Odysseus," declaimed the girl into the stillness of the hot afternoon. "Hear the song of the Siren Aglaophone—she who knows all things that have happened and all things that will. You will live, by the whim of the Mother. You will hobble home alone over land and sea. You will arrive in your own kingdom to discover your queen rutting with a hundred strangers—each competing to be her next year-king, as she revives the Mother's ways. Think of it, Odysseus! While you were roaming the wide world thinking to destroy Her, the Goddess was ruining you in your own home."

Odysseus groaned at her feet.

"So return, Odysseus! Enter your own palace as a lame, reviled beggar, and conspire with your effeminate son to regain through slaughter the kingdom and the sluttish wife that were once yours. Then hire a hundred bards to help you spin your lies of a life of pretended glory—of triumph over foul enchantresses and demon singers and giant, one-eyed cannibals—all, in reality, the innocent victims of your murderous hate.

"And thus become a legendary hero to a gullible and ignorant world ruled by war-happy men and their like-minded gods.

Triumph for three times a thousand years as admiring men spread your blood-stained fame.

"But always, ALWAYS, Odysseus, dream of Aglaophone the Siren, the woman you could not have nor kill—the woman who defeated you—the woman you will burn for and desire throughout countless lifetimes. Until one far-off day on a strange and distant shore, we will meet again—and then the Mother and I will surely put an end to you!"

Now turning her attention from the groaning man at her feet to his hangdog companions, she pointed to the horror on the gateway door.

"This man was the gentle leader of a gentle people. Look how you have used him! Did you know he was beloved of Poseidon, the Mother's consort? What do you imagine the Earth-Shaker thinks of the manner in which you have destroyed His son, a son in whom He was well pleased? Perhaps at this very moment, He is gathering His might to avenge this terrible crime. Perhaps, all it will take is a simple invocation from a priestess who has served this community to bring that wrath upon you.

"Or perhaps, He will be merciful to those who leave here now without delay, reserving His vengeance for this carrion who lies here whimpering in the dust."

With that, Aglaophone fell silent. The men on the walkway above looked at each other with an awe that turned quickly into a wild and frenzied hope. Then instantly there was a jostling scramble, panicky, hurried shouts, a jumbled gathering of horses, and a hasty, clattering exit from the village of the Cyclopes. Only a third of the men had mounts, though—and those who had arrived in a ship that now wallowed helplessly in the harbor faced a hot, dusty walk of twenty miles to the nearest port.

Within moments, the last of them had disappeared to the south in a riotous cloud of dust that gradually settled and cleared. A couple of the stragglers had made a dutiful effort to stop and lift their fallen lord, but with her sword raised, Aglaophone had sternly forbidden it.

"The Goddess told me only to spare his life, not coddle him. Let him make his own way back to Ithaca. Zeus can lend him a hand if He cares to," she said, waving them along.

Ignoring Odysseus, who continued to whine and fume in pain, the last of the Sirens started back toward the gate thinking she'd better check on the state of things inside the settlement. Then she stopped, unable to force herself to pass through the portal upon which hung the mutilated corpse of Polyphemus. Besides, what was the point? There were only more dead friends inside, undoubtedly scores of them. The survivors would have to manage without her. She had her own death to attend to now.

Turning back, she saw that Odysseus had roused himself enough to tear a strip of linen from his tunic and wrap it around the ugly slice in his calf. Within seconds, it was soaked through with blood. He began to work his way to his feet when Aglaophone, humming a haunting air, passed by and gave him a rough shove that tumbled him to the ground again. He yelled in fresh agony.

"See you in your dreams, Odysseus." Her spellbinding song would see to that.

As she walked out onto the promontory to view the remains of Peisinoe and Thelxepeia, she absently listened to her enemy revile her from the distance. Out on the plateau, the scene was a miniature version of the disaster at Circe's villa. The little stone house was pretty much intact, except for the thatched and timbered roof, which had collapsed within. Were the incinerated remains of her sisters buried beneath the smouldering wreckage? No. The monster had said they'd been thrown from the cliff. No reason not to believe him.

She walked by the little shrine of the Mother that the three of them had tended since the death of Ligeia a decade earlier. Odysseus's men had taken the trouble to demolish it, stone by stone, and, as at Circe's, the sacred image of the Goddess had been broken.

Then she was there—standing on the edge of the precipice. She closed her eyes and steadied herself. Finally, she looked down.

Oh!

Her heart broke. There they lay, a little off to her left, their naked, smashed bodies lying nearly on top of one another. From this height how tiny they looked. She couldn't even tell which twin was which. She walked over a few feet till she stood directly above them. At least she knew where her mortal remains would rest—till time and the sea washed the three Sirens away.

Aglaophone became all business now. She focused her consciousness with an intensity she had never equaled before, inwardly rehearsing Daisy's instructions with absolute concentration and flawless accuracy till she became distracted by something—the sword she still held.

The sword. While Daisy had been very precise about the last minute formula to effect the unprecedented transition to the distant future, she had earlier made it plain that Aglaophone was to maintain a questioning vigilance about the untested process and was presumably free to improvise any final adjustments she might consider necessary.

Now she lifted the familiar weapon and held it vertically before her, as she balanced on the precipice's edge.

"You've served me well, old friend," she whispered. "You who have long been my eyes to the future, come there with me now!"

She then re-entered the deepest regions of her unique and potent consciousness, this time factoring the sword into the psychic double invocation of the Triple Goddess which Daisy had rehearsed with her.

Almost ready.

. . . Now!

Clutching the sword, Aglaophone leaped upward and out—into forever.

Twenty-Two

Daisy was growing frantic. She needed to concentrate, to go deep with herself to prepare for the rapidly approaching moment of transition when she planned to be joined with her Dawn Time self. But now with the unexpected revival of Dulcie Abbott, there was no question as to where her moral duty lay. She must run for help if the young woman were to have any chance of survival.

Why? Daisy thought bitterly. *She meant to destroy me.*

And if she did get help, what would the medical team make of seeing the leading contender for next President of the United States moaning and writhing around on the sands of her own private beach with his hands turned to porridge? No question. She'd have to dispose of Dedwell now. But just how . . . ?

She saw Dulcie's eyes flick open. A moment later her lips parted with the effort to speak. Daisy bent over and put her ear close to Dulcie's mouth. Slowly and painfully, the whispered, rasping words formed and were heard.

"Forgive me, Great Mother . . . I didn't know what I was doing."

Tears sprang to Daisy's eyes.

Turning her head so that she could speak in Dulcie's ear, she said, "Go in peace, child. The Goddess is waiting for you and will make you welcome."

Gently, she kissed the girl's forehead and took her hand. In another moment, Dulcie was gone.

Oliver Dedwell screamed.

Now what? Daisy thought, with irritation. She climbed to her feet and approached the wretched man.

240

"What's the matter now?" she demanded. She saw that with his ruined hands Dedwell was clutching feverishly at his lower left leg.

"My leg!" he gasped. "It feels as if someone just slashed it . . . with a knife!"

"WHAT?"

Then it was Daisy's turn to gasp. She knew what this meant! Aglaophone!

As her spirit soared with elation, she found herself looking at the body of Dulcie Abbott. And it was then that Daisy Crandall came up with what had to be one of the greatest Plan Bs in the history of the world.

Forgetting Dedwell, she scrambled back to the side of the dead girl and sat down in the sand. Then she took hold of Dulcie's hand, and held it for all she and a woman who had lived thirty-two hundred years ago were worth.

Think! Remember! A minute for her dramatic little speech over her fallen foe, another two minutes, say, to threaten his men on the town walls with extinction, three or four minutes for the scrambled evacuation of the enemy. That made . . . seven. About five more after that. Two minutes to walk out to the cliffs, another two to mourn her dead sisters, one to get ready . . . Daisy was filled with an excitement, an exhilaration she had never known. How could she have doubted the Goddess? She had worked everything out to perfection!

Come on, Phonny!

Only a couple of minutes more now! Concentrate! Concentrate! She had to block out Dedwell, still moaning and cursing somewhere nearby. She clutched Dulcie's hand even harder, if possible . . .

Then impact! Daisy screamed in an agony she had never experienced! She felt as if her skull had been split with a double-ax that continued down through her thorax to her navel. She flopped back on the sand still shrieking but dimly aware of the need to hold onto Dulcie Abbott. She did.

I overstepped, she thought. *I offended the Mother. I trespassed in Her realm, and She has killed me.*

Daisy's eyes fell shut.

Aglaophone opened her eyes.

Owww! Doing so was all but unbearable. Her eyes felt puffy. Her entire body was consumed by pain. It hadn't worked. She had jumped and had smashed onto the cruel boulders below her home. But somehow she had survived. She must be hopelessly crippled. Now she would suffer a lingering death of intolerable pain—just lying there thirsty, boiling in the fevered summer sun. How the Mother must hate her—or, in Her guise of Persephone, Queen of the Dead, She would have come by now and gently claimed her.

Everything seemed gray, she noticed. Mist seemed to swirl around her. She couldn't see much of anything, and it hurt to keep her eyes open. She closed them. She'd rest for a minute, then open them again. Then she'd see if she could locate the bodies of Peisinoe and Thelxepeia. She must have landed very close to them.

Just another minute, though.

Then she felt something odd against her right hand. Something soft and gritty. With her eyes still closed she tried desperately to identity the substance. Then suddenly she did. *Sand!* But how could that be? There was no sand beneath the familiar cliff—only slick, hard, sea-sprayed boulders draped in brackish seaweed. Then she identified something else. A sound, this time. The sound of waves gently shushing and lapping back and forth somewhere just ahead of her.

All at once, from out over the water, came a low, mournful bellow, a terrifying sound signifying some great, unknown beast. Frightened, Aglaophone forgot her pain. She opened her eyes and struggled to raise her head. She was only momentarily successful before crushing agony forced her to slam herself back down. But she'd seen something in that instant that frightened her even more than the unfamiliar noise. She'd seen that she was dressed in an odd black tunic.

Black. The color of death.

Terror knifed through her! She was dead, after all! Then she put it all together. The waves she heard belonged to the dread River of the Dead, the Styx. The bellowing monster out there must be Cerberus, the huge, three-headed dog that guarded its further shore. Any minute now, and she'd hear the barge of Charon, Death's ferryman, scrape on the nearby shingle, come to pick her up. But she couldn't pay him! There'd been no mourner to place a coin under her tongue! She'd have to stay here forever in the dreary Fields of Asphodel with the restless shades of the unmourned!

But it got worse. Now she became aware of another sound that had been there all along but somehow hadn't registered before. Somewhere behind her a man was shouting and cursing in obvious torment. That could mean only one thing. She was in an even more terrible area of Death's domain than she'd thought. *Tartarus!* The dark, subterranean landscape to which only the foulest criminals were consigned, doomed by the angry gods to suffer eternal torture for their vicious deeds during their lives.

Now she began to cry. She'd been wrong all along. Zeus was stronger than the Mother, after all. She'd gone too far in her vengeful punishment of Odysseus, and now she'd been damned forever by the king of the gods for her mistreatment of a favorite son.

Then at the moment of her darkest despair, a warm sensation of comfort—something that, like the man's howling, had so far escaped her notice. Someone was holding her left hand. With a thrill of joy, she craned her head in that direction.

Mother!

Oh, her mother was here with her! So this couldn't be Tartarus! No god could find just cause to be angry with Terpsichore, the sweet, dancing little Queen of Aetolia! But her being here meant that her mother was dead, too, didn't it?

She saw that her mother slept. She'd forgotten, through all the lost years, how pretty she was. She was wearing a gown of a beautiful shade of blue. Aglaophone couldn't take her eyes off her. She decided to try to raise her head again, bracing herself for the wrenching pain it would cost her. She wanted to get a closer look. Ooof!

That's funny! She'd never considered before how much like Daisy her mother had looked! And yet she'd dreamed of Daisy for many years. Too bad their great plan hadn't worked out. How wonderful that would have been!

Still, with her mother here she felt a lot better. Maybe she could try to wake her up. With that thought in mind, she rolled herself onto her left side. Then she gasped with more than the pain. There, lying between her and her mother was a familiar dark object.

Her iron sword! She'd gotten it through!

Strange! She'd been allowed to bring a weapon with her into the Underworld! She lay down again, more pain ripping through her. Her right side seemed particularly bad, as if bones had been shattered. She put her hand to her face and winced at her swollen left cheek. Her mouth, too, was severely bruised by the feel of it. A couple of teeth seemed loose, as well.

Aglaophone was puzzled and lay there, trying to sort things out. If she had landed on her back, the position she'd found herself in upon regaining consciousness, why were all her injuries on her upper front and face? Why was there no pain in her legs? It was almost as if, instead of falling from a height, she had been . . . badly beaten.

Then she became aware of yet another area of pain and discomfort, and her mind recoiled in instinctive horror. This injury was centered at the inner juncture of her thighs. Tremulously, she reached her hand down and then up under the strange black tunic. With a sharp intake of breath, she discovered that she was naked underneath. Someone had removed her breech cloth! With a strangled wail, she acknowledged a crushing truth. While she had lain dead or dying, someone had stolen her very self. Like Peisinoe, Thelxepeia, and Circe, she had been raped.

Who? What monster would...? Then she knew, of course. The last man to see her alive, the man whose pride she had mortally wounded, the man who had shouted curses at her as she'd walked out to the cliff. Odysseus! He must have followed her, seen her jump, and, filled with such hate that he'd forgotten or ignored his severe wound, edged his way around the base of the promontory, found her, and violated her.

Now such was Aglaophone's rage that she forgot all the agony of her battered body and sprang to her feet. Suddenly, the loud, unhappy man behind her screamed, as if at the sight of her. Startled, she looked his way.

Him!

Even with the strange clothes he wore and the beardless face, she recognized her immortal enemy! Odysseus, King of Ithaca! The gods had granted her one final boon, after all—and had delivered him first to death and then into her hands for further punishment!

Reaching down beside the still sleeping form of her mother, she snatched up the sword. Ignoring the lancing pains that wracked her, she bounded to Odysseus's side before he could scramble to his feet. She noted in flashes his open mouth, his wide, terrified eyes, his bloody, misshapen hands raised helplessly to shield himself from her approach. She heard him babble frightened words at her in some mysterious, unknown tongue.

Then grasping the sword hilt in both hands, she raised the blade vertically before her and instantly plunged it downward into his chest. He bleated once and thrashed beneath her. She savagely extricated the sword and raised it again, intending this time to impale him through the groin. But as the sword reached its apex, two things happened with startling suddenness. Glorious morning sunlight flooded through the enveloping mist, and an iron grip closed on her wrist, staying her hand. Aglaophone whirled around to see her mother standing there, shaking her head. Effortlessly, the older woman wrested the sword from her and cast it aside.

Then she faced her daughter and said something stern in the same unknown language in which the girl had heard Odysseus raving. Then she smiled—the warmest, prettiest smile Aglaophone had ever seen. Terpsichore looked as if she wanted to embrace her but then held off, apparently noting her daughter's terrible injuries.

"Mother!" Aglaophone cried, ready to burst with happiness.

But the woman looked puzzled, as if SHE couldn't understand what was being said. She frowned, then brightened up again. She smiled and, raising her hand, tapped herself on the side of her head. She next made a similar motion toward Aglaophone's. Still not understanding, the girl gave a shrug. Then, stunningly, she heard a familiar inner voice.

(Hello, Phonny! We did it! You're here! . . . Darling . . . I'm Daisy!)

Aglaophone stared in disbelief at the woman she'd mistaken for her mother. She started to speak aloud then remembered.

(But how? . . . Did I misunderstand? I thought you said we'd be joined together as one being.)

(I *did*, Phonny! That was my plan until only a few minutes ago. Then, miraculously, the Mother showed me another way. A much BETTER way! Think of it! It would be very difficult for two women, each used to charting her own destiny, to inhabit the same body.)

Daisy grinned.

(Why, what if you wanted to walk left and I wanted to go right? See what I mean?)

The younger woman considered that then smiled and nodded.

(So what happened?)

Daisy heaved a great sigh. She pointed at the dead man at their feet.

(He did. You knew him as Odysseus, a powerful warlord. In this time, he was a man named Oliver, who was about to make himself leader of our country—a great land called America, many times bigger than either Greece or Sicily. But he was as ruthless and violent as the man YOU knew. I was fighting very hard to keep him from succeeding. He found out . . . somehow . . . about my efforts and came here this morning to kill me. But first he murdered a young . . . friend of mine who was working with me. He beat her to death then left her here for me to find. He was hiding nearby. When the girl surprisingly revived for a brief moment, and I was trying to help her, he attacked me. With the Mother's help, I managed to best him by crushing his hands, as you can see.)

(Phonny, then the idea came to me. You see, this girl was your age—and bore an incredible likeness to both of us. I knew you were on your way when Oliver started screaming about his leg feeling as if someone had just cut it. So I channeled you into the dead girl. The effort knocked me out.)

(That's why you were sleeping.)

(Well, that's one way of putting it! But, oh, my dear, look at you! It's a wonder you can stand. Here, I want you to lie down and rest. Just a minute!)

Daisy moved away a few feet and retrieved a large white piece of cloth. Laying it on the sand, she eased Aglaophone down onto it. The material was rough in texture but soft and comforting. Aglaophone sighed with the bodily pain she'd momentarily forgotten.

(Now you just rest, Phonny! By killing this beast, you've done me—and more importantly, the entire world—a vital service. But I've got a little cleaning up to do here—then we'll see about getting you some help.)

Daisy abruptly removed the beautiful blue gown she wore and stood there nearly naked, except for a tiny breech cloth and a similar strip of material covering her breasts. Daisy had told her once that she was ancient—fifty-four—but she certainly didn't look it. Maybe in this time people stayed young forever. It was a pretty thought!

Although she was lying down, Aglaophone positioned her head so that she could watch her savior's activities. First, after looking carefully around her in every direction, Daisy took the sword and, walking down to the sunlit waves, waded in up to her knees and threw the weapon as far out as she could and watched intently until it sank. Why'd she do THAT? Aglaophone thought angrily. It was a wonderful weapon! Didn't people have to protect themselves here?

Splashing ashore again, Daisy next seized the dead Odysseus (or whoever he was) under the armpits and dragged him also to the water. She set him afloat and guided the corpse with her hand till she was nearly up to her neck. Then she placed both hands on the body and forcefully sank it. Aglaophone saw her look all around her again with seeming anxiety. Maybe she was on the lookout for enemy soldiers.

As Daisy started back, Aglaophone found herself overcome by drowsiness. Her last conscious thought was that Daisy emerging from the water looked very much like a goddess—like Aphrodite rising from the foam . . .

Daisy began to tremble now with all the pain and strain and wonder of the past hour. She was halfway up the sand when she felt a premonition, a hollow giddiness in her head. Startled, she stood stark still. Then it came . . .

(Hello, Daisy.)

(. . . ?!? . . . Yes?)

(Do you know Me?)

(Great Mother?!?)

(Yes, although, as you know, I've gone by many other names throughout time—Gaea, Eurynome, Rhea, Hera, Demeter, Persephone, Aphrodite, Athena, Artemis, Tiamat, Isis, Ishtar, Astarte, Riannon—not to mention Semele, mother of Dionysus, and Mary, mother of Jesus.)

(My God!)

(I beg your pardon?)

(Sorry! My Goddess! I'm a little frazzled. It's been quite a morning so far.)

(I know it has, honey. But you've saved the world this day. You've done very well, all things considered.)

(Thank you, Mother. Is it all right if I call you that? It's simple—and right now very comforting.)

(Fine.)

(Uh, if you don't mind my asking, what did you mean by "all things considered"?)

(Well, Daisy, you made a potentially fatal miscalculation. You yourself forgot to take the advice that you gave to Aglaophone—about not tampering with the flow of history. As a result, you came within a few minutes of canceling out your own existence.)

(I guess I'm not following.)

(Honey! You made arrangements to have your Dawn Time ancestress leapfrog over three thousand years to join you. But in doing so you would have wiped out all of her interim incarnations, including YOUR immediate predecessor, Jenny Lind. Without her and all the others, there would be no Daisy Crandall. Where would Phonny have ended up? There would have been no YOU for her to join! She would have been converted to eternal ether.)

(Oh! . . . And to think something that basic never even occurred to me! What a fool I've been! What a presumptuous fool!)

(Well, don't be too hard on yourself. Conceptually, your plan and its implementation were brilliant. In addition to sparing humanity, you've invented time travel, Daisy. The details needed some serious last minute tweaking, though.)

(What did You do?)

(Nothing. I'm not allowed to. And I have to tell you, I was in a panicky funk when I saw how things were headed. Fortunately, the Fates got into it and provided you with the raw materials—Dedwell and Dulcie. It was YOUR inspired idea to shunt Aglaophone onto a different track, so to speak, by relaying her through yourself into Dulcie Abbott. That was quite a jolt you took!)

(That's okay. I'm just so grateful someone or something was looking out for me. So what happens to Dulcie? I promised her You'd accept her in spite of . . . You know.)

(Now THAT was presumptuous of you! However, for your sake, because you meant well, I'll go easy on her—although her genealogical line has been forever extinguished, of course. But it all works out beautifully.)

(What do you mean?)

(Let that go for a moment. Tell me, what are your plans now?)

(Well, first of all, I've got to get Aglaophone patched up. Look at the poor thing! It'll have to be done hush-hush, of course. I can't have her going to a hospital babbling proto-Greek and trying to deal with the bureaucrats in triage. That means fixing up a room for her, either up at the house or down here at the bungalow, and then pulling strings to get top orthopedics people and dentists to make house calls and to keep quiet afterward. Then I have to figure out how much to tell Brian and my sisters—not to mention how to deal with the crush Phonny is bound to have on Brian. And how do I explain Dulcie's temporary disappearance to the council? What if the FBI starts snooping around looking for her? What if Dedwell washes up on a neighbor's property?)

(Don't worry about that. There's a Great White honing in on him right now—courtesy of Poseidon. But, Daisy, these are all petty concerns you can easily deal with once you've calmed down. Let's look at the Big Picture, shall we?)

(All right.)

(Do you remember my saying a moment ago that everything had worked out beautifully? Let me elaborate. Aglaophone, as Dulcie Abbott, is now in position to project her own line of incarnations into the indefinite future. Also to replace you eventually as head of New Dawn.)

(Oh. I see.)

(See what?)

(I'm being taken out of the loop. You think I can't do the job anymore.)

(Well, yes, silly girl, I am taking you out of the loop. But not for diminished capacity. I'm the one with diminished capacity! Daisy, I've been at this job for over a million years—for as long as there have been people and semi-people on earth. I'm tired and I want to start winding down. Of all My daughters from Pandora and Eve on down the ages, I've decided with good cause that you are My Chosen One. You still have a great number of productive years ahead of you in your current role, but eventually, instead of transitioning to yet another incarnation, I want you to succeed Me as the Goddess. What do you say?)

(. . . Oh, Great Mother!)

Daisy felt as if she might topple over with shock.

(Is that a yes?)

(. . . How can I AGREE to such an honor? I wouldn't have any idea of what's involved! And I'm certainly not worthy of being worshipped!)

(Nonsense! As an actress, you're used to adulation—and you do love it, Daisy! But anyway it doesn't matter. As you pointed out to someone not too long ago, I'm not here to be worshipped and neither would YOU be. Like Me, you'd exist to be USED—used as a source of strength and guidance to anyone attuned to the world's eternal harmonies. Used to unlock the brains and the energy of a stunted humanity so that they may learn at last the Secret that has eluded all but a handful of the best of them for all these eons. Jesus of Nazareth knew it. And now Daisy Crandall knows it. What is the Secret, Daisy?)

(. . . I believe it's that You and God together are the ultimate manifestation of every woman and man who ever lived. That as a species we are eternally bound to grope haltingly upward toward You until, in some unimaginably distant future, the Truth, the Secret becomes obvious to one and all. That we ARE You—the Both of You—and that we have been You all along. WE are the gods.)

(That's IT, honey! That's all of it! And it will be your job to help lead humanity to that conclusion over many, many centuries. As for Me, I'm a bit burned out, as this era would say. So how about it? Will you accept?)

(But this is so overwhelming! What will I do for guidance? Where will YOU be?)

(Still with you, Daisy, I promise. Always available for consultation. I guess I'll be doing the Queen Mum thing. So now will you agree?)

(. . . Yes, Mother. I will.)

(Fine. Now turn around, Daisy Crandall, and just look at the sunrise.)

Daisy did as she was told, falling to her knees in solemn awe.

(That's YOU, Daisy! The world's hope, the world's solace . . . the world's Bright New Dawn. Bless you, My Daughter—and, for now, farewell.)

The Mother left her mind. For a long time Daisy remained on her knees in the sand, tears of wonder dewing her cheeks. Then, full of fright and exhilaration, she arose and gently awakened Aglaophone. Helping her to her feet and careful not to cause her any further pain, she tenderly embraced and supported her younger-older self. The two women smiled warmly at each other and began to walk gingerly up the beach. Then something occurred to Daisy, and she stopped.

(Phonny, how'd you manage to get the sword here?)

(Oh, at the last minute, I thought it would be a neat idea—you know, a comforting familiar object to accompany me on an uncertain journey. So I worked it into the invocation you gave me.)

(Just like that?)

(Well, yes.)

Daisy whistled.

(That's unbelievable! That invocation was painstakingly devised, I thought, only for your psychic transport through time. And YOU snuck a physical object through the space-time continuum as an afterthought!)

(I guess. By the way, Daisy, why'd you throw it away? I loved that sword!)

(Sorry, darling. Under the circumstances, it would have caused us tremendous problems eventually. I'll explain later. Besides, swords are antiquated and no longer necessary in this age. And then, of course, you and I have our OWN stockpile of unique weaponry.)

(What do you mean?)

Daisy waved her right arm. The sky over the water flashed with a loud bang.

Aglaophone jumped, then laughed.

(Oh! . . . Right.)

They resumed their slow and halting walk, Daisy steering their path toward the bungalow. Then she saw the door suddenly open and Brian emerge, undoubtedly drawn by the unexpected atmospherics he'd just heard.

Uh-oh! Daisy grimaced. Here's where things REALLY get complicated!

Great Mother, she pleaded fervently, be with me now!

Then, struck by an insight that was stark and profound and absolute, She realized She was talking to Herself.